Designing HAPPILY EVER AFTER

ELLIE HALL

Srishti
PUBLISHERS & DISTRIBUTORS

Srishti Publishers & Distributors
A unit of AJR Publishing LLP
212A, Peacock Lane
Shahpur Jat, New Delhi – 110 049

editorial@srishtipublishers.com

First published in India by
Srishti Publishers & Distributors in 2023

First Published by Ellie Hall

10 9 8 7 6 5 4 3 2 1

This is a work of fiction. The characters, places, organisations and events described in this book are either a work of the author's imagination or have been used fictitiously. Any resemblance to people, living or dead, places, events, communities or organisations is purely coincidental.

Printed and bound in India

This one is for my very own Viking beefcake with a beard. I'm glad that early on in our relationship you figured out the way to my heart is through my stomach (quesadillas forevah). All the meals you made while I wrote this book, a few feet away from me at the kitchen table (aka my office), are appreciated...as well as all the things you fix around here...and how you make me laugh...and, well, I'll stop now and spare readers all my mushy-gushy romance because there is plenty of that to come in these pages.

♥

CHAPTER 1

Christina

If you look up the expression *hot mess*, you won't find an explanation about a warm meal like a sloppy Joe that requires a stack of napkins while eating or a bunch of scrap-yard junk blazing under the sun on a summer's day. However, you will find my photo next to the definition:

hŏt mĕs

Noun

1. A woman excelling at mess-ology—the study of stitching a life together that at first glance doesn't look like it's in shambles, but if you adjust your gaze, it reveals a dumpster fire

Verb

1. A woman excelling at the art of mess-ery—the act of making it look like she has it all together, but underneath she is a stressed-out, untidy disarray of chaos

From a technical standpoint, there are various levels of hot mess-ism. I'm talking a rainbow spectrum of disaster. Let's see, there's:

- The hot mess upon waking up in the morning, coffee is her saving grace
- The walking hot mess most days excluding weekends
- The A+ hot mess student who excels rapidly to the top of her class
- The superstar who has hot mess-ness elevated to an art form

I'm quickly edging out of the waking hot mess classification because I can usually pull it together before I greet the public, but if I don't put on the brakes, I'll soon have a degree in hot mess-manship.

Am I winning at life or am I losing? That's the question I've been asking myself a lot lately. Forty-something, single, and now living in small-town USA leaves the answer up for debate.

You should also know hot, I am not. At least according to my mother and the few men from my past. Unless, of course, the hot part comes into play thanks to the scorching southern sun.

See, I thought I had this thing called my existence figured out —I'm an in-demand social media influencer and interior designer. But my grasp on my life feels like it's sliding out of my hands, if I ever had a firm grip on it in the first place.

If the question, *Are you winning at life?* were on a scale of one to ten, the number one side would be the #fail category. Lately, for me, it looks like this:

- Waking up after a close shave with marriage, caked in Cheeto dust in an apartment that smells like a litter box (even though I don't have a cat)
- My elderly neighbor coming at me with a broom because my eye makeup made me resemble a raccoon

(Mrs. What's-her-face has poor eyesight, so honest mistake)
- Packing up and running away from it all (including marriage number two)
- Entering a home improvement hostess contest on the HLTV network but losing

The ten end of the scale would cover #winning, including:

- Long brunches with friends involving nibbles of organic fat-free chia seed yogurt topped with mixed berries, gluten-free granola, and a sprig of mint (complete with a photo for social media) which is a mom-approved meal
- Sweaty selfies showcasing glistening abs (to be clear, I've never had abs, plural never mind a singular ab, but I work out like they'll miraculously bust through my fluffy abdominal wall)
- Videos of my most recent shopping haul from the latest sustainable, green, and fair-trade clothing brands (#paidadvertisement, of course)
- Ending up meeting three incredible women and taking a leap of faith and going into business with them and creating our own home improvement show: Designed to Last

The #ladyboss is who I'm supposed to be. That's the Christina Cricket Abernathy that I show the world on my @DomesticDiva Picto-Chat account—that's the gal everyone likes, follows, and engages with.

(Yes, my middle name is Cricket—a completely out-of-character naming convention for my well-to-do parents. But I have an affection for it because in some ways it speaks to the real me—the gal who's slightly less than the picture-perfect version I present to the world. Think of it like Beyonce's *Sasha Fierce*, but, um, the opposite.)

However, lately, I feel the need to reassess what success means. All my life, my solution is to go all-in with a fake it 'til ya make it mentality. If I can pretend that I have my head together long enough, my life will no longer be in shambles.

Sound logic, right?

No one can see the inner stress and slow unraveling behind the scenes because all I show them are the staged, curated, and glossy, Picto-Chat photos. Bonus: that's all they want to see.

At first glance, I thought it would be a win-win. Then why do I feel like I'm losing?

- The discarded wedding dress in a crumpled heap in my closet? No one needs to know it's there.
- The lunatic ex-fiancé who won't forget about Las Vegas? That's our little secret.
- The drawer full of unpaid bills, overdue credit cards, and unreturned calls? No one needs to know about those either. I can afford to pay them, but the hot mess thing I mentioned comes into play here

And those are just the appetizers. Overall, I'm not exactly where I want to be in life, except for right here with my three new besties at Ladyboss Headquarters. This new venture gives me hope (that I can get myself on track before anyone discovers the real me).

Only, if they could cool it on the chocolate thing for a minute, I might survive this meeting. Don't worry, I'm not some deranged monster who hates chocolate, but long ago my mother made it clear that my metabolism isn't chocolate friendly (or welcoming of anything involving sugar, fat, or carbs). She had me on Weight Watchers when I was eight. Jenny Craig at thirteen and threatened to cut up my credit cards prior to my sweet sixteen if I didn't fit into the dress she got me for the party.

The only time I eat other yummy scrumbos is if they "accidentally" fall into my mouth. You know, like the late-night solo date with a bag of Cheetos while binge-watching the latest Netflix series. I can't be a woman of steel all the time. Plus, mega marathons like that require fortification.

I must resist. I must resist. In a shrill voice of warning, the words repeat in my head. I take one of those deep cleansing breaths like my therapist taught me.

"You okay, Christina?" Mae asks in her sweet voice that sounds like it should be in a Disney movie.

"Yeah, for a second I thought you were 'making eyes' at those chocolates. Now it looks like you want to murder them," Louella Belle says, referring to one of Rhondy's famous terms—I've gathered it's like big cartoon heart eyes. Rhondy is the owner of the Starlight Diner and the woman who's become a surrogate auntie to all of us and maker of said chocolates.

If this were an alternate reality, I'd offer her my life savings in exchange for her mouth-watering creations.

Flustered at being caught, I wave my hand dismissively. "Oh, I was just noticing that one of them is in the shape of a heart." I point.

"That means you should eat it," Camellia says.

I must resist. I must resist. Growing up as the chubby girl in the family, I learned the painful lesson that if I want anyone to like me, I have to skip the sweets. At least, that's what my mother told me.

The ladyboss inside me wants to argue and refute Sylvia Lancaster's harsh judgment of my appearance, but I've never won an argument with my mother, so why try now? Of course, my inner ladyboss has an answer along the lines of accepting how I look, loving the gift of this body God gave me, and a whole bunch of other well-meaning words of wisdom. However, Sylvia's voice is loud in my head.

"Rhondy is still working on getting the form right. I suggested she order some of those silicon molds," Louella Belle says. "I guess she wants to free form them for now before investing until she's happy with the flavors."

"If you ask me, they're perfect as is." Camellia gestures with a chef's kiss.

I wish I could say the same about myself.

"I don't care what they look like. If you ask me, they're delicious." Mae plucks the second to last piece from the tin.

Aside from the one shaped like a heart, the perfectionist in me wants to march over to Rhondy's kitchen with an arsenal of all the chocolate-making molds and supplies so they can be uniform. But then she'd give me some to sample and I wouldn't be able to say no. Telling the ladybosses and Rhondy about my love-hate relationship with all things sugar and fat and anxiety is a story for another time. I open my mouth to get us back on track during this meeting.

Camellia cuts across me. "Is there anyone you've been making eyes at? After all, you did catch the flowers at the wedding."

Suddenly clammy, I smooth my hands down the front of my floral skirt. Today I'm wearing it with a classic white T-shirt tied at the waist. I was going to put on a pair of cute sneakers my mother would say I'm too old for. Instead, I opted for a strappy pair of sandals with a medium heel. I also have a straw hat and coordinating bag. Dressing for the southern humidity is a different animal than Manhattan, even in the summer. "Is the AC on the fritz again?"

Louella Belle's expression wrinkles in confusion. "It was never on the fritz. Aunt Fawn had the thing tickled to perfection because it was important to keep the flowers climate-controlled."

The four of us: Louella Belle, Mae, Camellia, and I currently occupy the Designed to Last headquarters. Formerly, this building housed Flora & Fawn, Louella Belle's late aunt's florist shop. We renovated and are using it to plan out the coming season of our show, hash out design plans, and eventually, it'll serve as a storefront and tourist destination—at least that's the plan.

The Starlight Diner, Rhondy's business, is on the left and a vacant building sits on the right. Also part of the plan is to buy it and open a coffee shop and confectionary—Rhondy will provide the chocolates and baked goods. But I don't want to think that far in the future. It's hard enough to keep things under control today.

"Back in college, there was a great French fry restaurant called Fritz in the town just off campus," Mae says.

Camellia lifts and lowers her eyebrows. "A restaurant just for French fries? Can we take a girls' trip there?"

"It's about fifteen hundred miles away, so we'd have to plan ahead. Anyway, they had about twenty different kinds of dips for the fries and free ketchup, of course, but I'd always get the flight of three—" Counting on her fingers, she names her three favorite sauce flavors.

"When I left my little suburb outside London and came to America nineteen years ago, I fell in love with three things. French fries and apple pie." Camellia sighs.

"I thought you said you fell in love with three things," Louella Belle says. "That's only two."

Camellia wrinkles her nose then looks away like she remembers something less pleasant than pie and fries.

I take her body language to mean there was a guy involved—trust me, I know what it's like to fall in love...or think I fell in love, be forced to love, basically everything but experiencing true love.

Mae bounces with excitement. "Back during my blogging days, I traveled around the country on the hunt for the perfect chocolate chip cookie—well, other than my grandmother's recipe which we lost. A tragedy, if you ask me."

"Did you find it?" Louella Belle leans in, practically drooling.

Feeling the hum of my mother's voice getting under my skin, I shift uncomfortably, eager to change the topic of conversation. When I was younger, she made it clear that fuller-figure girls like me couldn't eat anything sugared, fried, or carb-filled. End of story.

My heart simultaneously aches for younger me but cannot figure out how to let go of the hold that old story has on me.

"I got close. The second best cookie was from a little bakery in Alabama. Sadly, they're closed, but I have the recipe. I've tried and tried but cannot replicate it."

"Would you be willing to give it to Rhondy? She's a baking unicorn." Louella Belle sings her praises.

"Sure. Anyway, back to my idea. I won't travel all over the country, but I will find the best French fries in eastern Georgia."

"Easy, Starlight Diner," Louella Belle and Camellia say at the same time.

"I haven't had French fries in years," I blurt.

The conversation drops off and they all whip their heads in my direction.

Did I say that out loud?

Three sets of eyes bore into me.

"Christina, is what you just said true?" Louella Belle asks in a gentle voice.

My throat tickles in a way that warns me against lying. Caught up in my thoughts and my monster chocolate craving plus the mention of French fries, the confession accidentally slipped out. "Oh, I, um, yeah. Nope. Haven't been able to..."

My three friends and business partners must fill in the blank of my clumsy sentence with *food poisoning* because they respond with various amounts of understanding and pity. The tickle in my throat travels down and lands hard in my stomach—my dietary restrictions have nothing to do with food poisoning. In fact, I've only had a cup of coffee today. I've talked to my therapist about the little lies I tell to cover my tracks. She said the sooner I can get honest with myself about the things that are little to most people but are mountain-sized to me, the quicker I'll be able to be truthful with others, which means I'll be able to sustain real, long-term relationships—with friends and potentially a guy.

Not that I want to be involved. Been there. Done that. Have the wedding gowns to prove it.

Louella Belle's smile reaches her golden-brown eyes. Camellia blinks a few times as though still processing the travesty of my French fry-free life.

Mae reaches for my hand. "In time, I believe you can heal."

Of course, she's joking around, being silly about the so-called food poisoning that rids my life of French fries, but the comment goes deeper with meaning because can I heal? Is it possible?

I don't want to endure a daily minefield of whack-a-mole when it comes to eating—usually, I start strong but then end up eating something my mother dubbed "bad" or "off-plan." But how can that be when it tastes so good? Moreover, why can't I let myself be bad or go off plan?

These are important questions, but first, the meeting because I'm a ladyboss and focusing on the project will distract me from my silly problems.

I open my mouth again to get us back on track from my battle with food—the war my mother started. I'm an adult woman and understand I ought not to believe everything she said. The wound is deep. "Listen, ladybosses. We have a lot of work to do. Have there been any more applicants for Mr. Fix-It?"

"No one compares to Mr. Fix-It." Louella Belle's voice is dreamy with love.

The rest of us giggle while she remains in her swoony reverie.

"They're still in the honeymoon phase," I say, with a cynical drop to my voice.

Mae tilts her head in my direction. "Does that mean you don't think that level of adoration and affection can be maintained over the lifetime of a relationship?"

I snort. "I know it can't. But that's not going to fix the problem at hand. We have a show that's going live next week, and we don't have an onsite contractor aka a Mr. Fix-It."

"Right." Camellia drops a thick stack of applications on the table. "We've gone through these a half-dozen times, interviewed them all, and no one is the right guy for the mansion job."

"Is that because we're being too picky?" Louella Belle asks.

"You already found your Mr. Perfect, so of course, we're being picky," Camellia says.

"We're not looking for my future husband," I reply.

"We're not?" Camellia asks with an air of disbelief.

I cannot tell whether we're still in joke mode from the French fry thing or if they're serious.

"Christina did catch the bouquet at the wedding, just saying." Camellia with her long white-blond hair is gorgeous and ageless like Galadriel from the Lord of the Rings movie. She used to be a model when she was in her late teens. She has something of a regal bearing which lends a certain credibility, certainty, and finality to everything she says in her faint British accent.

"You've mentioned," I mutter.

"Do you believe in happily ever after?" Mae asks.

"Absolutely." But Camellia's voice cracks toward the end.

I give a slow shake of my head. "I believe in single-y ever after."

They laugh like I'm joking. I'm not.

"Ladybosses, I'm on the No-Man-Plan. I'm career-minded and want to grow my brand. Dating or a relationship would just slow me down. I have time to dominate the world. I do not have time to date."

The part I don't say is that historically, my only experience is with liars, losers, and cheaters. My love life has more than a few dents. My heart is busted, broken, kicked like a can down the street, so I married my first love—interior design and that's the way it will stay.

"That's a unique approach," "Interesting," "Huh," they all say in turn.

These three women have become my best friends in the last months, but we're veering too close to personal-emotional territory. These relationships are built on business and have to remain that way. I can't let anyone get too close, otherwise, they'll see that underneath the @DomesticDiva perfection is a woman struggling to keep control over her life. Yep, that's me.

On the surface, I'm perfectly put together. Below that, I'm a wreck.

But if I can resist chocolate, and if I can say no to French fries, I can do anything. At least, that's what I tell myself.

After Louella Belle's disastrous segment on the Mr. Fix-It Search for Miss Fix-It contest, she, Mae, Camellia, and I could've been fierce competitors. Instead, we became fast friends—mostly bonding over my sordid stories about Bo's previous wife (he's the former Mr. Fix-it on Home and Landscaping TV's eponymic show and Louella Belle's forever Mr. Fix-It).

Bo retired from the spotlight but wanted a project to keep his talented bride and her three friends busy, which gave birth to our brand new show: Designed to Last.

While HLTV's show Mr. Fix-It—now known as Miss Fix-It with its new host—is on hiatus, Bo's assistant Kim got us started in the business of buying, remodeling, and fixing up unique properties for television. We plan to offer the homes at auction to good causes—kind of like what Louella Belle did with her aunt's old house on Wayfarer Lane.

There are plenty of shows that feature your standard single-family detached homes. We're featuring the ugly ducklings, the houses and buildings no one wants—the story of my life. We're in the business of making transformations, turning eyesores into beautiful locations people enjoy, and creating comfort and leisure out of rejections.

After being single as I'd neared my thirties, my mother attempted to marry me off. When that failed, I tried my hand at finding my own spouse. Now, I realize that I'm better off on my own. It's less messy that way, and we all know that I need to steer myself out of hot mess territory, STAT.

With Louella Belle as the hostess and coordinator, Designed to Last will partially be filmed live to leverage social media visibility—especially with my massive following—and to keep us current.

Each season, we'll have a new project. I'm up first this

summer with a Georgian mansion remodel. In the fall, Mae is revamping a neglected farmhouse that's been in her family for generations, and Camellia, well, we haven't gotten that far yet. One thing at a time, as Meredith, my therapist, tells me—after we realized that I tend to take everything on at once and then pile up a little more for good measure—hence, the stress(ed) hot mess.

"Let's talk about why these candidates aren't a good fit for the project," Camellia says. "He was knowledgeable about historic homes." She points at the photo stapled to the application on the top.

"Because he was as old as the house itself."

She shrugs like it's no big deal and then points to another snapshot of a middle-aged guy smiling with his mouth closed. "I like his beard."

"You like beards?" I make a gagging face. "Ew. No. Yuck."

Louella Belle twirls a loose piece of hair. "I don't mind them."

"Yeah, because Mr. Fix-It's handsome face is beneath it." I shake my head. "Ix-nay on the eard-bay."

"What does that mean?" Mae asks.

"Pig Latin," I answer, trying to keep us focused. The best thing about working for myself and by myself was that there weren't any distractions, sidebars, or dumb conversations with chocolate. I mean *about* chocolate. No way is that stuff in the tin with its high shine and cocoa scent *talking to* me. I'm not having a conversation *with* chocolate. (Oh, but the sweet things it would say to me if such a thing were possible!) Anyway, I don't need that kind of therapist. I'd just rather it not be here.

In front of me.

Within arm's reach.

Looking all delicious and stuff.

My stomach grumbles and I cover it up by coughing, then saying, "We can't hire Beaver-Man."

"Beaver-Man?" Mae asks.

"Did you notice his teeth during his live interview?" I ask.

Camellia waves her hand dismissively. "That's nothing that a few thousand in orthodontia can't fix."

"In a week?" I shake my head and flip through a few of the other candidates. Hopelessness grows.

"We should give the project a name," Mae adds.

I pause on another guy with a beard and flannel, then shuffle his folder to the bottom of the pile. "Guys with beards, men who wear flannel, heck, even work boots are a solid *no* because they can be so disorderly. These are the kinds of people who eat with their mouths open, walk around with their shirts untucked, or track in dirt. We can't have that on my worksite."

The other three stare at me, agape.

I give my head a little shake.

Christina, stop narrating your thoughts out loud. Also, don't talk to yourself in the third person.

It's been a few weeks since I saw Meredith, my therapist. I should schedule a tele-appointment. The stress of this project and being out of my routine is probably getting to me.

To Mae's comment, I reply, "Of course, we'll give the project a name. I just haven't thought of it yet. Typically, all my interior design projects get a name, a hashtag, and the spotlight on all my accounts. This won't be any different." I speak confidently, trying to convince myself I can pull this off.

"Okay, Domestic Diva, what's it going to be?" Mae asks, using my social media handle.

I get to my feet, shifting my attention to the whiteboard with the as-is picture from the real estate listing, the plans, and elevation as well as the details for the first Designed to Last project. I tap the photo with my pen, thinking. "This old mansion is my cup of tea."

"I thought you didn't drink tea," Louella Belle says.

"I don't. Give me a latte with a double shot of espresso and topped with skinny oat milk foam." Before leaving Manhattan for Butterbury, as the queen of interior design with a highly successful Picto-Chat account, I was at the center of the world of high energy, high maintenance, and high production quality. Where am I now? The middle of nowhere and my inspo didn't travel well.

The diner next door only sells regular coffee, and they don't even have skim milk. Some days I ask myself what I'm doing here. Then I gaze outside at the Butterbury town square, surrounded by trees dripping with Spanish moss. The quaint library, stone church, and kids riding bicycles are like a Norman Rockwell painting brought to life. This town is the stuff of Picto-Chat perfection. But will it last?

Perfection is an ever-moving goal post, elusive, and impossible to grasp. At least that's what Meredith tells me. But I'll prove her wrong. I'll make everything perfect, and then...

...And then it'll be perfect, and I won't have to worry about chocolate or French fries or my figure. Coordinating accents and pillows and matching colors will come naturally and easily. There won't be worries, distractions, interruptions, or surprises. My anxiety will finally be gone when I get everything just right.

That dreaded hum starts up under my skin, leaving me feeling restless and uncertain, despite my ideal surroundings and best friends.

"Let's go over to the property. Maybe I'll get inspired," I say.

"And maybe a contractor in shining armor will ride up on his steed with his shield and sword lifted, ready to renovate the place," Mae says.

"A shield and sword? Don't you mean a hammer and saw?" Louella Belle asks.

The two laugh, then Louella Belle goes abruptly quiet.

"What?" we all ask at once.

She shakes her head. "Nothing. It was silly."

"Oh, she's imagining her Mr. Fix-It in shining armor, riding up to renovate with her."

Louella Belle's brow wrinkles. "I wasn't." Her tone isn't exactly one of denial. More like she thought of something else, about the project maybe, and quickly dismissed the notion.

Perhaps she was going to ask Bo to come out of retirement then thought better of it.

I check my Picto-Chat account and reply to a few comments in response to the hints I've posted about the upcoming project. My audience is pumped, but some have expressed unhappiness at me leaving NYC. There's a direct flight that's little more than an hour between Savannah, Georgia—the nearest city—and New York, so I'll be traveling there plenty for events. As a highly sought-after influencer in the domestic and home space, I'm invited to all sorts of parties, brunches, dinners, charity events, and I have even walked a few red carpets.

Louella Belle claps her hands together. "Great idea. Let's head over there. I have a stop I'd like to make in that direction, anyway."

"And I should take a few measurements." I gather up my three-ring organization binder with all my paint and fabric samples, ideas for the project so far along with fixture, appliance, and hardware inspiration—all color-coded with tabs.

"I might stay here and work on the website," Mae says.

"You have to come with us." Louella Belle's tone starts sharp then softens.

"So demanding," Mae mumbles, pushing off her stool around the wooden table Bo built and dubbed the Ladyboss Command Center.

"I have something I need your help with," Louella Belle adds.

"Actually, I was also thinking of staying back," Camellia says. "I wanted to make a call to one of the artisans I met at the spring craft fair. I think her textiles would be a nice touch to the boutique when we open up."

"We'll have plenty of time to do that. I need your help today," Louella Belle insists.

"But you have Mae and Christina."

"This might be a team effort."

I tuck my head because Louella Belle wears a look of determination cut with mischief.

Then the reason for their apprehension clicks. "You guys don't really think the mansion is haunted, do you?"

Mae and Camellia nod in unison.

"Nonsense. These old southern homes just have a lot of character." Louella Belle forces cheer into her voice.

"That's not entirely true. My grandparents' farm is definitely haunted. At least that's what my brother told us," Mae says.

"I am certain it's not haunted," I say.

"You haven't even gone inside yet," Mae counters.

"Last time we were there, it was dusk and the electricity hadn't been activated yet. I didn't want to fall or bump into something. As we all know, the real estate listing said it was for sale as-is."

Louella Belle snorts. "Come on, ladybosses, I'll buy us all French fries on the way back. I'll also see if Rhondy has any more chocolates for us to taste test."

Standing by the door, a breeze ruffles the loose pieces of my brown hair by my face. I catch a whiff of cocoa. I glance back at the heart-shaped piece of chocolate in the tin. A long sigh escapes. I can't let myself have it. Not today. Not ever.

If I didn't know better, I might think this place was haunted too—tormenting me with chocolate. It's Designed to Last's base of operations, and after Bo revamped it with our direction, transforming the place from a dark and dated flower shop to an open and spacious storefront and office, it has a much less spooky feel.

I follow the others, and we pile into the SUV that replaced Louella Belle's beloved minivan—that she and her aunt Fawn affectionately called Vanna-white—and hit the road. When we reach the intersection to take us toward the mansion, Louella Belle turns in the opposite direction.

"I thought we took a left here." Camellia points out the window.

I did too, even though I'm still learning my way around Butterbury and Willoworth county.

Louella Belle revs the engine. "Right. But I have a stop to make."

"Are you bringing us for ice cream again?" Mae asks, referring to the first day of summer when Louella Belle surprised us with a trip to a creamery at a farm on the edge of town.

Of course, I told them I'm dairy sensitive even though I accidentally got cream in my coffee last time I was at the Starlight Diner and didn't have any complications—but ice cream is definitely off-limits.

The three of them chat about the delicious ice cream flavors and the ones they want to try next time we visit. As usual, I keep quiet, not wanting to tempt a craving.

Nearly fifteen minutes later, we wind down a long dirt road edged by overgrown trees.

"Louella Belle, where are you taking us?" Camellia asks.

"Looks like the set of a horror movie," Mae adds.

Louella Belle stops in front of an intricately designed iron gate and pushes a call button on a keypad. "Think of it as a surprise."

The four of us are close, but there are a few things they don't know about me. One of them is that I don't like surprises. Not. At. All.

The uncomfortable humming under my skin sends my thoughts spiraling, threatening an internal tornado. I shift with discomfort but play it off like I'm adjusting my skirt and wish there was something I could do—instead of the long list of things I can't do: eat chocolate, fries, date, etcetera—to make it stop.

CHAPTER 2
Christina

Mae stares out the window, wide-eyed. Camellia frowns politely. Now that we're stopped, I unbuckle my seatbelt and poke my head between the two front seats of the SUV. "Seriously, Louella Belle, where are we?" Concern for our wellbeing peppers my voice.

"Inspiration struck, and I followed it." Louella Belle's throat bobs with a swallow as though her confidence wanes.

"Followed it to the middle of nowhere," Mae says in a small voice.

"Please say a fully restored Georgian mansion that we'll use as a comp lies on the other side of that gate and not an ax-murderer," I say.

"Bo and I have been out here loads of times. It's perfectly safe. No ghosts, ax-murderers, or ice cream, sadly," she adds, sounding like she could go for a scoop.

Me too. But if I can resist that and chocolate and French fries, I can handle this...whatever it is. You see, my mother taught me that it's all about control. If I can keep a tight grip on myself and my life, everything else is ancillary. At least I'd like it to be.

Louella Belle pushes the button for the call box again. A deep, male voice crackles from the other side.

"Hey, it's me. Ella Belle," she hollers her friends-only nickname into the box, infusing sunshine into her voice.

Whether the sun is still shining above or not is uncertain, because the trees remain closed around us as the gate opens and we pass through. I fight the trail of tremors traveling up my spine.

We continue down the dirt road that opens up to a clearing. Louella Belle parks next to a massive black truck with a lifted suspension and zombie apocalypse tires. Next to it is a large aluminum building with a metal roof. Random pieces of wood and metal lay strewn amidst weeds struggling to grow out of the debris. A massive metal dragon sculpture sits on cement blocks instead of the stately lions outside my parents' building on the upper east side. I imagine whoever lives here is Medusa's twin, except instead of transforming things into stone, their preferred medium is metal.

I briefly imagine a Dungeons and Dragons live-action role-playing scene. When I was a kid, I enjoyed LARP-ing, but when my mother found out about my involvement with the activity it came to an abrupt end—with no thanks to my sister who tattled and teased me, saying it's only for dorks. Never played again.

I also notice a shed surrounded by junk in the shadows of a large oak tree. My mother also said that goblins live in the woods and that they'll snatch little girls and eat them—I realize now she didn't want me to wander off, not that there are forests in Manhattan. But we're not in the city. The shed is probably where whatever goblin lives here hides its victims. Goosebumps skitter across my arms.

"No Georgian mansion in sight," I say. "We can go now."

"Please say this is a chocolate factory," Mae whispers.

"How about we leave?" Camellia adds.

"Ladies, do you think I'd bring us somewhere dangerous? Have a little faith."

We pile out of the SUV, but none of us other than Louella Belle march forward. In fact, Mae grips the door handle with white knuckles.

What sounds like a caged beast goblin from the bowels of the earth barks aggressively from behind the metal door to the building.

My body goes rigid like I've already been mauled and killed. My mother warned that wolves think chubby girls taste better and to keep my hand out of the cookie jar.

The door to the building opens and a hulking figure fills it—a Viking beefcake with a beard. He wears a leather apron and the tattoos covering his cut muscles glisten.

Louella Belle clears her throat. "Hi, Buck. We just happened to be in your neighborhood, so I thought we'd swing by."

What looks like a broom missing most of its bristles and standing on four spindly peg legs barks wildly as it streaks past the Viking's boots.

"Gremlin, be friendly," he orders.

The small, shaggy creature with black and gray fur in some places and bald patches in others, charges toward Louella Belle. It has big Papillion ears, a stubby tail, and a concerning underbite with several crooked teeth jutting upward. The thing is...homely, but stops short at its master's command.

The dog's tongue lolls out of its mouth as it sniffs Louella Belle, who praises it like it's an adorable little baby and not a freak of nature before the thing moves on to Mae.

If that thing comes near me, I swear...

"We most certainly were not in this, uh, neighborhood. Is that what you called it?" Camellia stage-whispers while cautiously eyeing the dog.

Louella Belle elbows her to be quiet. "Ladybosses, this is Buck McDermott, and these are my friends and partners on the new show Designed to Last: Camellia, Mae, and Christina. You may remember each other from the wedding. I hope this isn't a bad time." She lays her southern charm on thick.

With the harsh and aggrieved expression pinching the space between Buck's thick eyebrows, I don't get the sense our pop-in is welcome now or ever—or that he remembers us. However, I sure do recall Buck. He was Bo's best man and the kind of guy you avoid in dark alleys and forest clearings. Especially forest clearings.

Camellia, Mae, and I take a subtle step backward.

Gremlin sniffs Mae who looks like she's playing a game of freeze tag with one arm lifted partway toward her neck to swat a mosquito, but then stopped when the dog reached her so as to not make any sudden movements that might set the thing off.

When the dog, at least that's what I think it is, finally moves on, Mae goes on a swatting spree.

I squish up my face and brace for the attack I'm sure is coming. The animal's hot breath grazes my leg as it sniffs.

"I don't want to die today," I whimper, wishing I could alert the others to what's about to go down, but fear paralyzes my vocal cords.

The sniffing abruptly stops, and I feel a wet sensation on my shin.

My fear must've sent me into an adrenalized state and instead of pain, all I feel is the gushing blood as Gremlin takes a big, juicy bite out of my leg.

"We probably should've called first," Mae says apologetically, interrupting what I'm sure is a scene straight out of a horror movie.

"Or written a letter. Could've done that too," Camellia adds, putting more distance between her and the intimidating man with the denim and heavy boots.

Gushing. Damp. Moist. Blood. All the gross words in the English language come to mind, but I still cannot speak. However, I do look down and instead of the bloodbath I expected, the dog merely licks my leg.

"It's tenderizing me for the kill," I manage to say.

Buck gives a whistle and the animal trots over to him. "He only licks people he likes." Then he gives a stern yet polite nod, as if fighting the question we'd all like answered. *Why are we here?*

The dog stares at me with its tongue lolling out of its mouth and panting.

Yes, Louella Belle why bring me to my death?

I'm pretty sure the dog thing is smiling. Isn't that what happens in the story of the Big Bad Wolf? *My, what big eyes you have and such sharp teeth*? My mother wasn't the fairytale reading type, so I'm a bit rusty.

Louella Belle wrings her hands. "Buck, you see, the girls and I are in a bit of a pickle. A lick of trouble, you might say. We need a contractor for our first project, and we don't have one. Preferably, we're looking for someone with ironwork skills, what with the bars on the windows and all."

I try hard not to think about why there are bars on the mansion's windows and even harder to deny what Louella Belle, my best friend turned traitor, is about to say...because I think I know what little flash of inspiration she had back at HQ.

Do I like it? No.

Will I allow it? Absolutely not.

However, I also don't want Buck to come at us with a sword or whatever he uses to slay dragons.

Louella Belle winds up. I know it's coming. Buck too by the way his posture stiffens.

"How would you like to star as the contractor on Designed to Last?" she asks grandly, as if offering him a first-class, all expenses paid, round trip ticket to wherever it is Vikings like to go to raid and plunder.

This will not stand on my watch. "Louella Belle, you said 'star.' We need someone with actual skills. The mansion is a mess."

Buck's gaze lands on me.

My insides squirm, but in a different way than they do from anxiety. I'm suddenly all hot and shivery. Flushed and quivery.

"I have my contractor's license—it's a bit dusty, but I do know my way around a construction site," he says, countering my comment.

Buck pauses long enough for me to digest the low rumble of his coastal southern drawl. It's the kind of voice that could put babies to sleep, make women swoon…or if you match the face with the speaker, make both run away crying.

He goes on, "However, I'm sorry, Ella Belle. I'm busy. Don't have time—" He turns and starts to close the door.

Ella Belle—that's the nickname locals and those who know her well use. Where did our sweet peach find this beefcake?

Louella Belle throws herself between it and the doorjamb as if she trusts that it operates like an elevator and won't squish her to bits on the slam I'm sure is coming. "Wait, Buck. You didn't get Bo and me a wedding gift."

He thumbs over his shoulder. "I was just working on it. A custom piece like that takes time and I had to wait for Bo to finish the brickwork around the hearth before installing it, anyway."

She thrusts her shoulders back. "I, uh, don't want it."

He blinks slowly. "You don't know what it is."

"Give it to someone else. I want you to be the Designed to Last contractor…for, um, my wedding present." She's in a verbal flailing free fall. Now would be the time for her three best friends to enter stage right and use the 'ole hook to pull her into the safety of the wings.

But the three of us remain frozen, terrified of Buck the Viking, dragon-slaying beast-man.

"Please?" Louella Belle adds.

Buck's brow furrows as if he's fighting against lifting Louella Belle up and planting her on the other side of the door and locking it behind him…or giving in.

There is no way this Yeti-Big Foot-beefcake would fit the show —Designed to Last is inspiring, current, and clean.

His nails are filthy. He's sweaty. Then there's the beard. No, thanks.

He and Louella Belle engage in a staring contest. Turns out he's immature, too. Great. Just great. Here I am, dealing with another man-child. They can grow up big, strong, and surly on the outside, but that doesn't always match the slow-turning of plastic widget gears on the inside—no matter that he works with metal or whatever Louella Belle alluded to about the bars on the windows of the mansion. If we don't get out of here soon, he'll probably lock us up in his tin cabin in the woods.

I step forward, ready to break up this unexpected and unwanted little showdown, and take control—that's what I do. "No. None of that will be necessary, uh, Buck was it? We have a list of qualified potential candidates for the contractor position. Thank you for your time. I know you're busy. Ladybosses, let's go."

All of us except Louella Belle, still standing in the doorway to the murder building, back toward the SUV. She whispers, "Please, Buck. You'd be perfect."

At that particular word, I go still.

Buck's gaze fixes on me. Interesting, usually people react to sudden movements and not the opposite. I flick my head toward him, wondering why I caught his attention. His eyes are an alarming shade of blue. Almost like gems, crystals. I may be a diva, but I'm not the kind that responds to bling. Not really. Okay, maybe a little. A lot. Whatever. It doesn't matter that my parents got me a piece of jewelry every year for my birthday. Looking back, I think it's because they didn't have the time or interest to purchase a more personalized gift, but like I said, whatever. *Whatever* worked well until Dimitri, but that's another story and it's almost impossible to be in Buck's presence and not think about my ex-husband—memories of him are off-limits. Not that they're anything alike looks-wise, but there's a certain dangerous, forbidden mystique—that attraction that ultimately resulted in our lives coming apart in a deadly way.

Christina, don't think about that. It's in the past. You're safe now.

My gaze drifts back to Buck's as if he could provide a safe harbor, a place where I could come apart, but he'd be there to hold me together, rather than the web of deception that I fell through after I found out the truth about Dimitri.

I shake my head, trying to unglue myself from Buck's blue eyes. They're all sparkle. Jewels. Mischief. ...and knowing.

It's like he instantly sees right through how I'm friendly but keep my protective walls up and don't let anyone get genuinely close because my biggest fear is rejection. I should fire Meredith and pay Buck three hundred dollars an hour for that silent psychoanalysis.

The second look I get from him tells me he won't let me get away with shenanigans. My inner three-year-old mini-tyrant comes out. The girl whose mother ignored her no matter what she did to get attention, so instead of tantrums she shifted gears and tried to be as perfect as possible. That would be me.

The perfect plan continues to backfire but now it's so habitual, I don't know how to stop it.

Suddenly, the sun seems especially hot above the clearing in the woods. I fan my face. "This Georgia heat really takes its toll on us northerners."

Buck grunts as if criticizing my thick blood. I imagine that animal skins line his lair with chewed-up bones filling the corner —my mind grasps for anything to paint him in an unfavorable light just so I don't feel the *rightness* of his gaze, posture, and those eyes.

"It's probably the fire inside," Louella Belle says matter of fact. "Buck is a blacksmith. Have I mentioned that? He also got his contractor's license years ago and kept it up to date. That's what Bo mentioned, anyway."

Oh, there's a fire inside alright. It's been lit and it's at odds with how I should be feeling right now—concerned, terrified, angry. Any of those. Anything other than the warmth that creeps through me at Buck's penetrating gaze and the quirk of his lips. It scrambles up the order I try to create inside and out.

His expression is pure amusement hidden under a stony exterior. He's the kind of person to laugh at my discomfort. Yep. I know all about guys like him. Er, guys in general. I've never really seen a guy like him in real life. Well, not much. Not since Dimitri's goons.

At that particular memory, the heat abruptly leaves me and the world tilts. I reach out for something, but my vision blurs and all I see is a flash of blue rushing in my direction.

CHAPTER 3
Buck

My vision may not be as good as it used to be now that I work with flame and molten metal all the time, but I'd have to be blind not to notice how attractive Louella Belle's friend Christina is with her thick dark brown hair and her jade green eyes.

My brother would revoke my man-card if I ignored the cut of her V-neck T-shirt and the way her fluttery floral skirt hugs her curves.

However, my observation skills and reflexes are as tuned as ever when I notice the sudden change in her demeanor. She goes from fully present to fading like a sunset. The light leaves those striking green eyes as it appears that she starts to lose consciousness.

I cross the yard in a few swift strides, do a deep lunge, and catch Christina in my arms before she hits the ground.

She's soft in the right places, as light as a feather, and smells like lilacs. I tell myself not to breathe too deeply. It's me and the iron forge now. Nothing and no one else enters the metal fortress I've built around myself.

Louella Belle and the others gasp and cluck with concern like a brood of hens.

"What happened?" a soft female voice asks.

"She was standing right here, staring, and then—" says one of the women leaning over my shoulder.

"I think she's only had a coffee today. She skipped the biscuits, melon, and chocolate at brunch in the office..." Ella Belle says.

"And she didn't touch the bacon," the southern-toned one says as if that's criminal.

"If that's the case and I had to guess, I'd say she has low blood sugar," I say as Christina stirs.

"I thought she swooned," the one with the white-blond hair says. I think her name was a kind of flower. Calendula. No, Camellia. I detect a subtle English accent. The other one must be Mae because I definitely registered Christina's name.

"Does Christina have a history of losing consciousness? Fainting spells?" I ask.

"Not that I know of," Elle Belle says.

She mumbles something. "Cricket." Then groans and says, "Call me Cricket."

Also, I fibbed, a little. I recall her from the wedding—not the others—, but it would be impossible to forget a face like hers. As I gaze down, her almond-shaped eyes flutter. Her full lips and cheekbone structure suggest eastern European descent. Maybe some Russian. I used to be better at identifying characteristics. Then again, I don't need those skills anymore.

"I agree. That looked like a swoon to me," Ella Belle says. "And I know a swoon when I see one, having experienced it myself."

I fight rolling my eyes at how my best friend, Bo, and his wife are so smitten with each other. I swore off relationships long ago —entanglements like that were too dangerous in my profession.

Christina jerks upright and leaps out of my arms, patting and brushing herself like she suspects I stole her wallet. I may look like a Viking, but I'd never rob or plunder.

"Swoon?" she semi chokes out. "I did not swoon. And don't you dare call me Cricket."

She blinks at me a few times. "Okay, Cricket?" I say with a question and a tease in my voice and to lighten the mood because I can't tell if she's joking, but as they say, "Laughter is the best medicine."

She shakes her head, eyes wide, mortified. "Where did you—who told you about Cricket?"

We all collectively shrug. "You."

"You were muttering, 'Cricket' then said to call you that," Ella Belle says.

Her throat bobs with a swallow and she covers her eyes with her hands. "Oh. Well, forget I said anything about it. Can we please move on?"

I straighten and move closer in case she's still unsteady. Don't need her to fall, hit her head, and have a lawsuit on my hands. She's a city girl and probably not used to uneven ground or anything but cement under her feet.

Then again, with her in my arms, I felt a little wobbly myself. Not my nerves. They're made of steel like the metal in my forge. No, it was something else. Perhaps I need lunch too.

Mae shrugs. "A swoon? It's not out of the realm of possibility. What with the beard and all."

Color returns to Christina's cheeks. "I told you I don't like beards." Her gaze lands on me. "In fact, I detest them."

Affronted, I smooth my hand down my dark reddish-brown beard. "What did my beard ever do to you?"

Everyone but Christina giggles.

One of them whispers. "He's funny."

Another, "And cute."

"Right? I told you he'd be a great candidate for the show." That would be Ella Belle.

Oh, get them out of here. First, they were clucking. Now, they're giggling and gossiping. This is why I can't have women in my life, on my property, or in my vicinity.

"Ella Belle and her gaggle of girlfriends, thanks for visiting, but I have work to do." I turn to the forge door.

"Ladybosses," they correct in unison.

Gremlin stands sentry by Christina—his little doggy senses attuned to her immediately. Traitor.

Lord help me.

Louella Belle scrambles after me. "Wait, you said Christina may have low blood sugar. Do you have some juice or um mead, ale, or whatever it is Vikings drink?"

"The blood of their enemies," Christina mutters.

I sharpen my eyebrow in their direction. "I am not a Viking." While their history is interesting, I'm of Scottish descent.

"More like Sasquatch's cousin living out here in the middle of nowhere." That was Christina again.

"I see you've recovered. Feeling better, sweetheart?" If she's going to come here uninvited, pass out, and not offer so much as *thanks*, I'll return her fiery volleys.

She tosses me an arched brow this time. "I will be when we're out of here."

"Christina, manners," Louella Belle scolds in her southern accent. "We're Buck's guests."

"I don't recall inviting you," I counter, eager to get rid of them.

Give me a hammer, anvil, and three-thousand degrees Fahrenheit and I'm a happy man. I'll take a pass when it comes to women, humans, and relationships in general.

I may look like a Viking, but I'm more of a lone wolf. A sigma wolf.

Ella Belle crosses her arms in front of her chest. *Uh oh.* Bo mentioned she's a feisty one. He and I were friends growing up—I worked for his father before our lives abruptly changed and learned my way around jobsites, kitchen remodels, and basic carpentry. During summers and after school, the two of us engaged in friendly competition until he decided he was too good for blue-collar work and left for Hollywood. I guess I left too, but for the role of a real-life superhero. At least, I tried. I shrug off the shame spiral—no one, least of all these women, will see my weakness.

"Buck, we're desperate. We need someone to be the onsite contractor for this project," Louella Belle pleads.

I recall Bo mentioning the new HLTV home improvement show, Designed to Last. That's his domain, not mine. Despite our friendship, I don't want to be involved.

Wood rots. Glass shatters. Only metal has any lasting power. That's why I chose to work with it after I retired from the agency.

"We're not desperate enough to hire him," Christina chimes.

I narrow my eyes. "Why the hostility?"

She bristles.

"Could they fake chemistry?" Camellia asks.

Relief swoops through me as Ella Belle starts toward the SUV. Over her shoulder, she says, "Okay, then we'll have to go with Beaver-Man."

Mae leans toward me. "She doesn't mean you. One of our applicants has a rather unfortunate dental bite." She demonstrates by jutting out her upper jaw. "Nice beard by the way."

Save me. Save me now.

"No, we're not going with Beaver-Man either," Christina says.

"Then who is it going to be? You've vetoed all the guys. Do you have a contractor's license that I don't know about?" Ella Belle's southern accents comes out a bit too sugary—like a rattlesnake's warning.

"I most certainly do not. But I won't have this, this hot Viking beefcake on my project," Christina stammers then takes a sharp intake of breath as the rest of the women repeat a crucial part of her statement.

"Hot?" Ella Belle asks.

"Viking?" Mae says then adds. "Yeah, I get that what with the beard and all." She must have a thing for beards.

"Beefcake?" Camellia asks. "Like a hand pie or meat pie?" She rambles about the difference and how in the UK cookies are called biscuits so it's an easy mistake to make. "I'm starved. I thought Louella Belle was bringing us for an early lunch."

This hot Viking Beefcake? *Huh.* My pulse hiccups. I'm definitely hungry. Or something.

Christina's cheeks flame red.

Hot. For. Sure.

An ember stokes inside at the presence of this infuriatingly beautiful woman.

Mae clears her throat then whispers in Camellia's ear about the American English definition of a beefcake.

Camellia's eyes widen and then she grins. "Oh, my. Oh, yes. I see what you mean."

"Yes, hot. It's extremely hot out. I'm probably at risk for heat stroke," Christina stammers.

The muscle in my jaw twitches. Time for these broody hens to clear out. "Thank you for stopping by, uninvited, in case I wasn't clear the first two times I mentioned that. What can I do to get you to leave?" I say in my most polite voice.

"Buck McDermott, were you raised in a barn? Where are your manners? At least invite us in for some kind of blacksmith brew."

I scrub my hand down my face. "I have water or water."

"Yeah, likely story," Christina mutters.

"If you're hoping for some fancy double latte café caramel mocha milk thingamajig, you won't find that here, sweetheart."

"She can't have milk—it's an allergy," Mae says, using air quotes.

The others giggle.

The huff Christina exhales turns her lips upside down in a perfect bow. The shape a metal worker like me strives to create out of a hard, otherwise unyielding material. I turn my attention to the cage around my heart, reminding myself not to think about her perfection and definitely not her lips.

Hard not to notice.

That would be my brother's intrusive voice, coming to me from the past, nudging me with his elbow, reminding me, like

Ella Belle, to use my manners and at least try not to do the opposite of flirting. He always joked that I was flirtatiously challenged and was born during the wrong era—even our parents say I have an old soul. He was my wingman. Fortunately, I don't need one anymore because women aren't part of my life. I don't need companionship, relationships, or any kind of ship—that's why I live in the woods instead of by the coast like Ella Belle and Bo.

I take a few swift strides to the door.

Ella Belle says, "Wait. Buck, you asked what you could do to get us to leave..."

An internal grumble grows.

"Will you at least come out to the property with us? We've only been once and it's, uh, a bit hazardous. With your careful eye and quick reflexes as demonstrated by catching Christina before she fell, we'd feel better about being out there alone. Loose floorboards, sketchy shingles, dangerous electric wires..."

"Speak for yourself," Christina mutters.

Perhaps she's the feisty one.

"The place should be condemned," Mae says.

"Actually, that would be the inn back in Butterbury," Camellia says. "I was hoping to stay there when I first came to town, but—" She wrinkles her nose and starts listing problems with the old inn known to locals as the "Last Resort" because staying there is something you only do if you're desperate.

"The mansion isn't that bad. It was marketed as a hot property and was the right price. With a little TLC, I'll be able to restore the place to its former glory. Ladybosses, let's go." Christina marches toward the SUV.

"Great idea," I say, my voice flat. I'm a single step away from being one of those fabled old men with a beard to my knees, seated on my front porch with a shotgun, and chasing off varmints.

Christina is the opposite of a varmint, but I can't get tangled up in this business.

"There are bars on the windows," Ella Belle says, referring to the mansion.

"Not sure why they're there, but we can get those off, no problem," Christina says.

"There's probably a dungeon," Mae adds.

"It's a mansion, not a castle," Christina replies.

"Hang on. Are you talking about the old Easton place on the hill?" I ask curiosity piqued.

"Yeah, the Haunted Hill. That's what my brother called it every time we'd pass on our way to our grandparents' farm when we were kids." Mae shivers.

I rub my beard in thought. "That place has been shut up for years."

"Yep. And I'm going to be the one to fix it up." Christina edges toward the SUV.

"But have you heard the story about—?" Mae starts.

Ella Belle holds up her hand to stop her. "Nope. None of that. We don't need to hear any spooky stories."

I cross my arms and lean against the doorjamb, eyes locked on Christina. "Unless the bars were put on as a cosmetic enhancement, which I doubt because they're one-inch reinforced steel and connected to the studs with bolts, you can't just pop them off without shredding the window trim."

"Stud?" Ella Belle asks in a dreamy voice.

"There she goes, thinking about Bo," Camellia says.

"And that's our cue to leave," Christina says.

Yes please, but I can't help add, "I know a bit about the mansion's history, and the bars weren't to keep anyone in. Rather, it was an effort to keep people out."

"As I said, spooky," Mae says.

It isn't spooky, but I'm better off not trying to solve that mystery. I gave up on that sort of thing almost three years ago. Turned in my badge, part of my ego, and definitely a pinch of my dignity.

"If that's the case, please come with us in case we do

encounter any, um—" Ella Belle gives me a set of puppy dog eyes that I'll have to warn Bo about if he hasn't already faced them.

"If the mansion is haunted, I'm staying away," Mae says. "I'm nervous enough about the farmhouse project in the fall."

"We're a team," Camellia says.

"The place isn't haunted," I say.

Christina brushes her hands together. "See? That solves it."

The "ghost" of my brother nudges me again, turning my attention away from speculation and toward the sway of Christina's hips and the elegant length of her spine as she pivots and slides into the seat of the SUV.

Ella Belle lets out a long, defeated sigh.

Christina slams the door as if to close the argument.

My pulse jolts.

As I said, the Easton Estate isn't haunted, but it has a lot of history. Part of that history, includes a little bit of mystery that my grandmother said her mother shared on her deathbed. I don't need my brother's urging to follow my instinct about the legendary Sweetheart Stone that two prominent families feuded over—claiming the other stole it when they didn't bless a forbidden marriage between the rivals. It's been missing for ages.

Could've been stolen, sold, buried like treasure...or it could be almost in plain sight.

And seeing Christina leave tugs something inside. I should know better, but I blurt, "I'll go with you just to make sure the site is safe."

Keep telling yourself that, bro. There goes Theo again, butting his dead backside into my business.

Ella Belle throws her arms around me in a hug that reminds me how very long it's been since I've had human contact—not that I'm at all interested in my best friend's wife. Nope. Not at all. Not my type. Too short. Too fiery and wily. Plus, I like my women a little more substantial. Or *liked*, past tense. Women like Christina.

My brother would've thought Ella Belle was cute, but he

could fight Bo for her. Not me. I'm out here in the middle of nowhere and single for a reason. Theo might've argued that it isn't a very good reason, but the coal fire keeps me warm enough.

Still, my gaze trails to Christina's silhouette behind the SUV's window.

Ella Belle bounces on her toes. "Thank you. I knew this would work out perfectly. With your skills around wood, plaster, and metal, along with Christina's vision for interiors, this first season will be a hit."

"I didn't say I'd sign onto your show."

Ella Belle grins like I'm a toddler trying to get his way, but ultimately, she's the one in charge.

Poor Bo.

Despite my better judgment, I get in my truck and follow the SUV through the gates because I'm curious about the Easton Estate...and the woman with the jade green eyes. If I've learned anything about my instincts, they've never led me astray even if doing so comes at a cost.

CHAPTER 4
Christina

Even though Louella Belle has the air conditioning in the SUV cranked, I roll my window down, letting the fresh air slap me in the face. Slap some sense into me.

No, I definitely didn't swoon. Buck was partly right, mostly my blood sugar was low, but I also started to have a panic attack—the real kind, not the one I sometimes claim to have when I can't find my keys or phone.

I dipped too far into the past, the one I've tried hard to forget. The one that nobody, not even a strong guy like Buck, can save me from.

Yes, I noticed his beefy biceps when I was reclined in his arms. It would've been hard not to with how hard they were and all. Like boulders. And he has those forearm muscles too—not sure what they're called, but they're cut. And tattoos. A beard with full lips that hide underneath and blue eyes that spark and sparkle.

I blink a few times, lost in my thoughts as Mae says, "Are we lost? I've been out this way and I don't think the mansion is in this direction."

If I don't get a grip, I'm going to be lost alright—runaway hot mess express out of control on the tracks.

"I just checked my phone's GPS, and we should've turned onto Route 17," Camellia says.

I study our surroundings as we pass. Spanish moss drips from the Live Oak trees, which means we're probably still in Georgia so that's promising. However, I get twisted and turned around on these country back roads, so there's no telling where we might be.

Give me a room that's outdated or in disrepair and I can visualize a way forward to contemporary comfort. Show me a map with the interstate or local roads, and I get lost. Never mind the fact that I don't know how to drive.

Several Georgian-style homes sit back from the road—miniatures of the mansion that we're supposedly headed toward. They give way to stucco buildings showcasing small businesses—the Low Country Real Estate Agency, the public library, Mirror Mirror Beauty Parlor, Sunny Side Pet Salon and Boarding, and Car-verse Sales & Repairs.

When we reach the main street, there's McIntyre's hardware store, several restaurants, the inn that's beyond repair, and the Starlight, a classic diner that pumps out the delicious scent of fresh biscuits. My stomach begs for carbs.

"What are we doing back in Butterbury?" I ask.

"Figured we were all hungry," Louella Belle says. "What better way to begin our tour of the mansion than with lunch."

"The best way to begin the tour of the mansion, is at the mansion," I grumble.

She winks at me in the rear-view mirror.

"Louella Belle, what's gotten into you today?" I ask, aghast.

"Any southerner worth their charm knows hospitality." She sweeps her hand toward the diner.

"We've been eating at the Starlight for weeks straight," Mae says as if she too is eager for a change of pace.

"I mean for Buck. If he's going to be our contractor, we have to treat him right."

I open my mouth to protest.

Louella Belle slices her hand diagonally through the air as we get out of the SUV. "Just go with me on this."

"I would if you'd tell us what *this* is," I say. "First, you drag us out to the woods to a guy who may as well be the huntsman from Snow White—"

"I was thinking James Bond's buff brother, but whatever suits your fancy." Louella Belle giggles like she knows something I don't.

I give her an eye roll that my thirteen-year-old self would applaud me for. "Now, we're back where we started without a clue to your plan. Care to share what's next?"

"Yes, French fries."

I shake my head. Not today, sister. Not any day.

Boots crunch on the gravel parking lot, and I make a wish to go back in time to pick one of the contractors from our applicants.

Buck gives us all a nod then says, "I thought we were headed to the mansion."

"Figured we'd better gain our strength first and have some lunch," Louella Belle says smartly.

"You make it sound like we're going to fight crime or slay a dragon," Camellia says.

"Did you make that dragon sculpture outside your forge?" Mae asks Buck.

"Yeah—Bo, my brother, and I used to play Dungeons and Dragons in the woods," Buck answers without any hint of irony.

"Nerd," I mutter, sounding exactly like my sister—she went from toddler to preteen, skipping all the childish stuff in between and even though I'm older, I had to keep up so she didn't get into trouble—considering where she's at now, I'm not sure I helped, after all.

Buck grunts, and if I weren't on my No-Man-Plan, it would be sexy in an alpha wolf kind of way. Instead, I envision him with green skin, nerdy glasses around a huge bulbous nose with a knobby wart on the end. Flies gather around his beard, and instead of orthodontic perfection revealing pearly whites, his teeth are a mass of crooked, stained, and rotting stink—like a cave-dwelling dork goblin.

I must be staring while I create this stand-in because, with a twist of his lips, he gives me a little nod like he can read my mind.

It's a mess in here, stay out. No boys allowed!

I have to force the dork goblin picture to remain in the frame of my mind. This project isn't going to be easy, and that's not just because I'm in charge of remodeling sixteen-thousand plus square feet of neglected Georgian architecture. If Buck signs on, I'll go from being a doer to being a goner. No kidding.

In my mind, I permanently replace the real-life vision of Buck with the dork goblin image.

"Let's get this over with," I mutter.

The four of us girls slide into a vacant booth at the back of the diner. Buck grabs a chair and sits at the end of the table. I'm seated on his left and can't help notice his ring finger is bare. Not even a tan line. The black lines under his nails suggest why. Who'd want to be with a gritty, thuggish, roguish guy like him? Barbarian women, that's who, and I'm not one of those.

I'm a lady. A lady boss!

"In a high school play, I had the role of a barbarian woman who helped slay a dragon," Camellia says.

I slap my hand over my mouth, terrified I spoke my thoughts out loud. The others carry on the conversation, asking her about the private school she attended in England. Relief sweeps through me because I must not have spoken my thoughts.

I hope.

A pair of blue eyes spark. They drift toward me and land on my hand, gripping the menu. I've scoured the thing, and I don't think there's a single item on it that's not fried, cooked in butter, high in salt, or otherwise outside my dietary parameters.

I angle the menu toward Buck then realize he has one at his place setting. Was he looking at it? My hand? My ring finger?

No, no, no. That's not possible. And if he was investigating my marriage status, he'd probably have just told Louella Belle to get my husband to do the contracting.

I preempt him. "In case you're wondering, I'm divorced. Husband number one, Dimitri, it turns out would've been fine with the demo work. *Smash, smash.* Fiancé number two would try to lure the two single women in our party into a dark corner or closet—let's just say he didn't only cheat at games of poker."

Louella Belle, Camellia, and Mae's conversation debating Shakespeare's best play goes quiet.

"You were married?" Louella Belle asks.

"Twice?" Mae follows up, lips parted.

Having neglected to fill them in on these tiny details related to my past, I take a long sip of water. "Once. The second one was a close shave with disaster."

"I was too," Camellia says in a small voice.

I flash her a modest divorcee-club look of resignation. "Not something I'm proud of, but I just wanted to let Buck know that there aren't any other candidates for the contractor job."

"Exactly what I've been saying," Louella Belle says.

I squish my eyes tight as if that will protect me from how this situation is suddenly wildly out of control—hot mess express going off the rails. "That's not what I meant. We have plenty of candidates who applied and have been vetted. I thought Buck was looking at my ring finger and figured he wondered if I was married—if so, my husband could fill his shoes. That way he could politely get out of this mess." The words start measured then relax because maybe I just offered us a mutually agreeable way out of this madness.

He grunts again. "Anyone that would divorce you couldn't fill the kind of shoes I wear."

I hurtle on like the runaway freight train I am, "Right, because you have on dingy work boots. But what I'm talking about is they didn't divorce *me*. The first one—"

Never mind the table, I think everyone in the diner is quiet, listening to me ramble and wondering what else I'm going to divulge. "Next time I'm driving," I say to Louella Belle. "If we'd just gone to the mansion in the first place, none of this would've happened."

"None of what?" Mae asks in her sweetly innocent way.

"I thought you didn't know how to drive?" Camellia says before I can shove my foot further down my throat.

Buck remains so still that if it weren't for the heat of his skin so close to mine, I'd think he was frozen. He doesn't react or respond to any of the conversation other than what he'd said about his boots.

I sit back in the booth, belatedly realizing that his comment was a compliment. He was saying that if we were married, he wouldn't divorce me. Little does he know it was the other way around—well, I was widowed then dodged a bullet with Les because he was little more than a con artist.

Rhondy appears with her order pad and pen in hand. She gives me a wink. I think that woman can read minds and if not that, she doesn't miss a trick. I'm convinced she hears every word spoken, and unspoken, in this diner.

"Salad?" she asks me, having kindly added it to the secret menu on account of my dietary requirements.

"French fries for the table. Christina, you have to try them," Louella Belle says.

I want to be mad at her for tricking us into going to Buck's and now coming here when the original plan was to head to the mansion, but Louella Belle's southern heart occupies my northern one, and I just can't be upset. But neither can I eat a French fry.

"You've never had our fries? No wonder you're so thin." Rhondy's question sounds like she witnessed a travesty, however, the statement doesn't come across like praise the way it would in my mother's city circles where a woman's physique is a measure of her social standing.

And for the record, I'm not thin—then again, neither is

Rhondy. I suddenly feel small and not the way my mother would like to see me.

The truth balances on my tongue, but before I can explain further, Rhondy moves on to take the next order. When she disappears to the kitchen window to give the slip to Paul, her husband and the cook, Louella Belle follows her.

Mae and Camellia resume their discussion about theater.

Buck studies me for a long moment like he would a textbook —like he's measuring just how big of a mess I am. A big, messy mess hidden under designer clothes, professionally styled hair, and the best bath and beauty products money can buy—that's a bonus of my social media influencer status.

It's almost like he sees right through the façade, accurately seeing where I land on the winning at life graph. The look he gives me could be a reminder to get my act together and do better or that he'd like to stand by and watch me crash and burn, I'm not sure.

I should turn in the other direction, but angle myself to face him as if to say, *Fire away.*

The muscle in his jaw works under his beard. *Give me your best shot.*

Challenge accepted. My lips form a flat non-smile.

His brows lift as though surprised I'd engage in this silent stand-off—one I've only played with other women to establish dominance. The world of social media influencers can be cutthroat.

I mouth, *Game on.*

He silently replies, *I always win.*

You've never gone up against me.

Definitely not.

I arch an eyebrow.

His lip quirks at the corner.

I tilt my head at a sharp angle.

His eyes narrow slightly.

Then our gazes lock. His spark, and I will not break the stare.

I cannot. If this is a battle of wills, watch me not eat chocolate or French fries or give into whatever *this* is.

Gradually, my cheeks warm and I fear they match the red vinyl of the booth.

I watched Les play cards enough times that I glean Buck wears a poker face now, but what does he hide beneath it? Curiosity? Scrutiny? Hostility?

From my periphery, Louella Belle returns and the three of them talk about the Designed to Last show like they're trying to sell it to a producer. However, Buck isn't really listening given his focus on me even though he nods and grunts a few times in their direction.

Mercifully, Rhondy appears with an armful of plates. My eyes flick away from Buck and to the basket of French fries in the center of the table as Rhondy sets down my salad.

Louella Belle says, "Your assessment?"

Rhondy chuckles. "Definitely."

My brow wrinkles.

"Huh?" Mae asks.

Louella Belle whispers, "I'll tell y'all later."

As I pick at my salad and Buck takes a bite of his burger, I can't help but wonder if what she's going to tell them has to do with us.

CHAPTER 5
Christina

I've never wanted a bite of a big, juicy hamburger so much in my life. Never mind the fries in the middle of the table, my sights are set on the ones on Buck's plate. I simultaneously want to ignore and annoy him like a kid at the school cafeteria lunch table because I want what he has.

I want him.

No, I don't.

Yes, I do.

No.

Yes.

I inwardly (and maybe out loud?) groan. This is not good. Not at all.

To my surprise, Buck's napkin is in his lap and he takes manly but polite bites of his burger—I wasn't expecting table manners, especially not after Louella Belle's barn comment, which he didn't refute.

"Not the beast you thought I was, eh?" He sets his burger down.

"You're doing this on purpose."

"You started it."

"Started what?"

His head tilts a few degrees and he mouths, *Challenge accepted.*

"It was in reply to your—" I splay my fingers and give my hand a little shake in the general vicinity of his head. Instead of a poker face, Buck's expression is pure amusement.

My face falls. Does that mean he won? "I demand a retry."

As has happened a few times today, three sets of eyes land on me. So that I don't have to explain what I'm talking about I do something forbidden, something crazy. I grab the last French fry off Buck's plate and stuff it in my mouth.

The girls cheer as if they helped defeat my fake post-food poisoning fear-of-fries-dragon.

Buck leans back in his chair because he won something else altogether, and I'm terrified of what that could mean.

But there's no time to consider it because the slightly crunchy exterior of the fry melts into the soft, pillowy interior of the fried potato. My eyes close.

Oh, salty heaven on earth.

From somewhere nearby, Louella Belle says, "I was right, Rhondy. Only, when I caught the bug, pie was involved."

When I open my eyes, Rhondy mouths something to Louella Belle, but I only catch the word *eyes*.

Feeling all eyes on me and eager to regain my professional persona of perfection, I say, "If we're considering Buck for the position, I have a few questions."

I dig in my purse for my tablet and open a fresh document. I try to present myself as a perfectly put-together career woman who can do it all. Underneath I'm like that closet that you shove everything into, telling yourself you'll organize it soon.

However, I am nerdy for interiors, taking other people's spaces and making the old new again—just not when it comes to myself or my own space. I never host at my apartment in New York because I'd be shamed off the internet, canceled forever. The truth is, I'm faking it until I make it and I have the uneasy feeling Buck sees right through me.

"What's your biggest life goal?" I ask him.

"Honor my Creator," he says without pausing to think.

"Oh, um, that's honorable." And not what I expected him to say. "Okay, where do you see yourself in five years?"

"Right here."

"At the Starlight Diner?"

"No, in Butterbury."

I make a note, *Not ambitious or upwardly mobile.* "Next, why do you want this job?"

"I don't." He pops what's left of his pickle into his mouth.

Louella Belle gives me a pleading puppy dog look.

My lips purse as I try not to sass her. *See? He doesn't even want to work with us.* "Alrighty then, have you ever been convicted of a crime?"

"What? Is this some kind of inquisition?" Louella Belle asks.

I give my best steely cop glare. "Just answer the question, Buck. If that's your real name."

"No, I have never committed or been convicted of a crime." His gaze doesn't waver from mine, and he doesn't do any of what Les called *tells* in card games—gestures that give away a lie.

"You've never gone over the speed limit? Jaywalked? Stole a piece of candy from a bulk bin?" I ask with disbelief.

I get what looks like a well-practiced steely cop glare back. "Are we done here?" he asks.

I make a note about his pristine record and then ask, "Last one. Describe yourself in one sentence."

"I'm honest, straightforward, and don't do complicated, high maintenance, or drama."

"That's perfect. You'll fit right in," Louella Belle says.

Buck and I must both disagree, meaning we agree with each other, because we each give her matching steely glares.

"Who's ready to go to the mansion?" She claps her hands together.

"That makes us sound fancy," Camellia says.

"You always sound fancy with your accent," Mae replies.

"I'm afraid it's disappearing. My parents will be mortified. My cousins will tease me. I'm terrified to go home."

"Whatever you do, don't go back to London anytime soon. We need you here," Louella Belle says.

I'm not sure what I need or where it is, but I'm terrified too. The hum inside gets louder. To quell my unease, I open Picto-Chat and post a quick selfie then fuss with filters for five minutes while the others continue to talk about the project while we wait for Rhondy to bring the bill.

After paying and leaving a generous tip, which she always tries to return, we step outside into the humid Georgia afternoon.

"Are we really going to the mansion this time?" I ask as we get into the SUV.

"Promise," Louella Belle says, but I almost don't hear her because I cannot ignore the way Buck moves fluidly to his truck—it's ninja-like and at odds with his large stature. It would be way better for my inner swoon if he lumbered around like a dork goblin. He's six-three or four, at least. Six-five maybe? A well-built beefcake.

"Mmm. Hamburgers."

"What was that?" Camellia asks as she closes the other rear door.

"Oh, um, the Starlight Diner does have great fries so I imagine the burgers are good too." I want to be mad at myself, bracing to hear my mother's voice in my head chewing me out for eating one but instead, I feel something else. I'm just not sure what it is...

Relief? Rebelliousness? Ready... but for what, I'm not sure.

In the reflection of the rearview mirror, Louella Belle's eyes twinkle like she too can read the minds of the desperate and lovelorn.

Not me of course, but you know, women who've had one point five failed marriages and aren't looking for romance because they know they fail at happily ever after.

Yeah, that's me.

This time, Louella goes the right way to the mansion and we pull up to what's little more than a moldering dump. My chest sinks a little because the fact of the matter is, in order to pull this off, I need a contractor that I don't have to micromanage, who can finish my sentences, and is able to anticipate what the project needs. But also who listens to direction, is willing to tear down walls, and work hard.

Buck gets out of the truck a moment later and takes a long look at me before turning to the Georgian mansion perched on a slight hill.

Avoiding him, I snap a photo and rapidly type a caption into my @DomesticDiva Picto-Chat account.

Get ready to see a lot of this place. Here's a little history lesson: it's a Georgian-style mansion and although I'm in Georgia, its roots are from the early 1700s to about 1830 when four different British monarchs ruled. Yep, they were all named George. It's also worth noting that this style dates back to ancient Rome and Greece. And there's no one here who I want to date. Not even a little.

I press *send* before I can erase that last part. I'm about to take a video and narrate it, pointing out to my followers that the hallmarks of this style include brick or stone, symmetrical design, including window and door placement and decorative elements such as pediments, arches, and ogees, when a shadow crosses into the frame.

I frown and lower my phone.

"What are you doing?" Buck asks.

"Oh, you're growly today."

"I'm growly every day." Buck's gaze slides and settles on my lips, sending a shiver through me.

"To answer your question, I took a photo and the caption wasn't about you at all. Then I was about to take a video for my fans."

"Was I in it?" Accusation fills his voice.

"No, I'm not going to post a picture of you on my grid." A

little voice in my head suggests that would be for my private photo file.

Ew. Don't be gross, Christina.

I almost make a gagging face.

"If you took anything with me in it, erase it immediately. You can't use it." Buck's tone is stern, commanding.

Almost a second too late, I recall our showdown. Okay, mister. Game on. "Why? Because I didn't get your good angle? Or were you banned from social media? Oh, wait, I know. You're in the witness protection program. Bad news, Buck. You stick out like a sore thumb."

He chuckles. "Is that so?"

This time I want to grunt. No, growl. This man scrambles my thoughts, my words, my feelings.

"Keep at it on that thing and you're going to be the one with sore thumbs." The look of disdain at my device could melt metal.

"If you're so concerned about my phalanges, I'll have you know that I work with a chiropractor to do exercises that help prevent tendonitis in my fingers, particularly for my thumbs."

He has the nerve to make a gagging face. "Phalanges, really? Sounds like TMI."

I narrow my eyes, affronted because I think he's insinuating that I'm a nerd for using the proper anatomical term or was he joking? With the beard, it's hard to tell.

"If you must retain your anonymity and stay off social media, problem solved. That simply means you can't be our contractor."

"Who said I wanted to be your contractor?" he counters.

My phone forgotten, I cross my arms in front of my chest, "You're here, aren't you?"

"Prime opportunity to see the old Easton Estate."

"Are you a history buff or something?"

"Definitely *or something*."

I roll my eyes.

"Oh, and for the record, all my angles are good." He pauses as if to let that sink in.

Oh, it sinks, right down to my knees. They're suddenly weak. However, I stand by my claim that I didn't swoon before, but in the sunlight, Buck isn't hard to look at. And he's right. His angles are good. I discreetly fan myself.

He continues, "I'm not banned from social media, nor am I a member of the witness protection program."

"Then why no photos?" My voice starts out slightly higher than normal before I get it under control.

The corner of Buck's lip quirks as if registering the effect he has on me. "Occupational hazard. Dismiss."

I balk at the commanding tone. "Is that an order?"

He nods then steps forward and into my personal space. "Because if you take a photo, I want to be sure it's not one that you'll erase."

I blink a few times, trying to understand his meaning. At first glance, Buck McDermott doesn't look like the flirtatious type, what with his imposing stature, grizzly tattoos, and the beard.

Oh, the beard.

But I might have been wrong about him because if I took a photo, I'd pull out my flashlight, tent up my sheet, and stare at it all night as I did with the *Teen Beat* magazines my sister would sneak into the house. I give my head a little Polaroid instant photo shake. No, erasing it and any thoughts of Buck are the smartest move I can make. I'm on the No-Man-Plan and sticking to it.

I take one of Meredith's deep breaths which turns into a mistake because I inhale Buck's smokey, leather scent.

Oh, my alpha male.

Legs, don't go wobbly on me now. I can't show any weakness in front of this solid, two feet planted on the ground, unwavering wall of muscle.

My exhale is ragged and the kind that I need to get under control—starting with no more French fries.

"Hot property, huh?" he says, looking at me and not the house.

Ugh. I melt. Right here on this hill under the Georgia sun.

Why is this man making me malfunction? Causing my pulse to hiccup. Giving me shivers even though it's a typical hot and humid southern summer day. He has a beard, for goodness' sake! That should be reason enough to back away.

Get yourself together, Cricket. Inhale, exhale like Meredith instructed.

I stagger back slightly, only I'm still in Buck's shadow and too close for comfort, for control. When I find my words, I add a little edge. "I was thinking it was more like a moldering dump. Overgrown, weedy, probably riddled with mildew."

He lifts and lowers his sculpted shoulder.

His massive, muscly shoulder. The kind that can heft entire logs in one calloused hand.

"I see some potential," he says, eyes still sparking in my direction.

"Definitely a fixer-upper. Emphasis on fixer-upper. Lots of fixing and upping before it's habitable."

Buck's brow furrows because we both know that was a word salad and not the kind I had for lunch.

"I mean, what's with the bars on the windows?"

"The metal work adds to the charm," he says offhandedly.

"If you're a prison guard." I get prison guard, military, commanding officer vibes from him, but he's a blacksmith and a contractor and likely doesn't answer to anyone.

"With a little TLC, it could have some curb appeal."

"Hey, that's exactly what you said, Christina." Mae's sweet voice is like the brakes on the wildly out-of-control rollercoaster of a conversation.

I want to deny her claim because Buck knowing that I agree with him is akin to him winning the game. The one he started. I stop short of popping my thumb on my nose and waggling my fingers like a child. Not that I ever did that while growing up because it was all about comportment, order, and control.

Mostly.

Except right now, I feel torn between my anxiety and not

running away from this situation like a grown human adult. I grip tightly to perfection with one hand, and the other one is stiff and shaky. I've learned that the only way I can divert attention from the shaky one is to make everything appear perfect—at least that's what I tried to do with my sister whenever our mother turned up. Mom was absent most of the time. Dad was a drinker and had a temper, so we steered clear of him. I had to try to tame Katelyn, my wild child little sister. I figured if I could behave myself and take care of her, the famous Sylvia Lancaster would be around more often.

Buck's blue eyes capture mine as if catching me spinning away and into my lonesome, never good enough, thin enough, smart enough, or pretty enough thoughts.

The thing no one understands is that when my mind races like this, the solution is to make everything just right. I'm afraid if I don't, everything is going to fall apart because it always has.

That's why I'm a self-admitted Type-A go-getter. If there are goes to be gotten, I'm the one to get them.

Or something.

Buck's shoulder taps mine and stings like a slap across the face to get myself together. "You ready to go inside, sweetheart?"

"My name is Christina, not sweetheart."

"Not Cricket either?"

"Not sweetheart or Cricket." I exhale sharply, wondering why during the fog of my loss of consciousness I said anything about my middle name.

"I know, sweetheart." The corner of his lip quirks. Of course it does.

Oh, this man.

With fists clenched on the edge of a tantrum, I march across the overgrown lawn and not because I'm taking orders. I'm rallying because I'm going to fix up this mansion and make it a hot property despite obstacles, anxiety, and the lack of a contractor.

At my back, Louella Belle says, "Kim will email you the contract before the end of the day."

I falter. Does that mean Buck agreed to be part of this enterprise? I need to game plan, fast. What can I do to thwart him? To make him not want to go through with it? Then a second question floats into my mind. Why am I so dead set against Buck being the contractor? He's capable, available, and not hideous.

Except for the beard. Not a fan. Not really.

My shoulders sag as I chug up the hill because I can't come up with a good reason to fire him before he's even started. Well, except for the way he makes me shiver inside despite the heat of the day. That should be grounds for dismissal.

However, possibly, for the first time in a long time, I cannot say no.

CHAPTER 6

Buck

Christina strides ahead of Ella Belle, Mae, Camellia, and me as we walk along the cobblestone driveway toward the grand entrance to the estate. She huffs and puffs, and I have no doubt she could blow this house down but would rather it not come to that.

She does seem fit to burst, but I don't think it's just about me. I sense pressure building inside her—a truth or desire or something desperate to get out.

A big part of my former job was reading people—body language, the words between the ones spoken, the glimmer in the eye, the tic in the jaw.

A subtle scratch of the nose could mean someone was lying. The twitch of the fingers could indicate nervousness. It involved training as well as intuition—a science and an art, really.

As for the woman with the delightful curves that flatter her floral skirt, she's trying very, very hard to hate me. That old rusty thing in my chest tries to grind itself awake. It's best for me to keep the fortress surrounding it protected against invasion.

I'm not easy to like, so I've been told. I'm guessing the beard and tattoos don't help either. Christina seems like someone who thinks she wants a guy in a custom-tailored monochrome suit or at least khakis and a sports jacket. I'd venture to guess that she doesn't know what she needs. I've played many roles, but finally, this is me—big, hairy, built, and possibly hate-able. I guess.

But not Christina. Nope. She's very, very likable, nice to look at, and fun to tease—especially with the way her true feelings shine pink on her cheeks through the veneer of glossy perfection she tries to create.

"I'm so glad you've officially decided to join us, Buck." Ella Belle's voice cuts into my thoughts.

I clear my throat and am about to reply, thanking her for the opportunity, when Christina interrupts.

"Are you serious? I thought we were the 'Hashtag Ladyboss-es,' a team, meaning we discuss these things first?"

"Kim needs the contract by the end of the weekend. Demo starts Monday."

"What about the permit, doesn't the contractor need to pull it?" Christina asks.

"Technically, Bo already did that so we could stick to the schedule." Ella Belle bites her lip. "Buck here will take over since Bo can't be on the jobsite regularly."

Christina exhales sharply through her nose and her gaze lands on me. I blink a few times so I don't get lost in those jade green pools of wonder.

"And what made you decide to grace us with your presence?" she asks.

"Gut feeling," I say.

"Considering it's full of a hamburger and French fries, I'm not entirely sure it's a trustworthy source of information."

"Never steered me wrong. Plus, you ate one of those fries, so it couldn't be all bad."

Her lips form a thin line. "Okay, listen up. This is my project. My rules—"

I think twice about confessing that I'm known for breaking rules.

She holds up her phone, likely for her social media account, and says, "Watch how it's done." She focuses it on me for a long moment then pans to the house and narrates, "Take a good look, folks. This is the *before*...and I cannot wait for you to see the *after* in a couple of months. It will be a full-scale transformation. Tell me what you think about the ivy growing on the stone. I say it gives the building character, but we may have to remove it to restore the integrity of the stone—" She continues to outline her vision for the exterior, which mercifully doesn't sound like it falls too far outside the bounds of simple restoration. As for the landscaping—I hear the words *fountain*, *water elements*, and *koi fish*.

Perhaps I should've thought through my decision a little more carefully. However, there's lore about this estate that connects to my ancestors, and I'll do anything that might help restore the family name.

Ahead of me, Christina opens the front door with a loud creak. A surprisingly cool gust of air billows out of the house, contrasting with the humid afternoon.

Cobwebs feature prominently and there's a rare stillness inside. My gut tells me to be on my guard, but this isn't an investigation—nope, it's a restoration, a renovation. Okay, maybe I'll do a little investigation, but it's more family history than an inquiry into criminal activity.

However, old habits don't necessarily die so I take the lead, testing the floorboards and making sure there aren't any hazards as we proceed through the foyer.

Christina stands in the center and gazes up at the chandelier, green eyes twinkling even though the crystals above do not. "This is going to be a lot of work."

Standing by her side, I say, "But it'll be worth it."

She startles and slaps her hand to her chest. "Alert a girl that you're standing there. You're as silent as a ninja."

"Would you prefer I stomp around?" I tease.

"No, but I didn't even realize you were there. Actually, maybe that's a good thing. That way, you can stay out of my—" Christina cuts herself off as she brushes a loose piece of her dark brown hair from her face and pulls out her phone, using it as a mirror. "Ugh. This humidity and the frizz. How do I fight it?"

"Maybe you don't. Perhaps you just give in." My voice is low, lazy, a mere suggestion rather than a command.

"Give into frizz?" She laughs. "You do know that I go live every day."

"I doubt your audience cares what your hair looks like."

Christina rolls her eyes. "Clearly, you don't understand."

"I'd argue that you don't. Your hair looks great."

She sniffs. "Says the man with the small animal growing on his face."

I stroke my beard. "Seriously, why are you so against facial hair?"

"It makes you look—" She gazes at the ceiling again. "Unpredictable."

"Good. That'll keep you on your toes." I waggle my eyebrows.

Her gaze lingers on mine for a moment then she starts to storm off in her heels and I grip her wrist to say something else, but she doesn't stop and not because she's still walking. The high heel of Christina's sandal catches in a loose floorboard and she loses her balance. My grip is strong and I reel her in until we're toe to toe—only, more like toe to high heel.

"I'm stuck." Her voice is strained like there's some subtext, something else in addition to her shoe, but my people reading skills aren't honed sharply enough to delve deeper.

"I know." I inhale her lilac scent and if I weren't steady on my feet, I'd wobble too. I clear my throat before saying, "I was going to add that this building is unpredictable. We have to be careful. Consider it a work zone until the project is complete."

"That's my line. Remember, I'm in charge."

"Of course, I'm just doing my job and looking after—"

"Buck, I don't need looking after."

I glance down at her shoe. "Clearly."

She makes a noise of irritation. "Will you at least help me get free?"

Again, I sense something unspoken, an emotion that she needs freedom from. I study her for a long moment.

"Please don't look at me like that." She speaks in a strangled whisper.

"Like what?" I play dumb.

"You know what I mean."

"Like I'm trying to figure you out?"

She tucks her chin back. "I was going to say like you feel bad for poor, helpless Cinderella with her shoe stuck in the floor."

"Could've happened to anyone. Good thing you didn't go straight through."

"You just wait, Buck McDermott. This place is going to be perfect," she says as if I questioned her abilities.

She struggles to get her shoe off. Then balancing on one foot and using me as a ballast, she tugs it free from the floorboard. I won't lie, having her soft hand gripping my arm isn't a bad feeling. Her skin is relatively cool to the heat I give off—I've always run hot which doesn't do me any favors working with molten metal all day.

My voice rasps when I say, "About your goal to make this place perfect, I never doubted."

She straightens and confusion wrinkles her features. "Oh."

"You don't have to prove anything to me."

Christina's shoulders lower a fraction as though she realized I'm not armed—not anymore. Sure, I've enjoyed getting a rise out of her, but that's because I know she's hiding her real personality under the one she shows the world. I want to see the frizz, the bare feet, and the girl who steals a French fry because I get the sense a long-ago bout of food poisoning wasn't the thing that kept her from eating them. The salad for lunch at the diner with the best biscuits and home cooked food in the state was a clear indicator of what kind of city girl she is—although my mother raised me to eat my greens like a good boy and I won't turn my nose up at vegetables.

She replaces her shoe and then jerks her hand away from my

bare arm as if she realized she'd gripped the handle to a cast-iron skillet with bare skin. With a wobbly stride, she starts deeper into the house and pulls out her phone. "Everyone, this is *before* the magic happens on the inside. Can you imagine the transformation? I'm talking a complete renovation—of course, we'll be retaining many of the classical elements, but the kitchen is woefully dated. Let's go have a look."

For a moment, I think Christina talks to me, but the cheer in her voice wouldn't be coming my way. Nope, she's talking to the screen and presumably thousands of unknown people—and she's worried about me being unpredictable?

I'm as steady as they come. Ella Belle didn't need to call ahead —not that I even use my cell phone except for emergencies— because she knew I'd be at the forge working. And if I'm not there, I'm out getting supplies, dining, or hiking with Gremlin somewhere on the massive and secluded property.

I trail Christina and hear the others elsewhere in the house. Their voices echo through the dust and patches of sunlight shining through the muntin bars as well as the metal bars on the windows.

There will be plenty of time to explore the estate's many rooms and study the craftsmanship. Then I recall Ella Belle saying we get started on Monday. It's Wednesday. That leaves me with less than a week to see if any clues trace back to my family.

I hurry after Christina, dodging discarded furniture and broken fixtures. She pans her phone's camera and pauses on me in the doorway with a gasp.

"And what you see is not a ghost. Rather, it's the beefcake contractor, Buck. Say hi to everyone, Buck." She belatedly must realize she included a certain adjective.

"If I'm a beefcake, you're a lady cake. Oh, and hi, everyone." I lift and lower my hand in a stilted wave, ignoring the call to perform for her social media.

Eyes wide, she lowers her device. "Lady cake? Are you trying to mock me in front of my followers?"

I swiftly move on. "I have a few questions about the house."

She shakes her head like I'm deranged and then almost but not quite missing a beat, she lifts her phone again. "Fire away. Chances are if you're wondering about this place, my followers are too."

My expression reveals zero emotion because that's what I was trained for, however, annoyance pricks me. "I'd rather keep it between you and me."

"Ooh. A mystery. Intriguing. I'll report back, folks." Christina lowers her phone. "Why'd you have to ruin that shot?" she asks me.

She's not far off the mark when it comes to mystery. "Ruin what?"

"That would've been a great live conversation for us to have to get people more invested in the project."

"Isn't it being filmed for TV? That seems like a decent enough investment."

"My mother was on TV. That's going the way of the dinosaurs. Social media is relevant now. It's modern, the new pink. You should check out my Picto-Chat account. I'm @DomesticDiva. I have over a million followers."

I fight a roll of my eyes. "I'm more of a renaissance man. Literally—I studied that period of history while I was still in college. This house, though not built until the early 1800s, adhered to those principles and—"

"Then you'll be able to help with the restoration work."

"Obviously. But I'm more interested in the occupants."

"I hate to break it to you, but they're no longer with us."

"Obviously," I repeat.

"So—" Christina opens her hands and gives them a little wave, urging me to get to the point.

"My great-great-grandmother was a servant here. My great-great-grandfather became the blacksmith's apprentice."

Christina presses her hand to her chest as if touched by how romantic that is. "Is this where they met?"

I nod. Hopefully, she's not as skilled as me at reading people because there's more to the story that I don't say. I'm not sure I want the mystery shared with the world. I waffled about taking the job, but that only lasted the duration of lunch.

Cons:

- I'm busy at the forge
- I didn't intend to get back into general contracting
- After retiring from the agency, I told myself no more investigations

Pros:

- Ella Belle said I'd be helping her and Bo out—and I'll do anything for friends and family
- I thought Easton Estate was leveled for a golf course, guess the mayor, Gatlin Stoll, didn't get his way
- Christina. End of story

So there I went, waffling back and forth. In the end, my loyalty and curiosity about the mystery won...and meeting Christina (aka Cricket, another mystery) may have tipped the scale slightly.

Bo's father used to rate jobs as either dry (meaning, they were straightforward remodels or home improvement projects that involved textbook carpentry) or juicy. He lived for the latter—historic buildings with unique features, projects lesser carpenters claimed were impossible, and the truly challenging type of woodworking that could win awards if there were such a thing.

Easton Estate is on the juicy end of the spectrum...and so is the lady cake, slightly annoyed interior designer standing in front of me.

"Oh, come on. That would've been great material for my followers. Their love story started here? Tell me it had a HEA."

"A what?" I'm very familiar with most three-letter acronyms, especially governmental ones.

"HEA stands for happily ever after."

"Oh, right. Yes. I'm here aren't I?"

Christina snorts as if that's a debatable outcome.

My lip twitches because we're back to playing our game. This woman has walls built around herself—they're bigger and stronger than the ones that support this building. I've played many roles and I've broken many rules...and walls. I intend to find out about the past—both hers and the McDermott family mystery, including the Sweetheart Stone.

CHAPTER 7
Christina

Ignoring the ignoramus who didn't know what a HEA is, I return to my phone and record another segment, telling my followers all about my vision for the modernized kitchen. As I pass an old cabinet, I notice the knob is shaped like a heart. I trace my finger around it—ever since I was a little girl, I've always had an eye for hidden hearts. They remind me that love is everywhere. It's such a novelty for a working kitchen like this.

I open the cabinet and my finger catches when it doesn't budge. A yelp escapes when I feel my nail snap. My phone goes dark as I wave my hand, trying to diminish that particularly nauseating pain when a nail bends and breaks.

"Ouch. Ouch."

A large figure rushes over, coming to my aid for the third time today. I wave him away. This time I'm not falling. Nope. My feet are steady on the ground. In fact, I make myself a promise not to fall for Buck McDermott. No, I meant I will not fall *in front of* Buck McDermott. Never again.

What is it with me and prepositions today? To avoid brain fog, from now on, my morning routine will consist of an energy bar, a clear mind, and work boots.

"Are you okay? What happened?" His voice is even, calm.

I show him my finger with the ragged summer blue French manicured orphan as if that's explanation enough. He rubs his thumb over it.

I shiver even though a bead of perspiration rings my hairline.

"I have a file in my truck."

Hope enters my voice. "You have a nail file?"

The corner of his lip tugs to the side. "No, it's a metal rasp."

I huff at his teasing because obviously, I'm not going to fix my nail with a home improvement tool.

"Are you going to be able to manage this worksite? You seem like you might be one of those high maintenance, uppity nail polish people." Buck leans against the counter with his arms crossed and his legs splayed in pure cocky comfort on the jobsite.

My cheeks heat and I incline my head at a, *Did you really just ask that?* angle. I straighten to my full height, which is medium, especially in these heels. "Let me set something straight right here, right now, buster."

With an arched eyebrow, Buck squares off with me. If it weren't for his lingering smirk, I'd make a run for it. The guy is intimidating. But his gaze shivers my timbers...or something. I can't explain it. Nor is it fair.

I'm a single ladyboss and proud. No way will I let his eyes or his lips or the rumble of his voice chip away at my walls...or my nails.

"Yes?" he asks in a tone that is entirely aggravating.

I poke my intact fingernail into his chest then lower it because I risk another breakage. "This is my job. You got that? My work-site. You understand?"

"Perfectly," he answers.

Expecting a snappy retort, I dip my head back. "Perfectly?" I repeat.

His blue eyes spark in the low kitchen light and hold mine. Once again, I sense he's not carrying a sword, here to slay dragons. Rather, he's the kind of hero who'd admire and respect its scales, wings, and fire breathing abilities before convincing it to use those qualities and powers for good. I give myself a shake because I've been in the country (or clouds) for far too long.

"Okay." My voice is scratchy like my nail.

"Okay," he repeats and the corner of his lip returns to full-quirk.

"What?" I ask.

"I have to admit that I like seeing you flustered, impassioned, real, raw instead of the glossy city girl you portray on TV."

"Social media," I correct.

"And TV on the Designed to Last show."

"Fair enough, but we're going to set some ground rules, right here—"

"Right now," he finishes.

I click my tongue with annoyance. "Number one, please do not finish my sentences. Two, do not intentionally fluster me or seek opportunities for, what was it you want to see? Me—impassioned, real, and raw. There will be none of that."

"Is there a three?"

"Open your mouth again and we'll find out."

And wouldn't you know it? He does. He opens that mouth of his with those full lips. "There's just one problem. You're a Type-A personality."

I sling my arms in front of my chest. "So?"

"I'm the contractor—this is *my* jobsite."

I give a patronizing laugh my mother would praise me for. "That's adorable. You're an alpha dog and you know what's great about dogs? You can train them to obey."

He rocks back on his heels, eyes full-on sparkly and shiny with...with mirth? Like I'm the one that's adorable when I'm all puffed up and trying to be mean. "More like an alpha wolf, but fine."

Oh, this man.

And here I go, getting flustered again. From now on, I'm on a steady diet of energy bars in the morning, a clear mind, work boots, *and* Meredith's deep cleansing breaths to retain my patience. I will be unflappable around this guy.

"I cannot wait until this project is over," I grind out.

"Thank goodness for deadlines, but I have to tell you these kinds of things often take longer than expected."

"I know that. This isn't my first rodeo, cowboy." I narrow my eyes. "I bet you'd like it to take longer so you can make more money."

He shakes his big, shaggy head. "Not so. Just want to manage your expectations."

"And what do you think those are?"

"You want perfection, reliability, communication—and someone to deliver exactly what you want." He says each word slowly like he's selecting chocolates from a box.

Does he have any idea how much those traits turn me on? He must because my cheeks are hot, my pulse high, and the inner shivers intense. I need to get away from Buck McDermott because this kind of physical response is not normal and sets my anxiety up for a nice little melt down.

I open and close my mouth, waiting for something sassy to come, but I fear I'll spout off another word salad, so instead, I storm off, using the last of my phone battery's charge to illuminate the floor so I don't get stuck or stumble.

The thing is, Buck isn't entirely wrong about me. I am high maintenance on the outside, but that's mostly so I can hide the mess on the inside. Instead of being up half the night picking apart everything I said to my followers, it'll be my conversation with Buck that's the focus of my scrutiny.

The next morning, we're back at #Ladyboss HQ. Mae, Camellia, and I gather around the wooden table to review the plan for the

Easton Estate. I'm bubbly because I finally feel like I arrived at the cool-girl table.

Growing up, I was a chubby nerd—a disappointment to my fashionable, fancy, well-to-do, and successful mother. During high school, I waited for the day one of the pretty and popular girls would take me under her wing and give me a makeover like in the movies.

Suffice it to say, it never happened.

Instead, I started improving my surroundings—area by area in the massive suite in my dysfunctional family's penthouse apartment in Manhattan. Eventually, it caught on and I figured out that if I could style a desk area, I could do my hair, makeup, and clothes as well.

With these three women, I finally feel like I found my tribe—except I'm afraid they're going to realize I'm a fraud and kick me off the playground.

Louella Belle comes in with a container that wafts the scent of strawberries and cream. "I come bearing breakfast."

"I thought you were going to say good news—Buck is off the job," I mumble the last part. I can't endure another restless night thinking about him.

"It's very good news. Rhondy made us her famous strawberry shortcakes." Louella Belle opens the container.

"For breakfast?"

Louella Belle shrugs. "There's fruit included."

"I meant good news like Buck decided to bow out of the project," I say more clearly this time.

Camellia balances her elbow on the table and rests her chin on her fist. "Tell us more about Buck. The two of you were alone for quite a while yesterday."

Mae's features scramble like she's fighting a sneeze...or a smile. "Yeah, tell us about him."

"We're all eyes. I mean ears," Louella Belle says quickly.

"What are you talking about? Buck? You mean the alpha male

dog with the brownish-red hair, beard, and rough and gruff personality?"

"And a beard," Mae and Camellia say at the same time.

"I mentioned that."

"Doesn't this breakfast look delicious?" Louella Belle asks as if trying to keep us on track.

"You mean Buck the guy who's incredibly unlikable?" I counter.

"But he's the most capable." Louella Belle taps the air, making her point.

"He's a country boy," I say.

"A man," Camellia corrects. "Buck is all man."

"Man-licious." I. Said. That. Out. Loud. I hide my face in my hands—hopefully, they'll think it's because I'm flabbergasted at their insistence Buck is at all attractive. Because he is. "I don't know what that means. It just came out. I probably meant the strawberry shortcake looks delicious. Yeah, that sounds right."

It's official. I've graduated from waking hot mess in the morning to walking hot mess—I've gone off the rails.

"I don't think the red tint to her cheeks is makeup," Camellia whispers.

"It's hard not to notice Buck is man-licious—the guy in the black T-shirt that perfectly highlights his biceps, triceps, and what's this muscle called?" Mae points to her upper forearm.

I cannot deny how safe I felt in said arms. They were strong, capable, and looking up into his eyes was dreamy, a HEA for sure. "We're here to discuss the estate." My voice cracks, betraying my thoughts.

"Do we have a name for it yet?" Louella Belle asks as if purposefully ignoring my internal struggle because she knows eventually I'm going to break and come clean.

"The McDermott residence." Mae giggles.

"You think he's going to buy it?" I ask, feeling a little lost in the convo. The three of them toured the house, leaving me with my phone...and Buck.

"He'll buy it for his wife," Camellia says in her confident British tone.

The nervous hum under my skin gets kicked aside by an incoming shiver when the discussion detours in this direction. "He's married? I didn't see a ring."

Was my voice too high-pitched? Why did I ask that? Are they suspicious?

Camellia shrieks and points at me. "But you looked."

"Oh, she was looking." Louella Belle's tone is very, *I told you so*. "Sparks were flying."

"We all have to wear love-tinted glasses to protect our eyes," Mae says.

"I went to the soulmate store and they have a pair of love goggles in your size," Camellia says.

My lips part in shock and disbelief. "Is that a real thing?"

"In London."

My eyes must bulge.

"I'm kidding," Camellia says.

"Ladies, what are you talking about? I was not falling for Buck McDermott."

Mae opens her purse and passes Louella Belle a hair scrunchie.

"I was right. It was swoon at first sight. But I was smart enough to consult Rhondy for confirmation."

"If I knew about Rhondy's matchmaking skills, I would've had her confirm before I offered you my last scrunchie," Mae says.

"Well, lucky for me, I'm one pink velvet scrunchie richer."

"You bet a hair scrunchie?" I ask.

Louella Belle tugs her hair into a high ponytail. "I love scrunchies."

I slap the table. "Ladybosses, focus."

"Oh, we're focused alright. On the love heart eyes you and Buck made at each other over the sugar bowl at the Starlight." Louella Belle says in her southern accent.

"Heart eyes? More like hate eyes," I say.

There's a short burst of knowing laughter before Camellia says, "You swooned."

"I did no such thing." I will deny it until my last breath, but explaining why I actually passed out yesterday isn't possible because then I'd have to tell them my first husband was a criminal, leaving me feeling vulnerable because I'd trusted him.

"Then what happened?" Louella Belle singsongs.

"Low blood sugar." It's half the truth.

"What have you had to eat today?"

"Coffee."

"That's not food." Louella Belle takes a serving of the strawberry shortcake out of the container, sets it on a plate, and pushes it toward me.

The biscuits smell buttery and look divinely flaky. The whipped cream is like a heavenly cloud. I pick up a strawberry and pop it in my mouth to pacify them.

"The whole thing." Mae hands me a fork.

"You can't force-feed me."

"You subsist on coffee, salads, and what my daddy calls rabbit food," Mae says.

"So?"

"So this isn't the city and we're not your followers," Camellia says gently. "Meaning, we're not going to judge you."

I lean back, but not too far because I'm on a stool and truthfully, I've only had a strawberry today so I don't want to risk passing out again.

Their eyes are soft. Their expressions open, inviting me to speak honestly, speak my heart.

I study my hands, not sure what part of the story to tell. "If I look a certain way, everyone will think I have it all together."

"But you don't?" Camellia asks—a question and not a statement.

"No one does," Louella Belle follows up. "You should've seen me when I came home. I was the messiest mess. Seriously, I didn't even have a change of clothes. I was living in Vanna-white, had no job...and look, here we are. I'd say things turned out perfectly."

"That's the problem."

"What?" they all ask at the same time.

"Perfection." The idea of talking about it after the many hours I've spent with Meredith exhausts me. The V between my eyebrows deepens—my mother always warned me against making this facial expression because it causes wrinkles.

That should've been the first clue that, as Meredith says, control is an illusion. And that chasing it is like trying to grab a tiger's tail. There are two possible outcomes, either I'll never catch it or I'll get bitten.

I understand now.

"Ladybosses, I think I just had a breakthrough." My voice starts slow and small then builds as I tell them about how I struggle with anxiety. "Growing up, my mother was very controlling but largely absent. She liked everything a particular way. My younger sister never got that memo. It was up to me to take care of her and make sure she didn't upset Mom. In an effort to be the good girl so my mother didn't get more disappointed with me than she already was—because all she saw was a chubby and dorky nuisance—I've strived to make everything perfect then maybe I'll be good enough?"

"Including your eating habits?" Camellia asks gently.

I nod, feeling slightly embarrassed. "I originally blamed my poor eating habits on the fast pace of life, busyness, and fitting in, but realize it's a way to control outside what sometimes feels like chaos inside." I tell them how my father was an alcoholic and stole from his clients to support his gambling addiction. However, I leave out the parts about how I married an art thief and a professional card player and a cheat.

Mae says. "I was the baby in the family and to this day am treated as such."

"I didn't know my parents," Louella Belle says in a small voice.

Camellia remains quiet.

"Even though I struck out on my own and made a name for myself without my mother's help, I'm behaving just like her—trying to control and micromanage every little thing."

"Does that include things like chocolate and French fries?" Mae asks.

"Maybe." My thoughts come like lightning bugs and it's hard to catch them before my eye spies another.

"Wait, what do you mean making a name for yourself without your mother's help? What's wrong with receiving help?" Louella Belle asks, having learned this lesson recently.

"Who's your mother?" Camellia asks, having caught that comment even though I hoped we could carry on for the rest of our lives without mention of it.

It's a question I avoid at all costs. The tickle in my throat grows.

They all stare at me, waiting.

My choices are to answer or take a bite of the strawberry shortcake. I did that yesterday with the French fry and look where it got me. Right here, being interrogated by a group of #Ladybosses.

"Um, Sylvia Lancaster."

Camellia gasps. She's from England, of course, she recognizes the name. She was also very popular overseas.

"But your last name is Abernathy," Mae says.

"That's my father's last name. My mom became well known before they got married." I leave off that my last name was *Petrov* and that I narrowly avoided *Streckle*.

"Your mother is Sylvia Lancaster? I missed a lot of pop culture having spent so much time traveling abroad, but she's world-famous."

"Yes, I know," I say.

"But we didn't," Camellia says. "She's a celebrity, a TV personality. I remember when she hosted that chat show and—"

"The game show. I once tried to be a contestant, but they didn't pick me," Louella Belle says.

"Why didn't you tell us?" Mae asks.

Because I don't tell anyone. The list is long, but for starters:

- My mother has the obnoxious habit of dropping names of the rich and famous so whoever she's talking to knows exactly what kind of company she keeps
- I didn't tell them because even though she did the dirty job of creating emotional distance between us, I do my part to ensure the physical distance
- Because I don't want people to think I'm like her by proxy

The answer I go with is slightly hazy. "Because I didn't want it to change things."

Silence stretches between us as they process this news.

Louella Belle squeezes my hand. "It doesn't change anything, Christina. Not at all. We may have heard of her, but we know you and you're our best friend."

"That's right. If there's more to the story you want to share, go ahead, but whatever the case, we're here for you," Camellia adds.

"And so is this strawberry shortcake." Louella Belle waggles her eyebrows and wolf whistles the dessert for breakfast.

We all laugh and they dig in...and so do I because I cannot resist strawberry shortcake or the trust and understanding of my friends.

After a few bites, I swallow back my pride and I ask, "What exactly is making eyes?" I throw air quotes when I speak the last two words so they know I wasn't doing it—whatever it is.

"They say that the eyes are the window to the soul," Camellia says wisely.

"There's the casual glance, the fleeting glimpse, and then

there's 'making eyes.' It's a form of flirtation and is often a result of attraction," Louella Belle says as if she's a relationship expert.

I'm about to deny it, but Mae cuts across me. "The eye flirting game was strong between you and Buck."

"Let's role play. I'll be Buck. Camellia, you be Christina," Louella Belle says.

They demonstrate with an abundance of smoldering and eyelash fluttering.

I turn my head defiantly to the side and sniff. "We were having a war of wills."

"Who will give in first and admit they're interested in the other one?" Camellia says.

"Rhondy called it," Louella Belle says.

After a long moment, I breathe out and say, "That was why she winked at me."

"She's a professional when it comes to recognizing those kinds of things." Louella Belle goes on to tell us about Bo, a different booth at the diner, and a slice of pie that changed their lives.

With my mouth agape at the accusation that Buck and I were "making eyes" I can't help myself and take another bite of the buttery, sweet, and creamy strawberry shortcake. It's delicious and makes the hashtag *nom, nom, nom* scroll through my brain.

But if I let myself think this and react this way to dessert, what will happen next time I see Buck?

Because that man is a whole lot more than a tasty snack.

He's man-licious.

I try to convince myself to stick to the No-Man-Plan with the same fervor I've resisted cake since my mother stopped serving it on my eleventh birthday.

But Buck is just so tempting.

CHAPTER 8

Buck

It's Monday, the first day of Designed to Last shooting, which also means it's demolition day. I am ready to smash stuff after spending all weekend unable to get Christina out of my head. And man, did I try. Let's see, between Saturday and Sunday, I:

- Hit the heavy bag with a massive workout, hoping to punch thoughts of her lips from my mind
- Worked in the forge late into the night until my eyes crossed, trying to erase the memory of the glimmer in her jade-green eyes
- Took a long hike, thinking I could walk or run away from the way she felt in my arms when I caught her—both times
- Went to church with my parents and prayed the Lord would make me forget her laughter
- Read up on the history of Easton Estate and checked it against family lore—who am I kidding? That only made me think about Christina more

- And distracted in thoughts about her, I messed up the letters on the gift I'm making for Bo and Ella Belle—the metal isn't forgiving

And now, here I am, still thinking about Christina—the looks we exchanged at the diner, her vision for the estate, and her comments about me being unpredictable.

As I pull the truck down the long driveway that brings the mansion on the hill ever closer, I won't have to wait much longer to see her. And if I had any sense, I'd know that's not a good thing.

The parking area bustles with people, vans, and a lot of expensive filming equipment. I recall that Christina doesn't know how to drive. Maybe I can remedy that. Living out here, having a range of basic survival skills helps, especially during hurricane season—never mind simply knowing how to operate a motor vehicle.

Bo stands next to Ella Belle with his arm slung around her shoulders like it's always belonged there—I like her a lot more than his ex, but somewhat resent that she twisted my turkey into this situation.

For a fleeting moment, I imagine my arm draped casually over Christina's shoulder. Picture her head nestled into the spot between my arm and chest. Feel her warmth, softness...

I nearly bump into a young guy carrying a tray of pastries.

"Excuse me, sir. Do you know where the craft services set up is?" he asks.

Mae hollers in our direction and gestures for the kid. I spin and grab a coiled pastry topped with a cinnamon glaze. I haven't eaten breakfast yet and no one wants someone my size going down because of low blood sugar. There's no one on set large enough to catch me.

After taking a bite, I have a moment of disorientation—a rare flashback to when I was on a case in Vienna. The scent and taste of the cinnamon with the flakey crust reminds me that there's no safety net. No one is there for me if I'm taken out.

And that's by design, right?

I left the city and the agency to live a quiet life. When I was younger, it was Theo, Bo, and me—we were on top of the world, playing football, chasing girls, living life like red-blooded, southern American teenage boys were meant to. The robbery changed everything. Bo and I bounced back. I'd do anything for Theo to be here with us—trying to cope, he strayed down the wrong path and never came back. If only I'd seen the signs sooner and been able to help him. It's a regret that routinely battles for first place in the big list of my mistakes and failures.

However, Theo definitely would have called dibs on the brunette that struts toward me wearing a sensible pair of work boots. However, that's about the only article of clothing or accessory that doesn't demand my attention. I trace my way up her legs covered in denim to the plaid halter top, thin gold necklace, hoop earrings, and her hair in a high ponytail.

Christina holds what looks like a digital clipboard, only at a second glance it's the tablet she used when interviewing me and taking notes. She swipes it a few times then pulls her phone out, holding it aloft, and says, "We're live from the Easton Estate. Be sure to tune into Designed to Last on HLTV, but stay here with me to catch all the behind-the-scenes footage, including our planning process, demolition, and maybe some drama." She bobbles her eyebrows.

"Drama?" Bo asks, sounding dubious.

He and I exchange a look.

Ella Belle swiftly moves into damage control, assuring her husband there will be none of that. Bo has experienced enough on-screen drama for a lifetime. I've experienced enough real-life drama for two.

"Howdy, partner," Bo calls.

"Hey, brother," I reply.

We do the same not-so-secret handshake we've been doing since we were eight years old.

"You realize we've been doing that for nearly forty years?" he asks.

"Funny, I was just thinking the same thing."

"We're not getting any younger."

"Speak for yourself," Ella Belle says.

Bo kisses her on the cheek. "Darlin', you're getting sweeter by the day."

"You guys, I'm right here." I give them a good-natured groan.

"And so am I. In fact, I just caught that on camera." Christina smiles mischievously.

Bo brushes his hand down his face. "I'm never going to escape this am I?"

"You can head back to Lilypad Lane and I can take it from here," Ella Belle offers.

"And miss demo day? No way. I have to take at least a few swings to remind you how manly I am and you know, work out my frustration." He playfully flexes his arm.

"Yeah, me too," I mutter.

Christina calls for a team huddle, summoning what she calls her ladybosses and the rest of the crew. Numerous cameramen, including those for drone footage, are on set, plus the lighting crew, and others holding boom mics that look like they've skewered a small fuzzy animal on the end of a long stick.

The guys on the crew ogle her—some cast flirtatious smiles and others try to be more discreet. Either way, my blood suddenly burns.

Listening to Christina talk about this juicy job with confidence and enthusiasm, makes my mouth go dry. It's not that I'll have a hard time taking orders from her—I'm not completely insubordinate. Just a little. Also, I can't blame the Georgia heat. I'm used to it, plus working the forge built up my tolerance. It wasn't the pastry and I'm not under the weather. So why am I suddenly desperate to lap up water from the pond at the back of the property?

"If anyone has questions, please consult me or one of the ladybosses—Louella Belle, Mae, and Camellia. Also, remember, we're all on camera so even if you break a nail, no cussing."

Her eyes float to mine and she blinks a few times as if seeing me for the first time...or remembering that I was going to be here.

Overheated from within, it feels like sparks fly off me.

She stammers, "And, uh, if there isn't, uh, anything else—" Her cheeks burst like summer strawberries then she clears her throat and starts coughing.

The other three ladybosses follow Christina's gaze and land on me.

Mouth. So. Dry.

Ella Belle claps her hands together. "Alrighty, if there isn't anything else, let's get started. Easton Estate renovation, here we come!"

There's a round of cheering. Everyone moves in different directions until Christina and I are the only two remaining in the driveway.

"Good morning, Cricket," I say.

"Hi." She blinks awkwardly a few times like she has something in her eye.

"Did you get my message about the load-bearing walls?"

Her eyes widen into a stare. "Yes."

"And how I think we ought to preserve the stone hearths?"

"Mmhmm."

"What about the tile work in the second-floor bathroom?"

"Yep."

Huh. Where I expected her enthusiasm earlier to convey to our conversation, considering our last one wasn't a total disaster, she's monosyllabic, distant, quiet.

"Is there a reason you're giving single-word responses to my questions?"

"No."

My brow furrows. "Listen, if we're going to work together, we have to be able to communicate. Do you have any questions for me, Christina...or should I call you Cricket?" I tease.

Her complexion pales then pinks up, but she doesn't tell me not to call her Cricket. I have to admit, my curiosity for all things Christina-Cricket-Sweetheart-Abernathy is about as keen as a dog sniffing out a steak on the grill.

"Why'd you wear jeans?" she asks.

I glance down at my dark wash denim then at her outfit. "Why'd you wear those?"

"Closet."

"And there I thought you'd accuse me of being a caveman. At least I speak in complete sentences. Have you had breakfast?"

"Mmmhmm."

"Coffee?"

"Yeah."

Being the leader on this project, perhaps she has a case of nerves. "Are you okay?"

"Fine. Fine. Fine."

Counting off, I wag my two pointer fingers between us. "Hey, you said three things. That's progress. Well, I'm going to go bash some stuff. Care to join me?"

"Fine. Fine."

I step closer, studying her carefully. "You're regressing, Cricket."

"Fine."

I squint, staring into her eyes. Her pupils properly dilate given the amount of sunlight out here and they're the same size so I don't imagine she has a concussion. Placing a hand on her forehead, I test her temperature—it's average, considering the ambient air.

"Yep. You seem fine, fine, fine," I say, hoping to get her to crack a smile.

Her expression remains hypnotically blank.

I point my thumb over my shoulder. "I'm going to head inside and get started." I start toward the house then pause when I don't sense movement behind me. Maybe she needs a moment or perhaps she shouldn't be left alone. "You coming?" I call.

Her mouth opens and closes. No sound comes out.

A long sigh escapes. "Are you having a case of stage fright?" Unlikely, given her amount of time spent on social media. Yeah, I left out the part of my weekend when I reviewed her dossier, aka her social media account @DomesticDiva.

When she still doesn't move, I say, "Don't make me do this."

She stares dead ahead, unblinking.

"I'm left with no choice."

I crouch down a bit and then wrap my arm around Christina's thighs before hefting her over my shoulder.

I get a yelp and she kicks a few times before saying, "Put me down, you brute." Then she pounds on my back. "Feet. Ground. Now."

"Sweetheart, it was turn you upside down to snap you out of it or—"

"Or what?"

"And she's back. Or toss you in the pond."

It's then I remember that not too long ago my mouth went dry in her presence. Did we have the same reaction to each other? Were we both stunned stupid?

Lord, help me, please.

"Set me down."

"Not until we're safely inside and I'm sure you've regained your senses."

"The only thing that's going to be senseless is you, as in knocked senseless." She howls like a cat.

"I'd like to see you try."

She pounds my back. Then, as I take the broad stone front steps, her arms wrap around me like a vice. I inwardly chuckle.

When we get to the threshold, my breath catches. I pause. This isn't exactly conventional, considering she's upside down, but should I carry her over or set her down?

A few of the workers inside stop what they're doing and stare at us.

"Nothing to see here, folks," she calls.

Someone whistles. Someone else whispers the word, "Drama."

I slowly lower Christina to her feet.

Her eyes lift to mine.

"If only your followers could see you now."

Her hand darts to her hip. "Oh yeah, and what would they see?"

My mouth goes dry again. It's time to break some plaster because I cannot let someone into my life, certainly not a woman like Christina. Or let her see how I might be starting to feel about her, especially when our eyes meet, when I hold her close—even slung over my shoulder. This notion doesn't make my cheeks turn red—not yet, but heat does creep up my neck. Forget sparks, I'm on fire.

CHAPTER 9
Christina

Despite the odds, I somehow survived the first day on the Easton Estate project...and with Buck.

I only rolled my eyes at the way he took command of the crew, outlining the scope of the project and having answers at the ready when asked difficult questions about dismantling the tin ceilings without messing up the wallpaper. *Mister know it all.*

I also managed to overlook how when a couple of the guys struggled under the weight of the clawfoot tub on the second floor, Buck swooped in with a helping hand and encouraged them. *Show off.*

I did my best to ignore the flex of his muscles when he removed a rusted wrought-iron railing that belongs in a scrapyard.

He makes me feel—black and blue and red all over.

Black because he is indeed very easy to dislike—gruff, bearded, and grumpy.

Blue because of those eyes. I'm lucky I didn't pass out again this morning when our gazes met—I did have a protein bar for breakfast because being around Buck McDermott on an empty stomach is a workplace hazard. There should be a safety cone with a swoon alert caution sign on it.

Red because he has an uncanny ability to make me blush—his mere presence gets me flustered and bothered and shivered—but not because I'm cold.

I've worked good and hard at keeping any indication that I don't have it all together behind a wall of calm, ease, and perfection. He's not going to come in like a one-man demolition team and break down my walls. Nuh-uh.

I must resist. I must resist.

The mere thought of him sets those shivers alight. Forget carpentry, it's like he's made it his job to bring all my insecurities to the surface—another tick in the *black* column.

Seated in the back of the SUV as Louella Belle pulls away, I glance back at the mansion. A good name for the project hasn't come to me yet. Maybe I'll survey my @DomesticDiva followers. I get the sense the house has a story to tell. While the crew knocked down walls, stripped wallpaper, and demo-ed an unfortunate obsession the previous owner had with oak chair rails, I toured the house, trying to feel into the final look and shape it's going to take.

Do I go for traditional Georgian and do a full historical restoration and decoration or mix in modern touches? Unlike all the other projects I've ever done—from Manhattan penthouses to Brooklyn brownstones—I always have the vision from the outset. For the first time in my career, I'm not sure where this is headed.

And for me, that's a very bad thing. It intensifies the uncomfortable hum under my skin and makes me feel squirmy along with the confession I made to the ladybosses about my past. I'm afraid I said too much. I sit back here, picking apart their reactions to finding out my mother is Sylvia Lancaster. Does this change things between us even if they assured me it wouldn't?

I steal a peek at each of them—Louella Belle talks about Bo's recommendations for the show. Mae listens and nods. Camellia chimes in with an idea to interview locals and their thoughts on the concept of home, community, and household improvements.

Nope. They're not obsessing over anything I said. That's a *me* problem. Always has been.

Don't get me started on how my knack for interior design is a cover-up for my internal struggle—anxiety and I are old frenemies. I probably shouldn't think about my dysfunctional family either. Everyone has one of those, right?

My sister is on her third excursion to an Ashram in India to find her inner self. She's also been arrested three times. I think she's banned from setting foot in Malta. And then there's our imaginary sibling which we shall never speak of.

I also don't discuss how I'm officially in my forties and not exactly where I expected to be in life.

Widowed once—thanks, Mom. Distant from my family—thanks, Dad. And the whole runaway bride thing is all on me. During what I call the "Mess with Les" period, I wasn't exactly being the best version of myself. Meredith and I are working on it.

This brings me back to my mother—she's bound to see me on TV and have one hundred and one opinions on how I could (which translates to should) do things differently. She'd have kept the chair rail to preserve the original look of the house, but it isn't true to the conventions of the Georgian time period. From floor to ceiling, she'd tell me how to stage the house, what to say, how to dress, what to eat, and who to spend time with.

However, one thing we'd agree on is to get rid of those bars on the windows. I click my tongue in annoyance that it wasn't the first thing Buck tackled today.

"You've been quiet, Christina. Anything on your mind?"

"Don't worry yourselves. That click of my tongue wasn't for you. I was thinking about Buck." I squish up my face because a second too late I realize how that sounds.

The ladybosses chorus a long and suggestive, "Mmmhmm."

"I meant I was thinking about how he didn't remove the bars from the windows. That should've been task number one, but he had other ideas." I grumble.

Louella Belle pulls into the dirt parking lot of a low brown building with white trim. Several picnic tables sit haphazardly outside. A red, hand-painted sign says *BBQ*.

"I thought we were headed back to HQ," I say, feeling the hum start at the prospect of dining here—and not because it likely hasn't had a visit from the health department, ever.

"I figured we ought to have a little celebratory dinner, considering my husband had a vision for us after the Mr. Fix-It contest, here we are, making it happen."

"Maybe we could go somewhere with a wider variety of food. You know for discerning palates."

"When in Rome, er, Butterbury," Camellia says.

"Trust me, if Mae's French fry place impressed you with the twenty different dips, you'll be wowed by all the different flavors of barbecue sauce at Bubba's."

"Bubba's?" I ask.

"That's the name of this place," Louella Belle says.

"The sign says *BBQ*," I correct.

"Bubba Junior, or is he the third? Well, he's the pitmaster and the owner. He and his father, grandfather, and likely a few generations before that made this place a landmark."

"Yeah, it looks like it's been here that long," I mumble.

"It could use a Designed to Last makeover," Camellia says softly so as not to offend.

The three of us hesitantly follow Louella Belle inside. I sniff the air and cannot deny that it smells so good, if ribs were something my followers wouldn't be scandalized by me eating, I'd post and comment that I wish they had the social media version of smell-o-vision.

A chalkboard that's barely legible lists only five items:

- Ribs
- Slaw
- Collards
- Fries
- Soda

Another board lists the variety of sauces—some are smudged, so I can't read them.

Louella Belle lists them for us. "Honey barbecue sauce, hickory, sweet and spicy, sweet and tangy, citrus spice, mesquite, mustard, white sauce, red sauce, Buffalo, maple, bourbon, teriyaki, peach with Vidalia onion, and of course, the secret sauce."

"What's that?" Camellia dares to ask.

"It's a secret." Louella Belle winks.

"What's a secret?" a deep, guttural voice asks.

The four of us turn to face a ruddy, balding man. The buttons of his shirt strain against his belly as he pats it. A tall, thin guy wearing a suit enters at his back. When I glimpse his face, my blood goes cold. Frigid. Georgia froze over during the height of summer.

"This is Gatlin Stoll, Butterbury's mayor." Louella Belle grimaces and introduces each of us in turn.

He resembles a potato with arms and legs.

"Hello, girls." The older man's voice is greasy like he's been chewing on a wad of fat tucked in his puffy cheek.

"It's ladybosses," I correct, willing my voice not to shake in acknowledgment of the other guy.

He eyes us like a juicy rack of ribs. "Indeed, indeed."

"And I am very pleased to make your acquaintance." His eyes rove over us and land on Louella Belle. "I keep telling that husband of yours to come by my office so we can talk about the future of this town."

She shakes her head slowly. "He told you that he's not interested."

"Ah, but he doesn't understand the power of his influence." Stoll smooths his thick hand down his shirt and pauses on his ample stomach.

"That's exactly why he doesn't want to endorse your plan." Louella Belle snorts.

Stoll tsks. "I'll get him to come around. Now, where are my

manners? This is my new assistant Les Streckle. Louella Belle, he was acquainted with your brother back in Las Vegas."

"Then that tells me everything I need to know about him," she mutters.

Les's eyes hop between Mae, Camellia, and land firmly on me. I get major curly mustache villain vibes from the mayor. As for Les, I'm certain he's a lying, cheating bad guy.

"Pleasure to make your acquaintance." He stares at me long and hard as if that'll get me to look at him. I won't do him the favor. I won't acknowledge his existence, just like I refuse to answer his calls, texts, and emails.

Les Streckle no longer exists in my world. He hates that fact. I shouldn't be surprised he tracked me down, but what does he want? And why hasn't he come out and said he knows me? Then I remember he's always playing a game whether it's at a poker table or when running a con. The question is, what's his angle?

Oh, right. The last word. The non-existent trophy. A ring on my finger. Access to my mother's world. Not a chance, buddy.

"Listen, girls—" Les starts.

"Ladybosses," we all say at the same time.

"Of course, of course. I hear there's work happening over at the Easton Estate and I want to urge you to be careful. Construction sites can be mighty dangerous."

Camellia's eyes widen as if she's been scandalized. Mae's eyes narrow. Louella Belle frowns.

I offer a fake smile and avoid looking at Les entirely. I will my body to hold strong and not shake. The last time I saw him was when I was safely in a taxi leaving Las Vegas. He stood there shouting at me to come back. I say, "With all due respect, sir, we're fully capable of handling ourselves on a jobsite."

"You can never be too careful, especially at those old houses. Have you heard or come across anything unusual?" Les asks, overeager for the answer to be affirmative.

"It's not haunted if that's what you're suggesting," Mae says as if trying to convince herself of the matter.

"It's not," I repeat, certain.

"There are just some old stories that I've heard…" Les leers, trying to spook me.

"And that's it. They're just old stories," Louella Belle says confidently.

Stoll claps Les on the back. "Well, it doesn't matter, anyway. Because the real treasure is my pending agreement with Hydro-pro."

I tilt my head, wondering if he thinks there's treasure at the estate. "What treasure?"

He waves his hand dismissively. "Oh, you know, family jewels and riches. That kind of thing." He lifts and lowers one eyebrow. "Les can get carried away with his big ideas."

"I'm well aware."

"I'm just saying, I think the Sweetheart Stone is on the property," Les says in a low voice and looks right at me. I'm all too familiar with his schemes.

Stoll hisses, "And if it is, considering you're a direct descendent, you're the rightful owner. Simple as that." He smiles flatly. "You hear that, girls? If you should come across anything unique and shiny, be sure to let Les know."

"Our corporation bought the house, what's there is ours, fair and square." Louella Belle scowls. "Anyway, how can you stand there and call yourself mayor while you partner with Hydro-pro who plans to flood the reservoir, putting the entire town underwater?"

My eyebrows pinch together at this new information.

"Well, you could make it worth my while. I've always wanted to be on television and I'd hate to see anything go wrong with one of your little projects." Stoll steeples his fingers.

Louella Belle's hand flies to her hip. "I met my match with Adair and there's no way you're going to sabotage us."

"Sure is a shame that we can't play for the same team. As I was saying, Les, she's the brains. Bo is the brawn."

"And you're a buffoon," Louella Belle says, flustered.

"Now, now, let's be polite. I'm merely doing what's best for Butterbury. The residents are eager to receive their payouts when we get the funds from the state to pay for the homes and land that don't already belong to the town. Then the houses have to remain vacant for a period of time before Hydro-pro works their magic."

"You mean destruction."

Stoll shakes his head. "It's all for the greater good. You'll soon understand that those who play their cards right will have liquid gold flowing their way." He winks at Les.

"Swindling people out of their houses doesn't sound like it's good for anyone but you."

"And how would that be good for me? I love this town." He guffaws.

"Because Hydro-pro is paying you off."

"Prove it," Stoll counters.

"Challenge accepted," Louella Belle says.

Stoll chortles. "Come on, Les, let's get our ribs and get out of this dump." They stump to the counter.

If I could shrink into the greasy wood-paneled wall or hide in the kitchen, I would. I don't want anything to do with Les Streckle. But my ex-fiancé looks back at me long and mean. I'm sure this isn't the last I'll be seeing of him.

I can't help but wonder if he tracked me down—not hard considering my social media presence. I'd hoped he'd moved on, forgot about me. Then again, maybe I know too much, or perhaps his ego is too big to deal with the fact that I walked (okay, ran) away when I wouldn't go along with his plan to swindle casino-goers with a scheme he called the "I do redo." In short, we'd tell people we'd just gotten married and were robbed so they'd take pity on us and give us money, a wedding gift as it were. Meanwhile, he'd get their bank or credit card information and buy us a bonus gift for the big score.

To say I was scandalized when I found out what he was really doing is an understatement.

Just when I think I'm in the clear, Les, says, "Nice seeing you again, Christina. I'm sure it won't be the last time."

I shiver and not in a good way—definitely not in the way that Buck makes me go weak all over. Stoll is harsh and Les is my nightmare—not that the ladies know about our history—making me eager to leave. Instead, the four of us do a team huddle in the corner.

"What was that about?" Camellia asks.

Louella Belle explains that Gatlin Stoll is in talks to sign a contract with a hydroelectric company. "They find towns near their dams, get a government grant, vacate the area, and then flood it to generate electricity."

"That's awful," Mae says.

"And just when we get started with our show, we find out Butterbury is on the list?" I ask in disbelief.

"Bo heard from the mayor last week, but it won't stand. Not if I can help it. I've finally put down roots and the likes of Gatlin Stoll and his slimy underling aren't going to tear them out," Louella Belle grouses.

"Slimy is right," I murmur.

I can't imagine living here for the rest of my life, but I'd hate to see Butterbury go the way of Atlantis.

"Looks like it's time we call Wallace Fordham," Louella Belle says.

"Who?"

"My brother's fake lawyer. He'll need to draft up a cease and desist letter." She winks.

Mae shrinks. "That sounds illegal."

"Very." She smiles confidently.

"It sounded like Les knew Gannon," Camellia says, having heard the stories about Louella Belle's deviant sibling.

"And like Les knew you, Christina," Mae adds.

That terrible tickle starts up. I don't want to lie but can't bear to reveal the truth. Desperate, I say, "It's not fine dining and definitely doesn't have smoothies or green juices, but let's order some food." With each word, the hum under my skin gets louder. In Manhattan, there are plenty of safe and passable places to eat. Sure, some of the restaurants probably have rodent and roach problems, but this place is so bad we actually have to eat outside. As for the food, I doubt the kitchen has ever seen a vegetable that isn't fried or cooked in massive amounts of butter. However, that's not my concern. Rather, I'm worried about the lying, cheating, con artist that just reentered my life.

"What would you like?" asks Bubba, the bald man behind the counter.

"Uh, I'm not hungry." For once, it's the truth.

He frowns and looks sad at my response.

"Oh, come on, Christina, you have to try this barbecue." Louella Belle coaxes.

"Why don't you just order for me."

Everyone, including Bubba, smiles broadly.

"You won't be sorry. I remember Gram and Gramps bringing me here when I was little," Mae says, ushering us outside.

We sit at a picnic table in the shade and Bubba brings us soda and an entire ream of paper towels.

"Are those going to be necessary?" I ask.

"Very," Louella Belle says.

"So, you mentioned you were thinking about Buck before," Camellia starts.

For once, I welcome this particular change in subject. "Those bars on the windows are confounding. I want them taken down right away, but why were they there in the first place?" I ask then belatedly realize that wasn't exactly the question. She was calling me out on my comment before I corrected myself on the ride over here.

"What else were you thinking?" Mae asks in her sweet voice.

I look up from the straw wrapper I shredded while talking. "Is this really going to turn into another interrogate Christina session?"

Louella Belle laughs. "I have a feeling the barbecue will loosen your tongue."

They don't say anything else about Buck but do discuss the scope of the project, decreasing the nervous hum under my skin by half. As the conversation continues and I (mostly) forget about the moody blacksmith-contractor and the lousy-loser ex who suddenly invaded my life, the vision for the estate becomes less blurry. The entry comes into focus with a new hardwood floor inlaid with wood, marble, and mother-of-pearl in a compass rose placed into the center because I want whoever buys this place to feel like they no longer need a map and that they've come home. The stair risers will complement the compass with whatever material best fits our budget. The banister will be mahogany and I will personally restore the chandelier.

"He definitely made her blush," Mae says. "Me too with that beard and all. But I can tell he only has eyes for our DomesticDiva."

I snap to attention, about to defend myself when Bubba Junior brings baskets of ribs, fries, and several sauces, momentarily distracting me because it smells so good. "Dig in, ladies," he says. "And kindly leave me a review online if it's not too much trouble. Seems it's getting harder for customers to find their way over here these days and we need a new roof."

He needs a new roof, walls, foundation. The building sinks into the ground on the south side and it looks like one of the windows is broken.

"I definitely will and maybe we could get the crew out here for dinner a few times." Louella Belle beams like she's scheming.

Around a mouthful, Mae says, "This is even better than I remember."

Camellia politely wipes her mouth. "Perhaps you could cater our wrap party."

Bubba Junior snaps his fingers. "Hey, you're filming that new home improvement show. I applied for a repair on Mr. Fix-It when they were shooting around here, but businesses weren't allowed. We could sure use some fixing."

I taste a French fry and they rival the Starlight's. "You know, if we have any spare materials, we could probably donate them to you," I say around a mouthful.

"That's mighty kind, but if that's the case, I'd owe you free food here for life."

We all laugh.

Bubba Junior's straight face suggests he's not joking.

"In that case, we'll see what we can do," Louella Belle says.

Bubba Junior leaves us to our meal, and the others have greasy fingers and sticky smiles. I pick at the meat, not inclined to eat with my hands.

"It's done like this." Camellia, the daintiest of us all demonstrates by sucking the meat right off the bone.

"Do you think Bubba Junior has a fork and knife?"

The others give me a *they can't with me* look.

I head inside and ask all the same because I cannot eat like a...beast, like a man. The thought brings Buck to mind and I flush.

When I return with a fork and knife, thank you very much, the others are nearly done. I take a few bites and won't deny that it's good. Fine, this barbecue is delicious.

"Even though we're not back at HQ, let's review the wins and losses of the day," Louella Belle suggests.

They break into chatter, praising the demo team, Rhondy keeping us supplied with baked goods, and how the electricians and plumbers are on schedule.

"Now, any challenges, questions, or things we can do better moving forward?" I say.

"There was a strange situation this morning, actually," Louella Belle starts.

"Yeah, after giving quite an inspiring speech and then being left alone with the contractor, the lead on this project seemed to get tongue-tied," Mae continues.

"Perhaps we could discuss that," Camellia says delicately.

The flush deepens. "I don't know what you're talking about."

Louella Belle takes a rib from my basket and has a bite. "Mmm. I'd never tried the peach and Vidalia sauce before."

"Sure is tasty," I say, more inclined to talk about this non-health food than the "incident" this morning.

"Mmm. So is a certain bearded blacksmith," Mae adds.

My eyes widen. "You're single. Why don't you—?" I say.

Mae shakes her head. "He's almost ten years older than me. Plus, we've established that there's something between you two."

I set my fork and knife down. "Okay, fine. When he showed up today, I don't know what came over me. I got flustered then annoyed. He has this weird ability to stir me up and make me blush. I just can't seem to keep myself together around him. So I figured I'd try to make him blush the same way he makes me."

"I cannot imagine Buck blushing," Camellia says.

"The two of you stood in the parking lot a good long while. Were you successful?" Louella asks, wiping her hands on a paper towel.

The sauce and ribs must loosen my tongue because I tell them the ill-advised plan that left me oh-for-five.

"First, I tried batting my eyelashes, but wanted to try a new mascara for the camera today and with the humidity, my lashes got stuck together. Talk about awkward. I tried long, sustained eye contact and that came off as creepy, I think. I was going to compliment his, uh, elbows? But he was badgering me with questions about the project and I couldn't quite get the words out. Or any words for that matter."

"Interesting approach," Camellia says.

"There's more. I was going to nudge him with my boot, you know to make physical contact, but I was frozen."

"It's, like, ninety degrees out."

"Yeah. I'm aware." I try to smooth my frizzy hair. "The last thing I tried to do was imitate his body language and I think I just came off looking deranged. He was very concerned for me. Then he tipped me over his shoulder and all the blood rushed to my cheeks. I was red for the rest of the shoot." I press my fingers to my cheeks. "I still am."

"You looked normal to me."

"I have a lot of foundation on."

"Should you see a doctor?" Mae asks.

I wilt, sag, wish I could lie on the floor, alone, in an air-conditioned room. "Not yet, but why does he have this effect on me?"

"What effect? Do tell us." Louella Belle leans in.

"I think we know the effect," Camellia says. "I have to ask, where exactly did you get those ideas—batting your eyelashes and all that?"

"From my followers," I say then add at a whisper, "At least I didn't use any of the pickup lines on him that they suggested."

"How about talking to real people about this?" Louella Belle says.

My tone is defensive when I say, "They're real."

"So are we," she replies.

There are probably a lot of things I should talk to them about —my anxiety, my previous marriages, being a runaway bride, Buck...

But the sky clouds over and fat drops of rain begin to fall so we race to the SUV, leaving the conversation and regrettably, the rest of my barbecue in the bin.

The big question is, what will happen if I let go of my steely grip on my diet, organizational needs, the No-Man-Plan, and everything else in my life? Will I dive headfirst into a hot mess hole, or will I rise like a phoenix and begin winning at life?

As thunder rumbles and lightning strikes in the distance from this summer storm, I'm afraid I'll soon find out.

CHAPTER 10
Christina

I spend the rest of the week training for an Olympic medal in worrying. After the strange encounter with Mayor Stoll and his henchman, I'm afraid of something going wrong on the project. I fear the rest of my vision won't take shape. Tradesmen will fail to show up. That the house will collapse.

Although, we're nearly done with the first floor, so that's progress. However, I always have an outline. I never design by the seat of my pants. What if it comes out awful? What if it doesn't come together at all?

By night, I fret, pace, and run through everything in my mind from cabinet hinges to drapery to those stupid bars on the window.

Buck has been MIA the last few days—typical contractor behavior. Actually, that's not true. I've worked with many outstanding contractors and carpenters. A few bad seeds give the rest a bad rap, but Buck's name has been in my black book since we met—and I don't mean the kind Les had with the names of all the women he'd dated.

There's just something about Buck that makes me shiver like he sees beyond the veneer and is going to pull back the curtain and reveal that I don't quite have it all together.

But why would he? Oh yeah, because the other men in my life have stripped me to my core—made me feel vulnerable and used. I'll never let that happen again, so it's better to keep Buck at a safe distance.

No-Man-Plan activated.

Even though those blue eyes draw me in. The quirk of his lips hidden beneath his beard makes me want to see more. And how his muscles are works of art, carved from marble like the statues in the estate's garden.

I fan myself now as we gather in the driveway to review the day like we do every morning. Today, I refuse to embarrass myself again by attempting to make Buck blush. The clouds from the storm that started the night we had barbecue haven't dissipated so I can't blame the sun for the flame in my cheeks while I review the final list of things to demolish and haul away.

I have my phone poised so my followers get a front-row seat on how things work behind the scenes of the show, and say, "I know many of you like busting and breaking things, but tomorrow is my favorite day because we're going to start creating. So roll up your sleeves and let's get this done."

Without Buck here, I'm not tongue-tied at all. I've got zero fluster. No flaps. I am not flustered. I'm unflappable, and today is going to be a great day, I can feel it.

Then my heart leaps into my throat and my cheeks match the red shorts I'm wearing with a white, button-down tank top tied at the waist as a pair of blue eyes scan me from toe to head.

Buck's eyes spark and settle on me. The corner of his lip lifts. He steps closer toward me.

"Oh good. You're finally gracing us with your smug mug," I say without any humor.

He lifts his coffee cup in a toast. "Get used to it, sweetheart."

Set off like a flaming Cheeto out of a cannon I stomp over. (I know it's only seven-thirty a.m., but I'm having a craving—those cheesy puffs of yummy scrumbos are my weakness...and apparently, so is this man, but I can't let on about that). "Just where have you been?"

"Louella Belle didn't tell you?"

My jaw tightens because the way he looks at me erases the cheerful message I gave the crew today. "That you're a lazy dork goblin? No, I figured that out on my own."

"A lazy dork goblin? I've been called a lot of things, but that's a new one." He makes a sound I've never heard him make. It's a deep rumble of laughter. "You're fiery this morning."

"Get used to it, sweetheart," I repeat.

To my surprise, not only does the corner of his mouth quirk, the entire, beautiful thing lifts into a smile. He aims finger guns at me and says, "Good one."

"For your information, I don't enjoy this banter. Just be here when you're supposed to be here and do your job."

"I wasn't supposed to be here yesterday or the day before. It was in my contract. You can ask Kim." Buck's voice gradually softens. "I had some business to take care of in DC. I'm not lazy or a flake. I will be here on time and work hard. I'll get those bars off the windows. I just have to do some research first."

"Research? How hard can it be? I thought you were a blacksmith, an ironworker—one of the reasons Louella Belle said you were perfect for the job."

"I am perfect for the job...and so are you." With a sparkle in his eye, Buck winks and then strides toward the house.

A rant builds on my tongue and I'm about to sound off to the @DomesticDiva followers and anyone who'll listen, but I falter. For years now, I've channeled my nervous energy into trying to achieve perfection—with what I eat, how I look, my work, and my surroundings. If I showed them the unhinged side of me, it would be a sledgehammer blow to the image I've built around myself and cement my decline into hot mess-dom. Instead, I smooth my hair, plaster on a smile, and update my audience on the final day of demolition. When I watch the replay, it's almost, but not quite perfect so I record it again. Then a third time and I finally get it right.

The shrill voice in my head pipes up, reminding me that whatever I do isn't quite good enough. And why not? I ask myself that all the time. I've never come up with an answer. What do I want most in the world? To prove to my mother that I'm an independent, capable, and successful interior designer—not at all in her shadow.

I startle and not because something from inside the house goes *bang*. Rather, because I realize that voice inside that critiques everything I do and say, looks and sounds a lot like Sylvia Lancaster.

Designed to Last is allowing me to show my mother and the world that I can stand on my own two feet—except, it seems, when Buck is nearby.

Just then, he hollers out the window and gives me the thumbs up. "Hey, sweetheart."

I narrow my eyes. "Hey, dork goblin. Are you tearing those bars off?"

"Soon enough, sweetheart. Soon enough."

But I don't find out what he was going to say—I'd like to think he was acknowledging the second little breakthrough I had.

Despite my internal mini-mic drop moment, I spend the rest of the day avoiding Buck...and the ladybosses. Everywhere I look, things are out of place, askew, and messy. I repeatedly remind myself that this is part of the process. The problem is, I feel that way inside too, and no amount of photos or videos for Picto-Chat sets me right.

I breeze through the foyer, past the drawing-room, dining room, kitchen, ballroom, and into the library, which I haven't quite figured out the look for. After this, it's upstairs and I already feel relieved that the style and vibe for the house are coming together. All week, my mother's voice was heckling and criticizing me for not having a clear path forward. I'm nearly there though.

She and I haven't seen each other in months and have hardly

spoken during that time, but she follows me like a shadow, inspecting every little thing I do to make sure it meets her standards.

The little girl in me feels like pouting, and I kick the cabinet door to one of the built-in shelves. It doesn't budge. The hinge probably rusted. But that would mean there's a leak or moisture is getting in somehow. There are times when I want to throw my hands up and give up, give in. My thoughts start to spiral and I reel them back as I turn slowly in the library, admiring the elaborately carved wooden shelves with the dark stain, the parquet floor, and the close, cozy feel of the room. It's missing something other than books. I pull a sheet off a nearby chair and sit down. A rolling ladder leans against the shelf, locked in time to whenever it was last left there. This room was relatively untouched during the demo, but something is off about it.

I glance out the window and bristle at the sight of the bars. Pushing the notion of Buck out of my mind, I scroll through inspiration on my phone—lighting, chairs, woven rugs. The décor isn't the trouble. It's something about the room itself.

Leaning back, I take it all in then realize the bookshelves are off-center and asymmetrical. I get up to double-check from different vantage points then slump, regretting not instructing the team to remove them.

However, it would be a shame to destroy the intricate carvings in the wood. With the finger belonging to the nail I recently broke, I trace the ivy carved across the shelf's border, leading to flowers, fleur-de-lis, and whimsical swirls. My finger pauses on a heart shape.

"Almost done for the day?" A deep voice with a southern accent calls from the doorway.

Again, I startle and my cheeks threaten to shade pink in Buck's proximity. I force myself not to let out a grunt of frustration. Maybe he gives off the heat of a furnace and that causes me to flush. Yeah, let's blame it on that.

"Yep. Finishing up in here. Did you need something?" I ask without turning around.

"Yep," he repeats.

"Let's try to be mature."

"Says the woman who called me dork goblin."

I turn slowly and give him an exaggerated roll of my eyes. "What was it you needed?"

"For you to come with me." His voice is commanding.

"Sounds like you're making an arrest. Where exactly do you want me to go with you? You'll have to give me a little more information."

Buck's forehead wrinkles slightly and he shifts his weight. "Sorry about that. I wanted to show you something I found by the window earlier."

My eyebrows lift with surprise at the apology. "The only finding I want to do is those bars in the scrap heap."

"Yeah, about that. I did some research and if you don't mind, I'd like to keep them up for a little longer."

"Today is the last day of demo, meaning they come off now."

"Come with me."

"What's the magic word?"

He puffs out a breath. "Please?"

"Have you forgotten to speak in complete sentences?"

"No, that was you earlier this week. Now, if you don't—"

"Oh, you are not going to pick me up again, mister. Lead the way," I say, gesturing ahead of us.

Buck cannot put his arms around me because I risk exploding at his touch. It's solid and has a feel of permanence like metal, like the bars on the windows and the ones around my heart—like once Buck's hands are on me, they may never leave. The problem with that is I might not mind.

He leads me to a storeroom on the other side of the house.

"All the windows had bars except this one." He pushes it open then ducks through. "Except, if you look out here, it appears as if it once did."

"I'm not climbing out the window."

"Fine, but—" He grabs my hand, sending a shivery blaze through me, and brushes my fingers over what feels like holes for very large bolts—the kind that would've fastened metal bars.

I lurch back and lean against the shelving that's painted a hideous shade of green.

"What's the point, Sherlock? Are you trying to solve a mystery?"

Buck cups his hand around his mouth then drags it down his beard. "Something like that. But when I examined the exterior wall more carefully, I figured out there used to be a clothesline that extended from this window to a pole out there. I learned the housekeepers used to stand here and hang the clothes before they got an electric dryer."

"Wow. Laundry. Fascinating." My tone is as dry as the grass in the field beyond the window. "Good thing we don't have to bother with chores like that anymore. It's almost quitting time. I have a few more things to do." I move to leave.

"Like what, sweetheart? Lounge in the library?" He steps closer, his leather and smoke scent filling the small room, his eyes filling mine.

"For your information, I was envisioning." I drag my gaze away and it lands on the frame to the empty shelving. The same carvings as in the library scroll along the wood.

"Interesting that the original carpenter decorated the shelves in here the same as in the library." I bite my lip, wondering if I should mention what transpired with the mayor at the rib joint. "The other day, the ladybosses and I had a strange encounter with the mayor and his, um, assistant."

"Eh, don't worry about him. He thinks he's the big cheese around here. He's all bluster, no bite."

That may be true about Stoll, but I happen to know Les is bad news but don't want to let on. "According to them, there might be an unsolved mystery at this house...and maybe the potential for some foul play."

Buck tilts his head and says, "Yeah, there's a mystery alright and it's not just what's going on between you and me."

I squawk a laugh, brushing off the last part of his comment.

Apparently, he does too. "My great-great-grandfather was the Easton family's blacksmith's apprentice. My great-great-grandmother was a junior housekeeper when they met."

"Sounds like the beginning of a love story." My voice rebels and goes husky with longing.

"Something like that."

His eyes search mine. I cannot look away, so I tuck my chin back if only to put more space between us, caged in between his massive girth and the shelf.

Buck moves closer still and I imagine him telling stories around a campfire. His hand in mine. His lips...

How inconvenient that I can picture that in heart-throbbing detail but not come up with a plan to update the library.

My breath is shaky and I grip the edge of the shelf when all of a sudden it gives way. My arms windmill as I tip backward. Only this time, Buck doesn't catch me. I reach for him.

CHAPTER 11
Buck

My reflexes are quick, but it takes me half a second to figure out what is going on and why this beautiful woman's arms wrap around my neck, why she's breathing heavily in my ear, and where we are. It's not exactly the storeroom. The shelf shifted and now we're in another room.

"Are you okay?" I ask Cricket.

"Am I still alive?" Her voice is small.

By the way her heart pounds against mine, I'd say so. "Alive and kicking."

Only, this time, unlike when I tossed her over my shoulder, she's not kicking. Rather, she's clinging to me for dear life.

After I rapidly assess the situation and am confident we're safe, I wrap my arm around her waist, angling her toward the shelving.

Her expression shifts from fear to confusion. I'm stuck on the latter but am starting to make some sense of what just happened. And it's not only how good she feels in my arms, stoking that fire inside.

Christina blinks into the darkness. "I thought I broke the shelf and was going to fall into the basement."

"I think you just added a clue to the mystery." I pull my flashlight from my tool belt, shining it into the space opened by the shifted shelf. "It looks like you discovered a secret passage. They're not uncommon in old buildings like this."

Her expression flickers with trepidation. "Where do you think it leads?"

"Let's find out."

Her grip on my arm tightens. I peel her fingers free then twine mine between hers and lead the way along the narrow passage. The lower portion of the shelf opens inward like a door and I duck beneath.

"Watch your head," I call over my shoulder.

Cobwebs hang like drapes and our movement makes the dust dance in the beam of the flashlight. Christina's hand feels small in mine and she trembles slightly. Before I take a step forward, I test my weight to make sure the floor is solid. It creaks like the hold of a cargo ship.

Cricket tightens her grip on my hand.

"It's okay," I say, my voice soft.

We stand just inside the entrance to the passageway. Her eyes sparkle in the dim light filtering in through the opening. We gaze at each other for a long moment as if making a decision. There's no turning back.

My breath turns slightly ragged. This woman could be the end of me. I have to push away the incoming desire.

I discreetly close the door to the passageway, plunging us into darkness.

Christina yelps then frantically spins to the entrance. "We're locked in here. Oh no. On no! I'm trapped with a goblin Viking man."

"And there I thought that would give you confidence."

I can practically see her straighten and cock a hip. "And what makes you say that?" She goes from panicked to feisty in four seconds.

"What are you afraid of, Cricket?" My voice is low, scratchy.

Her breath catches and she doesn't answer right away. "Oh, you know. Just your run-of-the-mill ghosts."

"And if there were, you're with a—what was it? Goblin Viking man?

She shifts closer to me. "Do you really think it's haunted?"

"Definitely not."

"How can you be so sure?"

"If there were ghosts, they'd be more scared of you, ladyboss. But there aren't." I chuckle.

I sense she smiles like she appreciates the comment. I want to add, *And you have me*. But I don't. Just like I have no idea where this passageway goes. I'm not sure I want to find out where things could lead between us. At least, I keep telling myself that lie. I know well enough a person can convince themselves of anything if they try hard enough.

She pushes on the door and it pops open. "Phew. I thought we were locked in here."

"Wouldn't be the worst thing."

"What does that mean?"

"You. Me. An enclosed space," I hint, knowing better but unable to stop myself from seeing where she takes the suggestion. I'm like good cop/bad cop in one person, playing against myself.

She shifts so we're face to face. The dim light illuminates her smooth features, drawing attention to the shadows around her lips.

She snorts and pokes me in the chest. "Nice try, Dork Goblin."

Stepping backward, relief sweeps through me because nothing came of the two of us alone in the dark. She's not interested. End of story. If I had any sense, I wouldn't tempt myself because I know something between us will only end up in ruin and regret.

We take a few slight turns but mostly the path is straight.

"Do you think there are rats in here?" she asks.

"Probably."

"Bodies?" She shudders.

"I hope not."

"That doesn't inspire much confidence."

I squeeze her hand as we continue. Periodically, I press the surrounding walls when it looks like they might provide an opening. None do. I stop abruptly when we reach a dead end.

Christina bumps into me. "Oof. Next time tell me when you're going to put on the brakes."

"There's nowhere else to go. This wall feels solid."

"Seriously?" She lifts onto her toes and reaches over my shoulder and pushes on the wall.

The dim flashlight illuminates her features and like before, we're merely a breath away. However, in the storage room, I was studying the carvings that framed the shelves. This time, I'm studying the jade of her eyes, the soft tip of her nose, and the smooth curve of her lips.

Christina's lilac scent overpowers the musty air in this small space, and I breathe deeply, but being this close to her causes it to come out ragged.

She shivers like my exhale tickled her. Our gazes lock. I see the reflection of my own curiosity and locked-down longing.

She lowers flat onto her feet and says, "We should head back."

Neither of us moves for another long moment.

I give my head a shake, remembering that though my theory about the mystery may involve a love story, this isn't one. I'm not on the market. Christina is technically my boss. And we're inside a wall—not the most romantic place to make a mistake that we'd both likely regret.

I slide past her and our clasped hands drop, leaving me feeling unusually cold.

Once we're back in the storage room in the fading light of day, whatever spell captured us before we found the opening breaks and we stand at opposite ends of the small space. Christina smooths the cobwebs off her clothes.

I expect that we'll return to being all business and banter.

"Maybe they started making a passage but never completed it," I suggest.

She takes a few steps toward me and brushes her hand over my beard. The flames inside reignite.

She giggles softly. "I cannot take anything you say seriously if you have cobwebs on your face."

I brush my hand through her hair. "Likewise."

As ever, our gazes meet, lock, hold. We both start laughing.

"What is this—?" she starts.

I don't know and am afraid if I answer, it might pop like a bubble. "Whatever we want it to be."

That simple acknowledgment seems to blow us both back into our respective corners.

Christina clears her throat, getting back to business. "In response to your comment about the passage not being completed, that seems doubtful. This house was overbuilt, over-detailed. Whoever owned it had a lot of time on their hands to comb over every inch. I mean, you noticed the details on the wood frame around the shelf, right?"

"Oh, I noticed." And I notice the way the light highlights golden flecks in her green eyes. The way one of her ears is ever so slightly wider than the other. How her lips form a perfect pillow.

She raises an eyebrow and parts her lips.

I shift and clear my throat this time. "As you were saying—?"

"The carving is similar to the shelves in the library."

"Likely, they employed the same carpenter."

"True. But why would they have such an ornate shelf in a storeroom?"

"Because they could?"

Christina tilts her head at a thoughtful angle.

I'm the former detective and should be the one piecing these clues together, but this woman is distracting me—the main reason I never remained in a relationship or got married while still with the agency. Women have the ability to pull me from my work, from my responsibilities.

"I'm going to retrace my steps," she says.

"I don't want you heading back in there alone," I say.

"I meant outside the wall. See if I can figure out where the passage led—" She points toward the hall.

I snap my fingers. "Good idea. It did seem to run in a fairly parallel trajectory."

"But how far did we go?"

An idea comes to mind. "Do you have any string? Rope?"

She goes through a few drawers and pulls out a frayed clothesline. "Will this do the trick?"

I instruct Christina to hold it tight at the opening to the passage and then enter and walk until there isn't any slack in the rope. She meets me in the passage and we repeat the process until we've measured three and a half lengths. We repeat the process in the hall, approximating the direction we took.

"Look, we're back where we started," Christina says, opening the door to the library.

Twilight falls as we fuss with the shelves in the library, trying to find an opening, get the wood to budge, or discover a loose shelf.

Focused, I forget to indulge my desire to get Cricket riled up, to see heat rise to her cheeks the same way she stokes the fire in me.

"I always loved it when in movies, someone would shift a book and the passage would open to another world," Christina says in a dreamy voice. "Too bad these shelves are empty."

"Too bad we couldn't find the other side to the passage."

"Maybe it truly is a dead end." She sounds forlorn.

We cross the room to the big windows overlooking the estate. Now would be a moment to sling my arm across Christina's back like Bo so casually did to Ella Belle. Then again, we're not married.

What is this strange stirring that's taken over inside of me, stoking my internal fire, a desire for something I've never before wanted? Nah. It couldn't be a relationship. Maybe just human connection. Or comradery between coworkers. Yeah, we'll go with that.

I hesitate but then remember that I'm a man, have served my country with courage, and have never balked in the face of a challenge.

Christina is definitely a challenge.

I lift my arm and the movement must cause her to flinch as if afraid the house is haunted. She shifts away slightly. I give her arm a little squeeze then drop mine, feeling foolish and awkward.

She must be right about me being a dork goblin. I cough into my fist to ensure my voice doesn't crack like a heartsick fool. "Hey, I just wanted to say that I think we make a good team, after all."

She tips her head up and a mischievous smirk plays on her lips. "You still haven't taken the bars off the windows." Instead of speaking in a nagging tone, she's playful.

Even though the passage didn't lead anywhere, maybe we took a step in a positive direction.

My training and previous job taught me never to show emotion, but a smile rises inside and stretches toward my lips. I should proceed with caution. We're in relatively unfamiliar territory. When I was younger I dated, but after that, I led a James Bond life minus the women. Too risky to get involved—for both parties. I may have momentarily had feelings for Eddy, but we set boundaries and never crossed them.

Doors slam outside, jarring me from my thoughts.

Christina races toward the window and gasps. "The lady-bosses are leaving. Without me. Wait!"

I'm at her heels as the SUVs containing the crew and lady-bosses pull away.

She drops her hands to her sides then pats her pockets, searching for her phone. "Why'd they ditch me?" Her face falls dramatically and instead of turning pink, she pales. "Oh no, they're gone and I lost my phone. My lifeline. No." Clutching the sides of her head, Christina slides dramatically to the floor.

I crouch down, fully resting my hand on her shoulder,

surprised to see her unravel like this. I'm not a "tend and mend" kind of guy. My strengths lie in solutions. "It's probably in the storeroom or the passage. Stay right here. I'll go look."

I hurry down the hall and am back in less than a minute with the bejeweled thing in hand.

Her eyes brighten when the case shines in the last remaining light of day.

Christina rushes toward me like we're a couple reuniting after a long separation. Instead of flinging her arms around my shoulders, she reaches for her phone with desperate, grabby hands.

Eyes on her device, she staggers as she follows me outside. I lost her to the world wide web or wherever it is she goes on there —I was not the tech expert. That was my partner—Eddy.

"I can bring you home," I say, but Christina hardly pays attention.

Concern for her safety in the city—head down, buried in her phone, and a lack of situational awareness—flares inside. That'll have to be a lesson for another time. Right now, another idea springs to mind.

With heavy footsteps, I exit the mansion with Christina trailing after me, tapping away on her phone and hardly paying attention to where we're going. My truck, and it alone, remains in the driveway. The glow of the device's screen illuminates her features and the fire in me flickers—I wish she paid me that kind of attention. I make a noise of distaste at the notion. It catches her attention.

"This means I'm stranded," she wails dramatically.

"At least you've scared off the coyotes," I murmur.

Her lips pull downward with a pout.

I've led teams of men on covert operations. Solved mysteries and brought criminals to justice. Strategized and implemented plots to take down enemies. Right now, a plan develops in my mind and if I'm not careful, I'll be the one in trouble because this woman drives me wild—and I'm afraid I may soon lose my lone wolf status.

CHAPTER 12

Buck

Standing in the driveway as the moon rises over the trees in the distance, Christina continues to pound away on her phone. “No one is answering my texts.”

I recall her comment at the Starlight about not knowing how to drive, and this gives me the perfect opportunity to teach her the basic skill. Next, we’ll focus on personal safety. “How do you get around usually?” I casually ask.

Without looking up from the phone screen, she says, “In the city? Car service, taxi, subway, by foot. Preferably in that order.”

“We don’t have those options around here.”

“Clearly.” She shakes her head like that’s a travesty.

“So you have to rely on your own wherewithal.”

“There was never a reason to learn to drive.”

“Come on. Get in.”

“I’m not going with you in that zombie apocalypse monster truck hybrid.”

“Do you have a choice, Cricket?”

She heaves a loud sigh. “Fine, could you bring me back to town?”

“What’s the magic word?” I ask, teasing her with her previous request.

Finally, she glances up but schools her expression. "Please, pretty please."

The corner of my lips tug to the side and I dangle the keys between us. "Fine, but you're driving."

She gives me a swift and irritable shake of her head. "Buck, I just told you that I don't know how to drive."

"Time to learn."

"I can't."

"You can."

Her eyes widen as she stares at my truck. "No, really. I can't. What if I get it wrong? What if I crash? What if I—?"

"What if you get it right?" I counter.

She tilts her head as if that possibility hadn't occurred to her. The idea that I suggested it, fills me with warmth.

I open the driver's side door and hold out my hand to boost Christina up.

"You'll regret this," she says.

That remains to be seen. I cross to the passenger side and proceed to give her a thorough tutorial.

"Be afraid," she warned.

"Fear hasn't stopped me yet. Slowed me down a few times but never stopped me. Although, I do recall my mother's look of terror the first time my brother and I got behind the wheel."

"Your mom taught you how to drive?"

"She and Dad took turns."

Christina is quiet for a long moment. In a small voice, she says, "It's practically dark out."

"The headlight switch is here but will come on automatically." Leaning over Christina, I point to the dial by the door. Her lilac scent fills my nose, and I remind myself now is not a time for distractions.

"What about other drivers? Oncoming traffic?" she asks.

"These are country back roads. I doubt we'll pass a single car. I have full confidence in you."

Hands gripping the steering wheel tightly, she's quiet for a long stretch. "You have full confidence in the person who calls you dork goblin?"

I chuckle. "Sure do, sweetheart."

Another moment of contemplation passes, but my comment must light the flame under her because she turns the key in the ignition. I narrate instructions to ease off the brake then begin to give the truck gas. We lurch forward then smooth out as we wind down the long cobblestone driveway.

Christina leans close to the steering wheel, wearing an adorable expression of concentration. We only stall at two stop signs, otherwise, it's smooth sailing except she goes a bit too fast around a couple of turns.

"Take the next left." I gesture to a mailbox.

"Uh, I don't really know my way around Willoworth County yet, but is this a back way to Butterbury because if I'm not mistaken, this creepy road leads to your place." Trepidation shadows her features as she slows the truck.

"Ding, ding, ding. You got it right and you brought us here safely."

"I drove monster truck junior safely to your dork goblin lair? To my demise?"

"Definitely not your demise, sweetheart."

A robust laugh escapes because if I'm not careful, she may be the death of me—or at least the guy that clings to solitude. Being with Christina comes with a kind of comfort and warmth I've never experienced with a woman.

"I should make you a certificate of completion. A few more lessons and you could take the official driver's license test."

She cringes. "I'm just glad I didn't kill us."

"Sweetheart, I wouldn't let anything hurt you—least of all your new driving skills."

Her head turns slowly in my direction—half in and out of shadow from the floodlights outside the forge. My pulse drops because the look she gives me suggests she doesn't believe me, and I wonder if she's been hurt before. The wolf inside bares its fangs protectively should any predators dare to cross her path. Christina's gaze snaps forward as if she saw my inner ferocity. I want to tell her that it wasn't directed toward her but am not sure how. The best I can do is say, "I'll make sure you get home safely, promise."

In the half-light, her suspicious gaze softens.

"Do you mind coming in first so I can shower? I got into some old insulation earlier, and the itch is awful."

She clicks on her phone and grumbles. "Do you have Wi-Fi? The service here is terrible."

"I can turn it on for you."

"I have some Picto-Chat posts that I have to catch up on," she says as we go inside.

I ask, "How many times do you post a day?"

"A couple. A few. Four. Sometimes ten."

"That sounds like a lot."

"The more you post, the more likes and follows you get."

Now that we're here, I want to show her around the forge. "How about a technology break? Just for this evening."

Christina's eyes bulge. "What? I can't let the algorithm forget about me."

"The what-go-rithm?"

She snorts a breath through her nose like I'm hopeless.

The smell of smoke and metal and a dog that's too feisty for his own good, greet us as we go inside.

Christina stumbles back. "I forgot about that thing."

"How could you forget Gremlin?" I give him a really good scratch on the neck and around the ears. "He's a good boy. A very big and very good boy. Aren't you? Yes, you're my good boy. My little, lovey, good boy."

Christina's lips part like my hair is on fire and I'm the one who struck the match.

"What? You don't talk to your pet like he's a sweet big little baby dog boy?"

"He's big and little? Anyway, I've never had a pet. Are you

sure it's a dog? By the looks of him, he'd probably eat me if given the chance."

"Gremlin wouldn't hurt a fly, would you buddy?"

The dog tilts his head from side to side, knowing I'm talking to him but not recognizing his favorite words like *walk*, *treat*, or *snugs*.

However, just like when he first saw Christina, he identifies that she's one of his favorite people and trots over and gives her a lick on the hand. I'm not sure what his criteria are, but the only other people he likes are Bo, Louella Belle, and the UPS driver.

Gremlin's tongue goes wild, but Christina jerks away like he's about to slime her.

"He's just giving you kisses. He only does that with his favorite *boomans*." I pat him on the head.

"Before he murderizes them," she mutters.

I chuckle. "Seriously, Gremlin is as gentle as they come—a mutt rescue."

"What sewer did you scrape him out of?"

"He, uh, was my partner Eddy's. Her boyfriend took everything except Gremlin." Leaving it at that, I kick off my boots and hang my keys on the hook by the door. Even though it's been years, that wound is still fresh because I could've stopped it from happening.

"You live here, at the forge?" Christina asks. "Interesting."

"It's not much, but good enough for me."

Up until this point, the space she called my lair, had been a woman-free zone. Self-consciousness rises inside. I wonder what she sees through her interior designer's lens.

The main living space has an open layout with a leather couch opposite a massive stone fireplace that I've used all of twice—the forge heats this place up for the most part. Wooden beams span the ceiling along with the exposed plumbing. Modern tube lighting crisscrosses overhead lending a soft glow.

"This is home, huh?" she asks. "Figures you'd surround yourself with metal and cement."

It's not cold or sterile per se but definitely doesn't have a professional decorator or woman's touch.

"Mostly I work in the forge next door, hike around the property, keep up on the chores."

"Seems like a quiet life."

"That's by design. I'm going to grab a shower. Then we'll go grab some tacos."

"I never said anything about dinner with you, Dork Goblin."

"It's taco Tuesday."

"So what?"

I pull an *Are you kidding* expression? "You mean you don't eat tacos on Tuesday?"

Christina frowns like she tasted something sour. "I don't eat tacos."

"It's a day of firsts. You drove, and then we'll get a delicious meal. Also, it was our final demo day. It's a tradition to get tacos afterward."

"You promised to bring me back to my place."

"What kind of gentleman would I be to send you home hungry?" I wink.

"A gentleman? Ha. More like a dork goblin." Christina must concede though because she wanders toward the nine-foot iron and wood bookshelves I built against the far, brick wall.

I linger by the bathroom door, letting her draw her own conclusions about my books, including many on austere survival, metalwork, and a fair number of crime novels.

She pauses in front of a framed photo of Eddy and me at a gala—my partner dressed to the nines in a satin gown and me in a tuxedo. For once, it wasn't a role or a uniform. Nope, we were helping to raise money for the same animal rescue from where she adopted Gremlin. Ordinarily, I wouldn't hang onto something sentimental or that had the potential to identify or implicate me, however, that photo was taken the night before she died. It was a night we'd crossed a boundary she created and ended in a kiss.

I should lock myself in the bathroom and shower. However, I

can't help but cross the room. I cannot quell the desire to be close to Christina.

"I thought you had some pictures to post," I say in her ear.

She startles and my hands drop to her outer arms, stabilizing her. Her muscles tighten as if not sure she can trust my touch.

Leaning over her shoulder, I say, "Evidence that, dressed in a tux, I can pull off playing the role of a gentleman. Also, I have it on good authority that I looked rather dapper that evening."

She gawks and points. "That's you?"

I rub my hand over my beard. "Yeah, more than a couple of years ago."

She cranes her head in my direction. "Seriously? I don't believe it." Then she gazes into my eyes and back at the photo as if she sees me differently. "Why do you hide under the beard?"

"Never thought of it as hiding. Though I suppose the same could be said about you hiding behind your phone."

Affronted, she frowns then looks down at it, clutched in her hand. "I don't hide behind my phone. I broadcast my life to the world."

"The life you want your followers to see. Not the real you."

Christina's nostrils flare. "You can't say that because you don't know the real me."

"Because of all those walls you have up, keeping people out."

She gazes at her hands as if deep in thought. "We just spent a week knocking walls down."

"Have we?" I ask.

She tilts her head. "And you're one to talk, considering the composition of your surroundings. They literally reflect the fortress inside you."

I grunt because she's not entirely wrong. "I have my reasons."

"Maybe I do too. I learned the hard way that there's no such thing as a happily ever after for me, so why bother?"

I'm not a lovey-dovey type guy but hearing her say that pains me. My eyes probe hers, wanting her to say more. Her glare is defiant like I haven't earned my way into her confidence.

My voice is gritty when I say, "Is this another challenge? One thing to know about me is that I never back down and never give up."

"Obviously not." She taps her chin as if indicating my beard.

"What do you have against this thing?"

"It's unkempt, unpredictable."

On the dorkiest of goblin grunts, I saunter to the bathroom and say, "I'm going to shower." But I leave off the part about contemplating shaving. What would I do for this woman? It turns out, almost anything.

As if not wanting to let me have the last word, she calls, "What about me? I'm grubby from working all day too."

I stride over and tuck a piece of loose brown hair behind her ear and lift her chin. Sparks fly inside. "No, you're perfect, sweetheart."

Rosiness flushes Christina's cheeks and she looks away.

"I'll be five minutes, then we'll get tacos and check on the mortar of those walls you keep talking about."

I close the bathroom door, scolding myself for being so forward and argumentative. Theo and Eddy would tell me I was out of line and that's not how you work your way into a woman's good graces. Unlike me, Eddy had a hookup in every city—not something I condoned, but she wasn't the lone wolf like I am.

We were partners. She treated me like a sibling. I wanted more. She did not. Losing her still stings and makes me wary of getting close to someone again—even friendship comes with risks. Relationships, like with Christina, even more so.

I let cold water wash away these thoughts, but I cannot stop thinking about how I came out here to live a quiet life and to be free from the burdens of the past. I have a feeling this woman is going to pull me out of my comfort zone and all that I've worked for.

Being with Christina is new ground. It's like riding a unicycle with a blindfold and holding a hot poker. I've never shrunk from danger and I don't think I'm going to do anything to stop it now.

CHAPTER 13
Christina

Have I ever met someone who flip-flops my emotions so much? Actually, yes, I have and that's exactly why I need to be careful. Buck is the exact opposite of the kind of guy that I should be with—if I were looking. Which I'm not. Much.

I've subscribed to the No-Man-Plan, and that's the way it's going to stay.

Except there are those tattooed muscles, his blue eyes that have so much depth I could get lost, and the way he moves and speaks with the kind of confidence a girl could trust.

But I'm not that kind of woman—have never been into tattoos, and who cares about eye color. What difference does that make?

What I need to focus on is that Buck is rough, a maverick, and has a beard. Have I mentioned that?

Ew. No thank you. Not for me.

Although, his living space is tidy—no stacks of mail, dirty dishes in the sink, or laundry strewn around.

The only thing out of place is an open book with a pair of reading glasses tossed haphazardly over the spine and the dog bed next to it covered in fur and containing a bone-shaped chew toy.

Forget flip-flopping, I feel torn in two because the things I've told myself not to like are the very things my body and heart cannot ignore—at least when it comes to this particular man.

And Buck is all man.

Keeping an ear on the shower, I take a lap around the room. Gremlin trails me, nudging his head at my ankles for a pat every time I pause. I'm afraid if I touch him, I might catch mange or scurvy. But his puppy dog eyes are kind of sweet...

Being in Buck's space is interesting and not only from an interior decorator's perspective—this could be in a magazine spread about repurposed industrial spaces.

I've also learned that there's:

- Buck the reader
- Buck who probably eats oatmeal for breakfast—given the decorative glass jars on the counter
- Buck in a tuxedo—everyone should have a framed photo of him in their homes. I could duplicate it and make a fortune

I pick up the photo of him and his friend dressed to the nines. She's beautiful in an intimidating way—they're a power couple. I wonder what happened. Or not. A little dip in my chest tells me I'm better off not knowing.

To say Buck looks dapper is an understatement. Had I met him that night, I might feel differently about this man who suddenly takes up a disproportionate amount of my headspace. Then again, likely everything about him hidden under the suit was the same then as he is now—gruff, unpredictable, and well, not the beard, but...

But I am doing a real bang-up job trying to convince myself I'm not attracted to Buck McDermott in every single way it's possible to be attracted to someone.

Why? To protect myself from the double whammy of a failed marriage and a failed engagement. I don't want to be hurt again.

As I pass a closed door next to the bathroom, the shower flicks off. I realize I haven't pulled out my phone and am now super behind on my posts. My thoughts start to spiral about falling behind, being forgotten.

I take a deep breath, then it hitches when the bathroom door opens, sending out a billow of steam to reveal a living, breathing work of art.

My thoughts hang back, stuck on the question: is Buck any different from my past relationships? My heart shouts so loudly, I blurt, "Yes." Water droplets shine like jewels in his beard and his eyes sparkle as I continue, "Yes, I want that." It's a full-body *yes, please* and I cannot stop myself.

As if amused by my outburst and more than willing to tease me, Buck rests his forearms on the door jamb overhead. His tattooed muscles twitch. Dressed in denim jeans and with bare feet, he's male-model material. I start to suffocate. The room tilts. The first time we met, I could blame low blood sugar. This time, it's pure swoon.

"I'm sorry. I forgot to flip on the Wi-Fi," he says as if that's the conversation we're having.

I stammer, trying to replace the real-life vision of him with the image of the cave-dwelling beast I made of him in my mind to suppress my attraction. "Dork goblin."

"Huh?"

"Nothing. I said nothing." Feeling faint, I grip the doorframe and my hand brushes his elbow. The shivers inside go wild.

"Are you okay?"

"Nope. Not okay."

"Is it your blood sugar again?" His blue eyes fill with concern. "Christina, stay with me."

With what must look like the biggest, goofiest smile on my face, the world turns upside down then goes dark. I realize too late that I was holding my breath, making me faint.

The scent of onions and peppers frying rouses me and I press myself up on a soft leather couch. I blink a few times, getting my bearings.

A pointy face with whiskers stares at me, whining softly.

In a flash, Buck kneels beside me. "Good job, Gremlin." His voice is soft, gentle. "Hey, Cricket, take it easy. I checked your vitals and I think you may have experienced another case of low blood sugar. When was the last time you ate?"

The more appropriate question would be, *When was the last time I swooned*?

Never. I've never swooned in my life and while my poor eating habits may be partly to blame for my passing out, the sight of this man did something to my pulse that I cannot explain.

"I figured I'd make something for us to eat here instead of going out. I'm frying up peppers, onions, and I have some chicken. It's not the same as the *carnitas* at the taco place I usually go to, but it'll do." His voice with its hot summer night southern accent is like a comforting lullaby in the darkness.

All the same, I'm on guard. He can't be this nice. What happened to Broody McBroods-a lot? "Is this one of those Hansel and Gretel cottages in the woods? Are you preparing to poison me?"

"I don't think that's what happens in the story."

"Well, whatever it is, there isn't a happy ending."

"I'm not planning to poison you or eat you."

"Oh, right. That's the outcome. But you actually know how to cook?"

"Such a tone of surprise. Would you expect anything less from an international man of mystery?" Buck winks.

"You really could be James Bond's buff and bearded brother." I slap my hand over my mouth and flop back on the couch. "What I meant was Louella Belle said you were like James Bond and it just seems like maybe...she was right." About a few things. Dumb, stupid heart eyes. Ahem.

"And who said the part about me being his buff brother?" Without letting me answer and embarrass myself further, he adds,

"We'd better get fed then we'll work on brushing you up on some more skills."

"What? Like keeping my mouth shut?"

The corner of his lip quirks. "Nah. Don't do that. It's pretty cute when you speak your mind."

"If by cute you mean embarrassing." I hide my fully red face under my hands.

Buck peels my fingers away, sending a warm shiver through me—if such a thing were possible. With his hands around mine, I suddenly feel like anything is possible, including the things I'd sworn out of my life:

- Affection
- Relationships
- Domesticity
- A full stomach
- Happily ever after

"By cute, I mean cute," he says.

I ignore the hum under my skin. "Can, I, uh, help with anything in the kitchen?"

"Are you alright to get up?"

"I didn't swoon the first time I passed out in front of you."

His blue eyes widen in question then land on what truly happened the second time I passed out in front of him.

"But thanks for catching me both times. You should trade in your leather blacksmith apron for a superhero cape."

He grunts then says, "I'll never let you fall, promise."

That's the problem though, I feel myself falling for this unexpected gentleman.

His eyes search mine, likely assessing if I'm okay after my loss of consciousness. I suddenly want his arms around me again, holding me secure against the tornado that threatens my mind in a whirl of questions and uncertainties.

What if my hair is a mess?

My makeup smudged?

What if I burp in front of him?

"I can have you chop up some tomatoes, chives, and cilantro for *pico de gallo*." He holds up a regular, cotton apron that says, *Kiss the cook*.

Not a bad idea.

"Would you like to wear this?"

"Give me some cooking lessons, then maybe. Plus, you're the apron guy."

He grunts and hangs it back on a hook in the pantry.

My stomach grumbles and Buck sets a bowl of chips and guacamole on the kitchen island. "Help yourself."

Ordinarily, I'd pass, but my stomach grumbles, and I take a bite. My eyes close. *Oh citrus and salt, how I missed you*. The flavors are bright and wonderful. I have another bite.

As Buck moves fluidly from the stovetop to the counter, I stab the tomato with the knife and it mushes down on the side. I try again, practically slaughtering the thing. Buck comes up beside me and wraps one arm around my back, gripping my hand around the knife.

At his touch, my body goes cold then hot and my internal thermostat stays there. I fight against leaning into his hard chest.

"Were you raised in a bubble?"

A queasy kind of embarrassment comes my way. It's a sticky wad of shame that I can only dissolve with the truth. "Something like that. My father had a drinking problem that we ignored. Thinking about it now, that fits because I was largely ignored too. My mother was an uptight, uppity, social climber who rarely gave me the time of day. I was left to take care of my trouble-causing sister. I'm starting to see that the skills I learned involved the false pursuit of perfection." By the time I finish speaking, I feel out of breath. Although, that could also be a result of the proximity of this massive manly man.

Buck is quiet for a long moment as though allowing us both to digest what I just said. Then he leans down and nuzzles the crook of my neck and whispers, "You may not realize this, Christina, but you are perfect."

The hum under my skin disagrees and I squawk a self-deprecating laugh. "Don't tease me. I didn't exactly have a normal upbringing in the city."

"Does anyone have a normal upbringing?" His tone is deep, meaningful.

"If only you knew the extent of my family's seismic level of dysfunction."

"Considering this meal is just for the two of us, let's focus on the here and now."

Those words are so much like the kind of thing Meredith would say, my appreciation and affection for Buck deepens.

He grips my hand around the knife and shows me how to make smooth slices and then dices them into squares. When we're done, he spins me around so we're facing each other. Our bodies are barely an inch apart and his hands grip my waist, keeping me firmly planted and unable to focus on anything but his hands, his body heat, this moment even though my thoughts try to fly in every direction.

"Is it getting hot in here?" I ask.

"It's always hot in here."

"Sounds like a bad pick-up line." The words come out of my mouth slowly, dreamily as if this man has me in a swoony stupor all over again.

"He he. I don't think I need to use good, or bad, pick-up lines for that matter."

My inner diva who declared herself on the No-Man-Plan steps up to take a final swing because there is only one direction whatever is happening between Buck and I can go. But she won't back down without a fight. "Aren't you arrogant?"

"Confident. There's a difference."

Without shifting his stance with his body blocking me, Buck opens a window over the kitchen sink. Meredith's breathing exercise has the unfortunate result of causing me to take a deep breath of his smoke and leather scent. The nighttime breeze does nothing to calm my red cheeks.

"Better?"

I chirp a pathetic little noise that sounds more like the crickets outside than a confirmation or a denial. Standing this close, I'm a trillion degrees of confused longing right now. My brain is like, *No!*, but the rest of me is like, *I want that!*

When he speaks, I can feel his voice rumble through my body like thunder over barren plains, sending shivers along my skin that does the opposite of cool me down.

"However, I haven't had to use a pick-up line because I haven't been on the market for a long time," he says.

"Are you married?"

"No. Very, very single."

"On purpose?"

"A lone wolf. I don't do complicated, high maintenance, or drama. Or so I thought..." Buck glances sharply at the gas stove then hops over there and tosses a blazing corn tortilla onto a ceramic plate. "I forgot I turned on the flame."

Oh, he turned on a flame alright.

"There's always a casualty, every time. Whenever I cook tortillas, one inevitably catches fire without fail."

"I hope you don't fling hot pokers and metal tools around like that." I laugh, but mostly because I'm feeling like a tortilla in Buck's presence—on fire, and I can't say that I mind. The way he looks at me sets me ablaze, and that's on top of the hot and humid Georgia night.

The corner of his lip quirks as if he realizes the effect he's having.

What effect exactly? While Buck finishes putting dinner together, and now that I have Wi-Fi again, I turn to the internet to find out. After scanning a few articles about dating at my age, what to look for in a guy, and the top ten questions a girl should ask to determine if someone is boyfriend material, I decide to interview him the same way I did before he was hired as the Designed to Last contractor.

Hopefully, I'll find a flaw or ten so I can get back on track with the No-Man-Plan.

But that's the problem, Buck is one hundred percent perfect alpha man…and I'm Type-A, but that doesn't stop me from wanting him.

CHAPTER 14
Christina

We sit down at the long wooden table with metal legs. Buck bows his head and clasps his hands, saying a prayer. Yet another surprise from this man. Beneath the beard and tattoos, there's a lot more than meets the eye. Although, seeing him fresh out of the shower gave me an eyeful that I'll never forget.

Two tacos sit on the plate topped with the *pico* de *gallo* I helped make and an artful zigzag of sour cream. The hum under my skin makes my thoughts pitch like sails in a growing wind that cautions me against eating the taco. It's messy, I'll have onion breath, and there are probably a ton of carbs.

However, I'm hungry and tired, and it looks delicious so I take a bite, then another, and another. I finish off the first one without stopping.

"You were hungry."

I wipe my hands and mouth on a napkin, feeling ready to be scolded like my mother used to do. "Yeah, sorry. I guess so."

"Don't be sorry. That's why I made us dinner and it makes me happy you're enjoying it. When we first met, I was afraid you were one of those salad-only kinds of women." His eyes are so clear and so true, the truth rises to my lips.

I set my napkin down. "Buck, I am exactly that kind of person."

He chuckles like I'm joking...or he's seen more of me than I do when I look at my reflection. "You can't miss tacos on a Tuesday—that would be a crime."

Recalling Louella Belle's comment about Buck's James Bond style, I glance at the bookshelf containing the plethora of books on art, criminal justice, and suspense novels.

In the past, I've been with guys who aren't as they seem on the surface and I'm afraid Buck is no different. Like both my exes, he's cagey about himself. Doesn't say much about his personal life. Dimitri was secretive and bossy. Les told other people lies so often I started to question whether anything he said was honest.

The wind in my mind rises and I take a deep breath to calm myself. "I'm a list-making good girl. A people pleaser. I care what people think about me. Heck, I care about what I think they're thinking about me. Does that make me complicated? High maintenance? Dramatic? Yes. I'm buried under checklists and to-do lists. My guilt is crippling. My doubt is paralyzing. Living inside my head is exhausting. Listen carefully, if you know what's good for you, you'll take the tacos back and stay away from me."

Buck chuckles like he's facing down a kitten rather than the ferocious tiger running amok inside me.

I click my tongue like he's the hopeless one and say, "You've been warned."

"I'm not afraid."

"You should be," I mutter. Getting back to the research I did about conversation starters, I pluck one at random to see if I can tease out more personal info about him. "Enough about me. What about you? When you're not here working on metal, what do you do?"

He leans back in the chair and folds his hands behind his head. "I find myself in the unexpected position of overseeing an estate remodel, exploring secret passages, and learning that there's always more below the surface—especially when it comes to beautiful women."

I guess I have to live with permanently red cheeks from now on. Thankfully, Picto-Chat has filters. "I mean in general. What more do you want in life? What do you see yourself doing in five or ten years?"

He shrugs like he hasn't thought that far ahead. Meredith's suggestion that I focus on the present comes to mind.

"What are your goals?" I ask.

"Live simply, love well, create beauty if not functionality—" Buck's head tips toward the forge then he adds, "And contribute to my community and country however I can."

I nod, taking in this information, but waiting for him to provide details. "Can you say more about that?"

"I lived and died by commands and a strict timetable for years. Now, I'm seeing where life takes me."

"Is there a specific experience that impacted this direction in your life?" If only I had my tablet handy, I could take notes.

"Yeah, there was." Buck gets up from the table and clears his plate as if that's the end of the conversation. "I haven't dated in a while and missed online dating, speed dating, and all digital forms of dating, so I have to ask if this interrogation-like line of questions is common or if you're just nervous."

A rapid gunfire-like laugh escapes in response.

He spins around and leans against the sink as if catching me guilty. "What about you? When was the last time you let yourself get bored? Saw where the day took you?"

This time, I shrug. I'm unable to recall the last time, apart from right now, when every minute wasn't scheduled or occupied by work or my @DomesticDiva account.

"What is more important to you than your achievements, likes, and follows?" he asks.

"Easy, the impact I have on people, making them happy through transformed interiors and exteriors."

"That sounds like an *achievement* to me." His voice is steady, low when he adds, "Don't chase or settle for likes, Christina. Look for love."

I start to argue then realize he's correct.

"Tell me your most embarrassing moment," he says as if picking up where I left off in the interview process.

"Why are you getting so personal?" I cross my arms in front of my chest.

"You started the interrogation. I was just making it a little spicy. By the way, did you try the hot sauce? Got it from a little market in Texas."

I eye the stuff, afraid that it'll make my eyes water, explosively cough, or otherwise embarrass myself more than I already have.

"Are you going to answer the question?"

I refuse to tell him that my most recent embarrassment happened right here in this room when I swooned—I'm sure there's a medical explanation for my spontaneous lack of consciousness like it was as simple as me holding my breath. "It's hard to say. How about you?"

"Hmm. I'll only tell you if you go first."

I squish up my face. "It's dumb."

"According to you, I'm a dork goblin. I think I can handle dumb."

I stare at my plate and mumble, "When I passed out."

Buck crosses the room in a few strides and cages me between his arms. "I don't want you ever to feel embarrassed in front of me."

I glance up and our eyes meet. "Too late for that. Your turn."

He huffs and shakes his head like I'm hopeless. "My most embarrassing moment, at least in recent history, is something I can show you."

After quickly cleaning up, Buck leads me down a hallway and the scent of smoke fills my nose. He pushes open a door to a large room with a stone forge in the center. Coals fill it and tools line the walls. A workbench sits under a window with projects in various stages of completion.

I'm afraid I'll get dirt-smudged or fall on a sharp object just being in here, so I stay close to Buck. The space lacks any discernible mode of organization and makes my skin crawl. I spot sculptures, ornate garden gates, hardware, and horseshoes. My fingers trace a metal heart shape although I think it's meant to be a leaf that's part of a trellis.

A shield leans against the wall. The knight in shining armor the ladybosses mentioned comes to mind. "Do you have a sword to go with that?"

Buck chuckles and produces a sword that glints in the low light. "Several. But I came to show you this." He picks up a wooden frame filled with swirling letters *Bo and Ella Ball forever*. "I made it for their wedding gift."

"That's so sweet, but what's embarrassing about it?"

"Look again."

I do so then laugh and cup my hand over my mouth.

"Metalwork requires keen focus. I was working on this the weekend after we first met. Must've been distracted. When I'm handling molten metal, it's the only thing I can think about, otherwise—" He taps Louella Belle's misspelled name to make his point.

"Are there things you don't want to think about?"

He grunts. "Kind of like when handling firearms, they require your full attention."

"Much experience with that?"

"Yeah. Former job."

"Were you an armorer?"

"No. I was, a, uh researcher for a government agency." He doesn't say another word as if he already said too much then shifts like turning the page in a book. "I'll have to start over."

"That's not overly embarrassing. Not like passing out in front of the guy you have a crush on." My eyes bulge.

"Is that so?"

"Scratch that. I didn't say that. I meant a guy I have a brush on. A brush in your beard."

He rubs his bearded chin. "Hmm. Maybe we both need to work on our grammar."

"Honest mistake."

"I think you did say *crush.* It just so happens that I have a crush on you too."

"More like we're going to crush each other on the jobsite. You realize you and I are like fire and oil or water or whatever the expression is." Here comes the word salad again.

Buck grips my waist and tugs me close.

My mouth goes dry.

Our eyes meet and then my phone beeps in my pocket. I should ignore it but after years of responding to it like a dog whistle, I pull it out, ruining a moment that may have turned into a kiss.

CHAPTER 15
Buck

In the days after I gave Christina driving lessons, she "didn't" swoon in my living room, and we had tacos, it's nearly impossible to get her jade green eyes out of my mind. I start to notice the color everywhere.

I can still smell her lilac scent lingering in my house and have the sudden urge to learn to garden—perennial flowers in particular. I practically feel her presence, which leaves me with a longing I cannot sustain.

She always wears her long brown hair pulled back and I want to take it down, run my fingers through it—feel the silky softness on my rough skin. While in my kitchen that night, on more than one occasion, our lips were so close I imagined them pressed together.

Kissing that woman would be sheer perfection—how can I get her to realize that?

On the surface, Christina is a glossy, put-together picture of perfection. In my eyes, she is perfect, but beneath I see a kind of agonized overthinking that I want to claim and toss in the demo dumpster. I want to calm the second-guessing and churning in her mind. It's the kind of stress that makes her cautious, maintain her distance, and keep her walls shored up.

I know all too well what it's like when life feels out of control and and also what it's like to take on the exhaustive task of trying to micromanage and orchestrate every aspect of it—thinking if I just get this and this and this right, everything will fall into perfect order.

That's a surefire way for everything to fall apart.

I know that firsthand too.

It pains me to think Christina experiences any kind of agony, but how I can help her is as elusive as solving the mystery that prompted me to take the contracting job to begin with.

The next couple of weeks pass with taking the kitchen at the estate down to the studs, doing the slow work of remodeling all the bathrooms, and spending long minutes standing in front of the shelf in the storeroom, trying to wrap my detective's mind around the dead-end passageway.

Interspersed with that, by day, I come up with as many reasons as possible to find myself in Christina's presence—what color grout she wants paired with the bathroom tile, cabinet hinge style selection, and whether to go with a traditional or more modern bevel on the trim in the ballroom.

Christina and I find our groove, working like a team, partners. I think fondly back to my time with my partner Eddy. It took us a while as we tested each other and discovered how we could work to our strengths and compensate for each other's weaknesses. It's kind of like that with Christina, only there's an additional element—one Eddy didn't share with me.

She was a friend, like a sister, and at times, I wanted there to be something more, but we didn't cross that line—except that one time then she expressed that she wasn't interested. She made that clear. Work came first. Unrequited Love 101.

Eddy dated but didn't commit and told me that I was the kind of guy deserving of a good woman to settle down with and make a home, a family. Instead, I went in the other direction, more inclined to solitude and bachelorhood.

Christina is a friend, I hope. And should I be so lucky, perhaps she'll become something more—that we can grow in our relationship and have a future together. One that involves breakfast, lunch, dinner, and every second before, during, and after—filling in the answer to all those questions she asked and more while we ate tacos.

Deep in thought, I'm on the second floor of the estate, replacing an iron heating grate I fabricated, when the dream dissolves at the sound of Christina voicing complaint as she approaches from down the hall.

The problem is, I don't think she likes me like I do her. My only hope is that this isn't Unrequited Love 201.

For starters, Christina is a city girl and I've sworn off that life and returned to my country roots.

For two, I imagine her with a guy who thinks more about his appearance than simply tossing on jeans, a T-shirt, and calling it good. I was that other guy once upon a time, but I had to look the part—depending on what that was and got accustomed to finely made threads, luxury shoes, and designer accessories. Now, I'm just me.

Thirdly, given the fact that I have a beard, and Christina isn't a fan, I'm not holding out hope for us.

Lastly, she said she doesn't believe in happily ever after.

Why not, and do I? Am I willing to change (or at least shave) for her?

Her voice echoes through the empty hallway. "Buck, there you are."

"Your best friend, at your service."

She rolls her eyes while wearing a smile on her lips. "More like my *beast* friend, but fine. Listen, I've been looking all over for you. For the gazillionth time, when are these bars coming off the windows?"

"Gazillionth time? Isn't that a bit of an exaggeration? I think you're only on a million. Maybe a million and one." I bop her nose.

She lets out an adorable huff. "And I have a million and one things to do. Could I please have your help?"

"Of course." I'm here to help in the ways she wants but maybe also the ways she needs.

I recall the presence of the film crew at her back and slip into a role—one I'd sometimes have to play while on a mission. *Pacify the enemy while figuring out how to solve the mystery—this message will self-destruct in ten seconds.*

In this instance, Christina isn't an enemy, but she's not happy at the moment and there is a mystery that I'm determined to solve but need those bars in place, at least for now. In my line of work, I often had to solve riddles, ciphers, and code. I learned that leaving everything at the scene of the crime or mystery, as it were, and untouched for as long as possible resulted in answers more often than not, so I'm reluctant to remove the bars—plus, it would mean we're closer to finishing. I'm not ready to say goodbye to Christina. Not yet.

"You look lovely today—cute shirt-skirt-shorts, skort?" I tug on the hem of her summery blue garment that would look somewhat like a mechanic's suit but has ruffles and lace trim.

Christina snorts a laugh as if tickled by my attempt to be charming, but in typical guy fashion, fall short—no pun intended. The arched eyebrow I get tells me I haven't escaped her wrath at not yet taking the bars off. I have my reasons. Rather, a theory of a reason.

"It's designer and called a romper. You didn't answer my question. The deadline is closing in on us. We have work to do, and I can't have anything hold us up." Stress tightens her features.

I'd like to wrap my arms around her and melt that stress away. I also don't want to think about this job being over. Granted, we have two months, but we're that much closer to saying goodbye.

"Well, good morning, Little Miss Sunshine," I say in response to her cloudy tirade.

"It's almost lunchtime, Buck. We're nearly halfway done with the job, and those bars are still there. Can we get started on removing them, please? Not to mention the tile guys are behind, the wallpaper glue is melting in this heat creating clumpy blobs, and—" She presses her lips together and gives a quick side-eye to the camera as if tired of being trailed by it.

I want to smooth her brow, but risk getting bitten with the way she's acting today. Instead, I place a comforting hand on her arm. "Yes, the bars will be off soon."

"Great because I'd like to look out the windows without feeling like I'm in a prison. Can you imagine what it was like to live here, caged in like that? I'd like to know why they're there in the first place. Strange, right?" She slows her roll as if recalling the secret passage—just one of the strange things about this place.

I've been researching the history of the Easton Estate and trying to connect the dots between what's on record and the stories I've heard passed down through my family. With the cameras rolling, I'd rather keep this off record. Plus, it's better not to speculate until I gather all the information possible.

"Speaking of strange things, Bo told me you found a key the other day." Perhaps this will help fill in some of the blanks in my research.

"I almost forgot." She digs in her purse, checks a message on her phone then produces an iron skeleton key.

Our hands brush as I take it, stoking the embers in me. Her eyes lift to mine and I cannot help but think about the night, a few weeks ago, when we almost kissed. I trace my finger around the bow—that's the part you hold and imagine tracing her lips—then lift it up to the light. The camera follows my gaze. "It's shaped like a heart."

I notice Christina sees hidden hearts everywhere, from the heart-shaped leaf made of iron in my workroom, to a heart-shaped rock in the driveway, a flower petal in the garden, the shape traced in the dust on a window, a cloud in the sky.

She either sees love everywhere or she's seeking a way to mend her broken heart. That's another mystery I intend to solve. Mostly, I can't take my eyes off her but not in a creepy way. The power of observation used to be an essential part of my job, but I'd call this more a labor of love—or something like that.

"Where'd you find it?" I ask.

"Second-floor bedroom. I was trying to open the window—"

"By that do you mean you were cursing my name for not removing the bars?"

A flicker of laughter crinkles her eyes. "Possibly. It wouldn't budge. Then I noticed something irregular about the extension jamb. I ran my hand along the wood casing and then removed a small, metal object lodged inside."

I turn the key over a few times, contemplating what I've learned so far, which isn't much but don't want to talk about it on camera. Old habits die hard. As if both of us are secretly longing to have this moment to ourselves, we drift slowly away from them and relatively out of earshot.

"Unusual, right?" she asks then looking up at me she says, "I wonder if it could be the key to someone's heart."

"Or someone's freedom..." I mutter then think about how they could be the same thing.

I press the key back into Christina's hand, lingering there as if to remind her she can trust me, including with her heart if she'd let me hold it.

The moment between us tightens as we step closer together—there are enough hidden nooks and alcoves in this house that if we were actually alone, I might just pull her close, disappear into one, and pick up where we left off before her phone interrupted on Taco Tuesday.

"Wouldn't it be something if this old house had a love story to tell," she whispers.

If I could stop recording and pause this moment, then help Christina step outside the role she's created for herself, I'd like to show her that she doesn't have to do it all. She can ask for help or do less or just do what she can and none of it has to be perfect. That she has me.

That *this* could be a love story.

I'm more of a man of action than of words but with the cameras on, neither come to me before Christina spins away from the moment at the sound of a notification on her phone.

If it weren't for the bars, I'd throw that thing out the window.

She holds it up like an antenna and answers while complaining about the terrible service in this part of the country. "I never had bad reception in the city." She strides in the opposite direction from the way she came and toward where the plumbers had to remove part of the subfloor to refit pipes in the cavity between the floor up here on the second level and the ceiling below.

I'd been doing a good job of keeping people out of there and hurry after her, hollering, "Christina," but she's distracted and it's too late.

With a loud crackling, all of a sudden the floor starts to cave in.

She shrieks as her arms spin wildly, trying to regain her balance then grappling for something to hold onto.

I lunge for her, but not quickly enough for me to stop us from falling. I wrap myself around her, pulling her close as we rapidly drop through the floor that vanishes beneath us.

CHAPTER 16
Buck

Christina's fear-filled yell is in my ears then goes silent as a massive sheet of protective plastic spanning part of the ceiling in the ballroom that's beneath us on this level slows our fall.

For one hopeful second, it cradles us with a false sense of safety before it's stretched too thin.

She clings to me and I grip her tight as the plastic gives way and once more we descend before landing in a tangle of canvas drop cloths, plastic, and a teetering gallon of paint on a plank of wood.

My back hits the ground first with a dull pain that's sure to sharpen later. Christina's eyes widen with fear and confusion and disbelief.

Louella Belle appears on a ladder and grabs the handle of the teetering paint can at the last second. "Is Adair here or was that just good luck?" she asks, scrambling down to meet us.

"More like bad luck," Christina says, out of breath.

Her head rests against my chest from me buffeting her fall.

"Your heart is thundering." She lifts and cranes her head in my direction.

Hers is too. I'd like to only blame the drop, but my pulse also has a lot to do with her proximity. "If it's still ticking and you can hear it, that means we're both still alive."

Taking a quick survey of the situation, it's clear that the plastic sheets around the upper levels of scaffolding acted like a hammock, breaking the worst of our fall. Looking up, we barely avoided a massive chandelier but in the process, completely ruined the freshly painted ceiling and tore some of the original wallpaper we'd preserved.

"What happened to the floor?" Christina asks.

Sharp pain hits my gut, heart, and throat in that order, but it has nothing to do with the crash landing. Rather, the fact that we fell in the first place is my fault. I'm to blame.

I explain how the plumbers removed the subfloor because there'd been a leak that degraded the wood, making that section little more than moldy, mushy plaster. "The beams were more than two feet on center, making the span big enough for us to slip through. Thank goodness for the work going on in the ballroom otherwise that kind of fall could've been deadly. All the same, it was scary and I'm sorry."

"Who was the idiot who didn't put up caution tape?" Christina asks.

I clear my throat. "That would be this dork goblin."

"You could've killed us or anyone here."

"I was working right there, blocking anyone from going down the hall. I wasn't intending to move until the plumbers were done. Then—" Then she distracted me and she could've died. That hits far too close to home considering what happened to Eddy. I get to my feet. "I apologize, Christina. No excuses. That was bad judgment on my part." My voice is low, forceful.

I knew I didn't belong here—I moved to the woods for a reason and that's because I cannot be trusted. Not with a simple job and certainly not with lives.

"This is a major worksite violation," Christina hisses then she blinks slowly, tilting her head as if looking up at something on the wall.

"Anything broken? Injuries?" I ask, concerned and feeling wrecked by guilt.

She slowly gets up, understandably distracted as Louella Belle scurries over. A few others enter the room, likely having heard the clatter.

Commotion ensues as questions are asked, assessments made, and film rolls. I'm sure this will be a shocking turn of events for the show and likely, I'll receive my walking papers.

From above, several faces peer through the hole in the floor. My gut churns with how much worse it could've been. How I'm not worthy of this beautiful woman or capable of taking care of her.

I turn to leave when a man in a slate gray sports jacket strides into the ballroom. Slick as a son of a gun, he removes a pair of sunglasses. He looks around the room as if it's his jobsite. "Well, it seems progress is being made...or something like that."

Christina and Louella Belle go quiet along with everyone else because he acts like the kind of man that stands on stages and commands rooms. But I'm not convinced. Maybe he's the producer or a Hollywood type who noticed Christina's talent and is here to make her an offer of some sort. Perhaps he has other designs.

I'm wary. On watch.

There's something about the tilt of his smile that makes me stay put. Maybe it's the way his gaze lingers on Christina. Or it could be jealousy. A violent, ballroom wrecking, kick this guy back to whatever hole he crawled out of suspicion seizes me.

"Hey there, Miss Abernathy," he says.

She lifts her hand in a little wave. "Oh, hi, Les. How are you?"

"I'm fantastic now that I get to see your beautiful face again. Listen, you're going to want to file a workplace safety incident report."

Christina pales. "I know. It was—"

He plants a pasty hand on her shoulder. "I'm jokin' darlin'. The line is...You're going to need to file a workplace safety report because I just fell for you." He chortles.

More than a few pairs of eyes dart to the gaping hole in the ceiling.

She shrugs out from under his grip, eyes wide with terror—or it could be that the reality of our accident sinks in.

"If you recall, I was with Mayor Stoll a few weeks back when we were discussing the future of Butterbury. I also mentioned this was my grandparents' home."

"I don't recall you saying that." Her eyes narrow. "I thought your grand—" She abruptly cuts herself off. "Never mind."

"Ah, well, it was probably overwhelming meeting the mayor for the first time." Les smooths his hands down the lapel of his sports jacket.

"Not really. Can I help you with something? This is a closed shoot." Confidence grows in her voice.

"I was hoping to help *you* as a matter of fact." He reaches for her hand and kisses her knuckles.

Christina blushes.

Something inside me crushes up like a tin can. That's my job —I'm the one that makes her blush. My fists tighten by my sides. But in addition to being red-faced, a sheen of perspiration glistens on her skin like she's nervous—the adrenalin catching up with her from the fall or something else?

"And how do you intend to help me?" Her expression is half perplexed and half intrigued.

How I wish those eyes were on me. Then again, I just blew my chance by being irresponsible and nearly sending us to our deaths.

"I'm going to make you an offer that you cannot refuse," he says, pacing a slow circle around her and studying the room before meeting her gaze.

"This is the ballroom, right?" He takes her hand in his as if ready to tango.

The wild dog in me builds toward a growl, protective if this guy so much as breathes at Christina the wrong way. But the voice of reason reminds me that it's my fault she fell through the floor. She could've died or been seriously injured. I have no claim to calling her my own.

"Sure is. We were nearly done with it until that—" She gestures vaguely toward the hole.

"Will you have this dance with me and I'll tell you my proposal?"

She looks around confusedly as if wondering where the music is then laughs. "This is a worksite and as mentioned, a television production. My three partners and I, the ladybosses, have a show called Designed to Last, so if you have a proposal, you should set up a meeting and talk to all of us."

That's my girl. Now, throw a pie in his face and we'll call it good.

Les chortles again. "I've gathered, darlin'. I figured since you're the DomesticDiva, you'd be the one in charge." He stops a few inches from her ear and lowers his voice. "We both know they're riding on your coattails."

Christina shifts from foot to foot as if something he said landed.

Les resumes his pacing. "If anything, this place was definitely designed to last. But as it was in my family, rightfully, it belongs to me." He gives her a long look that seems to convey something—a command? A threat?

"We bought it for the show." This time her voice is small.

"Shame about that, actually. I wasn't made aware of its sale."

"It had been on the market for three years—our lawyer assured us all heirs had been properly contacted during the probate period."

Les's lips tug smugly. "Yes, well, that was in error. However, I'd like to offer you double for it."

"We've already invested that much into it, if not more with the show, the team, and everything. I'm sorry, but—"

He takes her hands in his. "I want it as is. This place is already perfect. Well, minus that hole up there. I always wanted the family home back in the family. You can stop production and I'll just take it off your hands. And pick up where we left off and take your hand in mine..."

Christina pulls hers out of his and searches for Louella Belle and the others. She shakes her head and backs away. "That's not my decision to make."

He pulls out a card and flicks it to her. "You sure about that, darlin'?"

"Very, very sure."

"Oh come on. What can I say to twist your pretty little arm?"

"There will be no twisting of arms or taking of hands, Les." Christina's tone is firm.

His lip lifts in a snarl. "I assure you, partnering with me is the best decision to make. I have a lot of, uh, history here and couldn't bear to let it slip through my fingers." He flashes his slick smile. "Call me tonight with your decision. I'll be waiting." He strides away, then stops, and his eyes land on me. "Oh, and you should fire whoever caused that. Someone could've died."

Yeah. I'm aware.

Christina takes a deep breath but doesn't look in my direction.

My chest threatens to crater with shame. That dreadful emotion took up residence inside me for a long time before I gave it the heave-ho and looks like it's making a rapid return.

I leave the ballroom as the girls chat about Les and Camellia calls from the second floor about peeling wallpaper.

I tail him as he gets in a shiny red sports car with Nevada plates. He speeds down the driveway. Something about that guy didn't sit right—the obvious reason is the way he looked at and touched Christina, not that I have any right to be possessive or protective.

He said he was related to the Eastons, but I don't recall any mention of him in the family tree. Additionally, Les isn't a family name. If there's anything I know for certain about the Easton family and the Quigleys, it's that they always passed down family names—I'd know, being the recipient of one myself even if I'm on the wrong side of their favor. I also don't recall Les's name on the list of relations from the will. Then again, I wasn't paying much attention back then.

After going upstairs and making sure the hole in the floor is adequately protected and the plumbers are almost done, I leave the jobsite, certain that I won't be welcomed back.

That evening, I have a meeting with one of my blacksmith customers. After consulting them on a gate for their entryway, I think some more about the bars on the window, the secret passageway, and the unexpected visitor—Les Easton.

I return home and get some work done in the forge then settle in after dinner. It's none of my business, but I enter his name into a background check database I'm not supposed to have access to now that I'm retired.

I learn that Les Easton's real last name is Streckle and glean little more than his vital statistics, that he lives in Las Vegas, and worked for an antique appraisal company—not entirely surprising given his interest in the old house. Next, I pull up the family tree, trying to find his name or a cousin I'm not familiar with.

No Les or any variations of that name. I contemplate this for a long moment and come up with two possibilities. He either has a legitimate interest in returning the estate to a member of the family or he's heard the same story as me—however, if that's the case, I'm not entirely sure that we share the same intentions.

Except perhaps when it comes to the brown-haired, green-eyed beauty that's heading up the restoration project.

I won't lie, it's become routine for me to keep up on the progress we're making on the estate via Christina's @Domestic-Diva account. I'm not a creeper or a troll (nope, just a dork goblin doing dork goblin things) and would never send her a message that says something gross like, *Hey babe, check out my account so we can hook up*, mostly because I don't have an account on Picto-Chat.

I've observed three things about Christina:

1. She's as charming in real life as she is online
2. She's passionate about what she does
3. The way her account coordinates from top to bottom with color to style to graphic design, the level of perfection she strives for must be depleting

Okay, there's a fourth thing. I have feelings for her I never thought I'd have for anyone—the urge to comfort her, be a companion, and loosen her hold on perfection because, beneath her put-together veneer, she's struggling inside. I can feel it. I can see it. I want to free her from it.

But is that really any of my business? Especially now that we fell from the second story of the house because I was careless? In my defense, I was being incredibly careful, acting like an armed guard in front of a vault by not letting anyone go beyond where I'd been working in the hallway. However, I still came up short. I still failed in the line of duty.

I sigh at the same time I notice Christina hasn't updated her Picto-Chat feed in a few hours, reminding me of her comment about the bad reception at the house. From the table by the door, my own phone beeps, a rarity.

Hoping my parents are alright on their cruise, I click it on to see Christina's name scrolling across the screen. Here it comes, she's going to fire me.

"Hello," I answer.

"Buck. I'm at the house. Please, come quick. I need your help. There's a—" Her tone rises in panic.

At least that's what I think she said. There was crackling on the line and her voice cut out more than once. I instantly revert to my training to keep a cool head while responding to the situation

—by dashing out to my truck and driving eighty-five miles an hour all the way there.

Thankfully, there's no one else on the road, but that doesn't keep my mind from racing about what could've happened to Christina.

CHAPTER 17
Christina

My heart pounds in my chest for the second time today—only, this time I'd argue it's worse. Much worse. Flappy, flippy, bitey worse.

When I tell this story to my grandchildren someday, if I survive, they'll wonder what could be worse than falling through the second floor and into a ballroom.

Let's just say that during the Twilight craze, I was not on team Edward.

I peer through the crack between the edges of the cardboard box. Yes, I'm holed up in an appliance box in the space between the dining room and kitchen. I'd been nagging the crew to recycle the cardboard but for once am glad they didn't listen to me.

After I saw the predator and was scrambling for safety, I threw on as many lights as I could and the house is mostly ablaze. Thankfully, I don't see any movement, but that doesn't mean it isn't out there, stalking me, waiting for the right moment to swoop down and attack.

Sealing the opening of the box, I scuttle to the corner. My ears tune to the sounds in the vacuous, echoey house.

Was that more wallpaper peeling off the walls or was that thing on a flight of fancy terrorizing me?

I'm practically shaking and click on my phone to call for help again, but just then the light goes out and it dies. I drop my face into my hands.

Worst. Day. Ever.

Why has it been so bad? Let me count the ways:

1. The wrong bathroom faucets were delivered
2. The ongoing problem with the HVAC—it blows cool air on the heat setting and vice versa
3. Wallpaper not sticking, leaving great, goopy gobs of glue on the wall
4. The crew lost some of the footage of the kitchen cabinet *before*, making the *after* less impactful
5. Unfortunately, they have the entirety of Buck and me falling through the floor
6. I FELL THROUGH THE FLOOR
7. My ex-fiancé appeared, offering to buy the place and making veiled threats
8. Buck disappeared without so much as a goodbye
9. I stayed late to catch up on things and it's Taco Tuesday, but I'm trapped because...
10. There's a bat loose in the house

Ten epic fails and that's just today. I won't go into yesterday and don't want to think about what tomorrow will bring. I dare not think about earlier this week or last week, starting with how the ladybosses abandoned me, making it so I had to learn to drive.

I surprised myself (and probably Buck too) by being okay at operating that beast on wheels. For instance, I didn't careen into a ditch and we arrived at Buck's house safely. Had I realized we were going to his lair, I may have driven off the road. On purpose. But it wasn't so bad either. The tacos he made were exceptional. I forgot how good a proper meal can taste—especially when guacamole is involved.

Did I swoon that night? I swooned so hard. Took a trip to

swoon city, I did. However, I haven't had a chance to properly process the experience with my ladybosses because we've all been so busy on this project.

Everything feels like it's spiraling out of my grasp. That and the rat with wings flying around the house makes my skin buzz louder than ever.

Curled up in my Fort Knox box, I'm probably one big wrinkle. I even wore a cute outfit today, hoping it might lift my spirits —newsflash, it didn't.

Sidenote: the romper I'm wearing has pockets, which is a major plus. But if you've ever worn a one-piece suit like this, then you know that using the ladies' room is a chore…so I haven't gone all day. TMI? Too bad, I'm getting desperate.

However, Buck noticed my frilly romper that paired surprisingly well with my work boots. But my hyper-analytical mind hasn't stopped obsessing whether he was criticizing my non-compliant worksite attire or complimenting me.

He's so stony and stoic it's sometimes hard to tell. Okay, he's like that all the time.

And where is he? Probably not coming because why would anyone come to my aid?

I listen carefully to my surroundings. Was that the *flap, flap* of a pair of wings, or more than a pair? Did the flying rodent invite friends to feast on my blood? I cower in the corner of the box, wondering if I'll make it through the night.

Am I being a diva? Yes, but it's not like I didn't disclose that from the outset—after all, I go by the Domestic Diva. What can anyone expect?

What might be a muffled growl comes from somewhere beyond my hideaway. Are werewolves on the hunt too? I start to tremble and say a prayer. This might be my last. From somewhere in the house, a deep voice bellows.

I sit up and knock my head into the box, no doubt revealing my whereabouts to the enemy.

"Hello," the voice calls from far away.

A terrible thought seizes me. What if Les is a vampire—I wouldn't be surprised. They're usually handsome and slick when in their human form. In the past, when we were first together, I felt flattered by the attention he gave me but didn't like the way he feasted his eyes on me earlier.

I think there's supposed to be a full moon tonight. Maybe now that it's risen, he transformed and is searching for me. A whimper escapes.

The shifting of floorboards alerts me to someone's presence. If only I'd grabbed something I could use as a weapon before I hid under here. My phone is of no use. I'd used my last lifeline to call Buck but doubt he'd go through the trouble to come here at this late hour.

"Christina." A male voice booms.

My eyes widen. It's him. I think. I hope. Or what if the bats got to Buck and are now imitating his voice to trick me?

"Cricket, it's me. Where are you?"

As I see it, I have two choices:

1. Risk revealing my location in the hope that it's actually Buck
2. Stay here all night and hope the vampire bats disappear by morning. If I make it until morning because my ankle itches from a mosquito bite (they're practically as big as bats around here)

I don't dare move a muscle. Then a loose piece of my hair tickles my nose. I want to brush it away. I have to brush it away...and scratch my ankle.

"Where are you?" he growls. "If anyone so much as laid a hand on you, I'll—"

The itch and tickle grow. This is totally unfair. Also, my romper is bunched up and digging into my thigh and now my foot is falling asleep.

Another whimper squeaks out of me.

"Christina." A pair of feet stop somewhere outside my hideaway.

Please be Buck. Please be Buck.

I hear the shifting of fabric and then smell woodsmoke and leather.

Relief and longing swallow me up and I feel as safe as I did while he held me tight after landing on the ballroom floor earlier. It's then that I realize this man will fall through floors for me. He'll race to my aid in the middle of the night...

I shift the box flap only enough to pick out a pair of blue eyes, peering inside.

"Quick. Come in here. It's not safe out there." I slide my hand through the slit in the box to grip his shirt to pull him to take shelter.

"I don't think I'll fit. More importantly, what are you doing in there?" he asks with concern as he pokes his head through the peephole in the flap.

"Hiding, obviously and sure, we can make you fit. It'll be cozy. Welcome to season two of Designed to Last—this is my latest project."

"If that's the case, it gives new meaning to a tiny house. What are you hiding from?"

I gaze above his barely-visible shoulder. "You're not safe out there, sir."

"Are you okay?" he asks like I may have hit my head earlier.

"No. There's a bat on the loose."

Buck straightens and looks around, leaving me with nothing but a sliver of his denim-covered legs. I wince because no doubt the thing has him in its crosshairs.

This is how the beginning of our love story will end. I'll be hiding in here and he'll be out there, bravely protecting me, then the thing will take him down.

"I should've told you my actual most embarrassing moment while I had a chance," I say.

From beyond the box, he asks, "What do you mean?"

"I didn't tell you the whole story about not having a happily ever after. I was married once and ran away from my second wedding. Both rival for first place in the humiliating failure department. When everything else I touch turns to gold, why not my love life?" Tears pierce the corners of my eyes.

Buck reaches through the cardboard for my hand. "Christina, come on out."

"As I said, it's not safe. If you were smart, you'd come in here with me."

He picks up the box, exposing me curled up in the fetal position then draws me to my feet. "I don't think a quarter-inch of cardboard is going to protect you."

"From the bat?"

"No, from what this is really about." His southern accent is soothing, gentle.

"This is really about a bat. Mostly." I glance up, taking in the chiseled jawline of a man with a pair of full lips, blue eyes. I gasp. "Who are you?" I ask, terrified the night went from a paranormal romance film to Twilight Zone.

"Buck McDermott. Your contractor."

"Where's the beard?" I ask, eyes widening at his freshly shaved face.

He brushes his hand along his smooth jawline. "Shaved. After the accident upstairs today, I figured I needed to change. I'm really sorry about what happened, Christina."

Horror fills me at his handsome face—and a little bit of that dreamy, heady swoony feeling too. Not going to lie. But the horror comes from the fact that he felt like he needed to change.

"Why did you need to change? Nothing needs to change." My tone rises a few octaves with panic because earlier when I was staring at the chandelier sparkling on the ceiling in the ballroom, I realized I like Buck. A lot. Just the way he is.

"Christina, I practically killed you." His voice rasps with pain.

"No, the bat is going to kill us both if we don't take shelter." I tug his hand, but the man is like a monolith.

He grips my arms and gazes into my eyes with a gravity that could cause us to fall through the earth. "I cannot risk anything happening to you."

"Thank you. But right now, there's a bat on the loose and we're not safe."

"I'm not afraid of a bat. I'm afraid—"

From elsewhere in the house, a door slams. I startle and leap into Buck's arms.

"The wind picked up on the way over. I left the front door open. If there were a bat in here, it probably flew away, but I won't let a little bat hurt you. What you have to worry about is me."

I frown. "How so?"

His brow tightens. "It's a long story for another time. Let's clear the house and make sure it's bat free and then I'll take you home."

"I still have work to do."

"It's late." Buck's voice is like a lullaby, a reminder that he's right.

Like a human blanket, he holds me protectively close to his chest and gazes at me with so much care I imagine this is what the earth's core feels like.

"Is this really about a bat?" he asks.

"This is really about a bat," I answer. "Mostly. I mean, it was lonely here by myself this late, but I'd never fake a bat-scare to get you to come over. Bats are no joke."

"How were you going to get home, anyway?" he asks as we walk slowly away from my safe haven.

Bye box, I mouth. *It's been nice knowing you.* My voice shakes a bit out here in the open and I answer, "I was going to call one of the ladybosses—they went out for taco Tuesday."

"Without you?"

"As I said, I had stuff to do." I bite my lip. "Plus, you disappeared this afternoon after, um, Les stopped by and I didn't want to do taco Tuesday without our contractor."

He grunts. "I'm sorry about what happened with the floor. It won't happen again because I'm no longer your contractor. I'm off the job."

"You can't do that."

"Decision made. End of story."

My arms cross in front of my chest. "Why don't I have a say?"

"You'll have to find someone who's more responsible. Who can keep you safe."

I tuck my chin back. "Buck, you're that guy."

"Nope. It was my job to block off that area upstairs, and I failed." Defeat enters his voice.

"Yeah, but you broke my fall with your body. You risked your life to save mine." I pause in the hall, in enemy territory, but I have to make my point.

"That shouldn't have been a thing, to begin with." He grimaces like the real damage was done to his pride and not his back or whatever other parts of his body that took the impact of our landing.

"That was an accident. I was the one who wandered over to your work area, not looking where I was going, and with my head buried in my phone. What matters is that you came here tonight. If you were careless or irresponsible, you would've stayed at home in your dork goblin cave doing whatever dork goblins do when they're alone. Instead, you showed up here like a knight in shining armor."

The corner of his mouth lifts in a smirk and scrambles my brain. I tip my gaze to his. His eyes sparkle in the fully lit hallway. It's like we're back in his kitchen on Taco Tuesday. If I lean in a little bit more our lips will connect and...

The lights go out.

I shriek and say, "The bat is coming for us." I want to add, *Save me*, but that's a tad dramatic when, in fact, I should be over the top dramatic and yell, *Save me from myself!* Because as Buck clasps my hand and leads us to safety, I'm having a hard time sticking to my No-Man-Plan.

CHAPTER 18
Buck

With Christina's hand in mine, I rush toward the door and exit into the night. The stars blink vibrantly overhead and the moon hovers over the line of trees in the distance.

"The bat turned out the lights." Her voice is a staccato of panic.

"Bats can't do that, sweetheart," I say, infusing the words with affection.

This night has taken an unexpected turn and I don't want it to end. I grab a flashlight from my truck. "Let's go investigate."

"We're not going back in there." She backs away.

"I thought you had work to finish."

"Not with a bat on the loose."

"Is it too late for tacos?" I ask.

"Is that even a question?"

My lips tug toward a smile. "Do you want to drive?"

"I'm still a bit shaken up from my ordeal. I'd rather you take the wheel."

"My pleasure, sweetheart."

"My name is Christina Abernathy."

"I know. Christina Sweetheart Abernathy."

She giggles. "That's not my middle name."

"Then what is it?"

"You'll laugh."

"Try me."

She clears her throat and makes a sound that she repeats, "Cricket. Christina Cricket Abernathy. On top of being the chubby girl, with that name, my parents doomed me for dorkdom."

"That's adorable and millions of people would disagree—you're definitely not a dork, but it's not so bad."

"What's not so bad?"

"Being a dork. A dork goblin."

"Oh and you're one to tease me? Your parents named you Buck."

"Yep, and my sister is Doe," I say matter of fact.

She narrows her eyes. "You're kidding."

I pop a smirk. "Yes, I am. But you should've seen your face. You were scandalized. I don't have a sister. My brother was Theo—Theobald. And I'm Buckminster."

"Stop teasing me."

"I'm not, Cricket." I pull out my ID and show her.

"Buckminster James McDermott," she reads in an awed whisper. "And your brother is Theobald."

"Theo for short." I try not to wince when talking about him.

"Makes sense." She smiles like we now share a secret about our names.

In the dim light of the truck, it feels safe to talk about these kinds of things. "Are your parents coming out for the grand reveal when we're done? I wouldn't object to meeting the people who middle-named you Cricket."

"I could say the same about Mr. and Mrs. Buckminster. But no. They wouldn't travel for this. For me. The only reason they attended my high school and college graduations was that they were like reunions for their well-heeled friends."

"But the renovation and the show are a big deal. I'm sure

they're proud of you and would want to see all that you've accomplished."

"Buck, they don't even know that I'm doing this. My mom and I are very different. Like a book and a movie. She's a classic and I'm somewhere between modern and goofball, or dork if you prefer."

"I don't think that's an official Motion Picture Association of America classification and I don't get goofball vibes from you."

"You just found me hiding in a box."

I chuckle. "Fair enough."

"I don't think my mother has ever so much as laid eyes on social media."

"Truthfully, mine either. But I find it hard to believe your mom hasn't seen the @DomesticDiva in action."

Christina scoffs. "She has people who run her accounts..." She trails off then says, "Wait, does that mean you've seen my account?"

"I've, uh, checked it out..." It's my turn to trail off. "Every night since we met. I'd like to say it's an occupational hazard—like doing a background check, but I wanted to get a better understanding of your style. You know, for the estate project. Also, I noticed you never wear your hair down."

"It gets frizzy."

"And I noticed you skirted the topic of your mom not looking at your social media account. Makes me wonder what other parts of the glossy life you portray to the world remain hidden."

I pause at a four-way intersection, and the streetlight illuminates Christina's smooth features. Her expression is pensive like she's pondering what to bring into the light.

"I keep a lot of things offline. Namely, that I'm terrified of bats."

"And that your middle name is Cricket," I supply.

"And that I've been married once—engaged then unengaged once too. Well, the second one made it onto my @DomesticDiva account a few times, but it's amazing what a delete button can do. A few trolls remember him, but most everyone has moved on."

"Have you?" I ask, feeling the dual emotions of protection and caution—my heart is behind iron bars like the ones on the estate's windows for a reason.

She squawks a laugh. "Oh please. He cheated on me twice. Lied to me more times than I can count. Turns out he was in it to make a move on my mother—not the way you're thinking. More like for her connections and collection. I made a hasty exit. Trust me, I'm not pining over unrequited love. He was a roach."

It's my turn to laugh. "What about the first one?"

"Unlike cockroaches, he's dead." A hint of sadness tinges her voice.

"I'm sorry."

"I'm used to getting that response, but people give it for the wrong reason. Believe it or not, it was an arranged marriage. My mother thought I'd been single too long and feared I'd become an old spinster or something. She had big ideas for our families. Anyway, it turned out he wasn't a very good person either." She goes quiet.

I leave the conversation there, not wanting to pry.

But Christina continues, "There's one thing I know for sure, even though the show is called Designed to Last, relationships don't. At least not for me. I've tried twice and failed both times at getting a happily ever after."

"I wouldn't count those as personal failures."

"But they're failures all the same." Emotion strains her voice.

"You don't really believe that do you—about there not being a happily ever after?"

A long beat passes, and all I can hear are the tires on the road and the pounding of my heart at the possibility of not having a chance at a future with Christina.

"When we were back at the mansion, you said the thing that I have to worry about is you and how that's another story for another time. Any relationship skeletons in your closet?" she asks.

I turn down the wooded road to the forge. "Nope."

"Do you mean *nope* as in you're being tight-lipped and don't want to talk about it even after I just bared my soul or—?"

"I mean *nope* as in I've never been in a long-term relationship or married."

"Define long-term."

"A month."

"You've never been in a relationship for longer than a month?"

"Never. I didn't have time. My career was my focus and adding someone else to the equation complicated things. Significantly."

We pass through the gate.

"I understand that. After my ex, I declared that I was single and proud. In fact, some of my online friends joke that I'm married to @DomesticDiva—the brand, not myself. That would be weird. But it took a lot to dig myself out of the rut after becoming a widow and then the whole runaway bride thing. My work helped me a lot. Although, my therapist says that I'm a workaholic and need to find a new hobby."

"I could teach you how to work with metal. Female blacksmiths are hot."

I park the truck and under the exterior light of the building, Christina's cheeks take on a reddish hue, reminding me of sparks and embers—what I feel whenever I'm around her.

Inside, the conversation shifts to the safe topic of the estate project while I whip up dinner, careful not to burn the tortillas again. Christina makes the *pico de gallo* and guacamole this time.

Starved, we both scarf them down.

"Save some room for dessert." I wink.

"I'm already full. That was delicious. By the way, where's that apron you had last time?"

"The one that says *Kiss the Cook*?" I waggle my eyebrows. "Is there something you want to tell me, Cricket?"

"As I mentioned, I'm considering a new hobby."

"Tell me more..."

"Well, making guacamole isn't as hard as I was led to believe. I think the trick is the avocados have to be perfectly ripe."

"Hmm. Is that really what you were thinking?"

She laughs. "Of course it was."

I'm pleased to see she's not squeamish around eating a regular meal like the first time we met nor is she terrified of my admittedly shabby-looking dog. Despite Gremlin's appearance, he's a love bug at least for Christina. I'd like to think I am too.

"I have some scrap wood from the jobsite to burn. Want to go outside and look at the stars?"

"What were you saying about dessert?"

I shake a bag of marshmallows.

Her eyes light up. "Do you have any chocolate or graham crackers to go with those?"

With Gremlin seated between us, hoping for crumbs, we spend the next thirty minutes building the fire and debating how to roast the perfect marshmallow. Naturally, Christina goes for the slow and low lightly browned method. I char mine to within an inch of its life for the perfectly molten center.

Christina leans back in the Adirondack chair and tilts her head toward the stars. "While we've been renovating and decorating, I try to imagine who'd live in the estate after we're done."

"A big family, a working couple, a single guy who hasn't found the right girl yet."

"It's a big place. How could one person or even a couple make it work?"

"I bet they'd find a way. For instance, I'd convert the building behind the garden into a man cave."

She laughs like the notion is absurd. "I was thinking it would be a she shed."

"Imagine us living there," I risk saying.

She snorts. "I'm too old for a relationship. That ship sailed."

"I find that hard to believe."

Her gaze leaves the sky and lingers on me. I turn to meet her green eyes, dazzling in the firelight.

Christina clears her throat and says, "As you may know, before Louella Belle became Mrs. Fix-It she was in a tight spot financially. She knew it was bad when she could no longer afford chocolate. But she came up with a system. She'd do without in order to pay bills and be responsible, but as soon as she has extra cash, she has a chocolate affordability classification method she uses."

"No, I didn't know this about her. So she's been working hard all for the chocolate, huh?"

Christina laughs. "Actually, it's more of a measuring stick that she uses. If she can afford a single store brand candy bar, she's just scraping by. If she can get a bag of chocolate chips, she's a step up and so on until she can walk into a homemade candy store and select her favorite chocolates from behind the glass. That's the big leagues."

"Are you telling me this because you're concerned about my finances? The truth is, being single so long and working so much, I hardly spent a cent and invested my earnings well. I could afford a yacht if I really wanted one."

Christina tilts her head from side to side as if not sure whether I'm joking.

"Or I could buy the Easton Estate." My thoughts skip to Les and I wonder about his intentions. "Money isn't an issue."

"I meant, can you afford a relationship?"

"That depends if the woman is one of those uppity nail polish people. That could get expensive."

"What if she could afford the nail polish herself and wasn't all that uppity after all?"

"I see. In that case, I'm thinking candy store, behind the glass, one of those deluxe boxes with all the flavors—except brandy. That doesn't belong in a box of chocolate. Where are you at on the chocolate scale?" I ask.

Her gaze leaves mine and focuses on the stars. "I just realized something Meredith would be proud of. I guess the real reason I've avoided French fries and tacos and chocolate is that I just don't ever want the box to be empty, you know?" The pain in her voice at being left, at the idea of there not being enough for her, pierces me.

No one has properly loved Christina. From the sound of it, her parents are distant and cold. Her first marriage sounds like a disaster and the engagement almost worse. I can't claim to be the best candidate for the job or even qualified, but I'd never purposefully hurt her or leave.

"Come here. You need a hug. Some snugs." I reach for her to join me in my chair.

A smile ripples across her lips. "Snugs?"

"Yeah snuggles."

She giggles. "Sounds strange coming out of your mouth."

Gripping Christina's waist, I settle her on my lap with her legs draped over the arm of the Adirondack chair. Pulling her close, I inhale her lilac scent, soft and smooth on this warm summer evening. She rests her head against my chest.

"A bottomless box of chocolates, huh?" I ask absently. "What about a bottomless plate of tacos? S'mores? Kisses?" I dare asking the last part.

Christina looks up at me through her long eyelashes. My gaze flicks from her eyes to her purely kissable lips and lingers there. They part slightly as if poised to ask a question.

I have one of my own.

My thumb absently caresses the spot behind her ear and the rest of my hand cradles the nape of her neck before I lean in, drawing her a measure closer.

"I'll admit that I'm a bit of a fixer-upper," I say.

"I'm whatever the opposite of that is. Overly fixed up?"

We both laugh, but our mouths go quiet and the question remains in our shared gaze.

Christina bites her lip.

The corner of my mouth hitches into a smirk.

"I want the expensive chocolate," she whispers.

"I'm here for the marshmallows," I reply.

My pulse heats a few degrees as the space between us closes.

Her fingers land on my cheek and brush what was a smooth shave only a few hours ago. "I already miss the beard," she says.

"I thought you hated it."

"I love to hate it, Buck."

Then our mouths meet.

Forget the three-thousand-degree forge. This is hotter. I'm burning up inside in the best way as we find a balance between curiosity and confidence in the kiss. Between soft searching and a demanding hunger for each other. Between the past hurts and trust in what we're creating.

My body, mind, and heart bends and molds like molten metal to the shape of this kiss—of what Christina and I could become.

As the kiss deepens, her hands trace the muscles across my shoulders and back. Mine tangle in her hair, desperate to take it down.

But mostly, I cannot fathom how anyone could leave this woman—not for a minute, a day, or a lifetime. I was right, everything about her, including her lips, is absolute perfection.

CHAPTER 19
Christina

On the ride over to Buck's house, the familiar hum under my skin warned me to keep control over the situation and to avoid anything that could paint me in a bad light. Granted, I didn't give him all the details about my previous spouse and fiancé—I avoided naming names and detailing crimes—but I said more to him about Dimitri than I told Les about my first husband. That's progress. Although, the fact that Les has reappeared in my life has me on edge.

Buck means more to me than the other two combined, and I can't imagine losing him. All of this is to say I trust him.

However, instead of the dreaded hum inside, a delightful shiver works its way from my toes to my chest as the kiss continues. It's like the stars rain down and send little flashes of delight everywhere Buck's lips touch me—namely on my lips, but then he pauses and trails little pecks along my cheek to my jawline, behind my ear then back again.

"Buck," I whisper, hardly able to believe this is happening. "Best box of chocolate ever."

His chuckle is low and manly.

I breathe in his wood smoke and leather scent before diving back in to continue the kiss. My heart races, reminding me of when we went through the floor earlier. How was that earlier today? It's like I'm in a free fall, never landing, but if I did I know I'd be safe in Buck's arms.

His large hands roam—twining with mine before wandering to my back, my neck, and my hair.

The kiss deepens and so does the demand. I want to call this man my own—gruff, unpredictable, and bearded.

I'll admit that I haven't exactly minded him calling me Cricket. It's like our own little game of tug-of-war, push and pull, love and hate. Emphasis on the former.

His pulse meets mine when we pull apart, eyes shining. Then we both lean in, wanting more. As the bonfire turns to embers, the fire between us grows. Forget the two failed relationships. I can't help but wonder if I'm getting a third chance at love.

I'm starting to really like the big dork goblin and his killer dog too.

It's late when Buck brings me home to my rental in Butterbury. I should go to sleep because there is a lot of work to do tomorrow, but like a teenager, I lay awake listening to the crickets, the night birds, and my own heart that's still hammering.

I think about his eyes, his lips on mine, and how much I miss the beard. Who'd have thought I'd marry an actual bad boy (Dimitri), then rebound with a guy who wanted to be a bad boy (Les) and then fall for a guy who looks like a bad boy but is as melty inside as a marshmallow. A long sigh escapes as I drift away on marshmallow-soft dreams.

I wake with a start to a sharp honk. My phone explodes on the bedside. I overslept!

Scrambling, I grab a change of clothes, my makeup pouch, and hairbrush. One of the upsides of not driving is I can get ready on the way, which I took advantage of only a few times back in

Manhattan. However, I've never appeared on camera or online without a full face of makeup, hair styled, and completely put together. But there's no time.

Louella Belle, Mae, and Camellia are going to question why I'm running behind. I race outside, shoving my work boots on my feet as the three of them wait in the SUV.

Louella Belle says, "You look bright today."

"If by bright you mean overtired, sure," I mumble.

"Any particular reason?" Mae hints.

Ooh, they're onto me.

"I didn't get a call last night, asking for a ride home," Camellia says innocently.

"Me neither," Louella Belle says.

"Nope," Mae adds.

"That could only mean one thing," Louella Belle says. "Someone else must've played chauffeur for our @DomesticDiva."

"Hmm. Let's see, as far as I can tell there are only two contenders. That slick fellow who stopped by yesterday. Les, I think his name was," Camellia says.

"Or the one who stopped her fall," Mae finishes.

"Oh, I've fallen alright."

There's a collective gasp.

Louella Belle nearly drives off the road as she steers to the shoulder. "You and Buck? I knew it. Y'all owe me. Pay up."

"Another bet?" I ask, aghast.

"This has been one slow burn romance I saw coming," Mae adds, sounding wistful.

"I told you, I wasn't wagering. I see the looks these two love birds exchange on the jobsite." Camellia coos.

"Speaking of the jobsite, we'd better get over there." My phone continues to beep with notifications, but I'll have to answer all my fans and followers on Picto-Chat later. They cannot see me like this—half my eyelashes done, no concealer, and raging bed head.

"Only if you tell us what happened last night on the way there," Louella Belle orders.

"I have to get ready." I gesture to my makeup pouch.

"Then multitask," Mae says. "I've been in the mood for a good love story."

I fill them in on what happened last night, starting with the bat and leaving out the details of the kiss.

"He's your knight in shining armor," Mae says.

"A real hero," Camellia adds.

"Fate, especially since Buck was Bo's best man and you caught the flowers at our wedding," Louella Belle says.

"Ladybosses, I have a career and all my followers. I'm not looking for love."

"No, love found you." Mae gets the last word as we pull up the long driveway of the Easton Estate. I admire our work so far, repointing some of the brick, replacing damaged trim, and the new roof.

Then it's my turn to gasp.

"What is it?" Camellia asks. "Did you see the bat?"

Louella Belle slows the SUV to a crawl.

"Something is missing," I mutter then jump out of the vehicle and run onto the lawn. The bars on the windows are gone. I jump up and down because no matter what challenges we face on the inside, at least on the outside, the house looks complete.

Cupping my hands around my mouth I holler, "Thank you, Buck!"

Before I can track him down and properly express my gratitude, the camera crew starts rolling and we resume yesterday's work on the first floor. I'm pleased as a peach because the La Cornue CornuFé range in Roquefort with stainless-steel and polished chrome is in position plus they installed the coordinating ventilation hood in the kitchen. The sconces in the hallway are now functional, and I just saw an email that the dining room furniture that was back ordered is now on schedule for delivery.

I do a happy little hop and update my followers as I move

from room to room. When I reach the ballroom to check on progress after yesterday's disaster, my cheerful update drifts into silence.

The original wallpaper, which we'd tried to preserve and was partly damaged after the ceiling cave-in, hangs from the wall. The glue failed, revealing something underneath. I noticed the tear yesterday but figured it could be fixed.

This is an absolute disaster. The final piece curls up in front of my eyes and then drops to the floor. I rush over and drop to my knees. "No. Just when everything was going so well." I gripe about now having to find a new product, clean this wall, and start over. This is a ballroom, so it's no small feat. Plus there's ornate trim that's sure to add a complication. When I glance up at the wall, I blink a few times, not sure I'm seeing things correctly.

I study the piece of wallpaper in my hand and then return my gaze to the wall itself. A large mural of a tree sprouts up from the center with branches growing in every direction. In the center are the name *James Easton* and *Mary McNally Easton*. From them, sprouts entire families, including a couple of unique names that I recognize...

Pounding the screen on my phone, instead of reporting to my followers, I call Buck.

"Hey, I'm upstairs. I heard you liked my surprise. I literally heard you but was removing a set of bars in the rear of the house."

"I loved your surprise and have one of my own."

"Starting the morning juicy. I like it." His voice is a deep distraction from the issue at hand.

"I need you here now."

"You need me or you need a kiss?"

My cheeks heat and I whisper, "No smooching on the jobsite, mister. I'd rather keep this between us for now."

"Professionalism, of course." He sounds slightly disappointed.

"Not in front of the cameras or ladybosses, either. They'll have a field day."

"When can I kiss you?"

"When we're by ourselves."

"Will I find you alone right now?"

"No. There's a problem."

"Is the bat back?" Concern etches his voice.

"Thank goodness no."

"Les?" Buck has an edge to his voice like he doesn't like the guy.

"You're getting warmer."

"Is it about the hole in the floor?"

"Warmer still. I just think you should get down here." I look up and he waltzes into the ballroom then tucks his phone away.

"You're hot actually," I blurt as he strides into the room.

Stubble already grows along his jawline but after the kiss last night, seeing him today, makes me breathless all over again. He is no longer just my contractor or someone I could call a friend—we gave each other a part of ourselves that's otherwise kept under wraps, behind bars, closed up. We opened ourselves to each other in a way that makes me feel connected like we belong to each other.

Then inch by inch, doubt creeps into my mind about it being too soon to think that way coupled with a second voice that reminds me that relationships never work out for me so why bother? I shoo them away as Buck chuckles and reaches for me. With the cameras somewhere in the vicinity, I step back.

"It's going to be a long day." He rakes his hand through his hair.

"I was thinking we ought to check on the secret passage, but first, I cannot work like this."

"What do you mean? I came right away. Are you being a diva, Cricket?"

"It's no secret that I'm a diva, given the fact that I go by the Domestic Diva, but although you're hot freshly shaved, I have to insist you grow the beard back."

"Is that why you called me down here?"

"No." I point to the family tree on the wall. "What do you have to say about that, Buckminster?"

It's his turn to gasp, only it's more of a slow inhalation of air. "That would be my great, great, great, uh, grandmother and grandfather?"

"Look, the name Theobald is there too," I say, referring to what Buck said was his brother's full, given name.

He stands there for a long minute, staring at the wall as though lost in thought. His eyes sparkle when he meets mine.

"Can you explain that?"

He snaps his fingers. "I knew it. This house does tell a love story, but it's not mine to share with the world." He leans close. "I'll share it with you, but not on camera."

He takes my hand and leads me to the library. It's one of the last rooms in the house that we have to complete, but I haven't quite cast my vision for it yet. Do I want it dark and moody to compliment the wooden built-ins or a light and airy oasis? Maybe somewhere in between.

Framed by the window, Buck holds both my hands in his. "James and Mary Easton started this family. As you saw on the tree, it grew and grew. There were brothers, sisters, uncles, aunts, cousins, and a few rotten apples."

"The original dysfunctional family."

"Something like that. Their great-grandson, Winslow, fell in love with a girl from a family that wasn't quite up to the Eastons social standards. Her name was Franny Quigley."

"Please don't tell me it was a Romeo and Juliet situation."

"Almost, not quite. However, the Eastons and Quigleys didn't get along much like the Capulets and Montagues from Shakespeare or the Hatfields and the McCoy's, if you prefer. The Eastons thought the Quigleys were beneath them and the Quigleys thought the Eastons were full of themselves."

"Were the Quigley's wealthy as well?"

"In their own way, I guess you could say that. It depends on how you define wealth—notoriety and riches or close family bonds and a self-sufficient homestead. The Eastons had old money. The Quigleys earned every cent through working smart and hard. You'll notice both family names all over local history, especially buildings, parks, and other things in the area. The Easton family funded projects and the Quigleys built them. It was a mutually beneficial relationship, but that's where it stopped. Neither wanted to marry into the other family."

"A stubborn refusal?"

"And a commitment to tradition. You see, as the oldest male, Winslow was in line to receive the Sweetheart Stone—the engagement ring that was said to always produce a successful marriage and plentiful offspring. But the Eastons didn't want a Quigley to wear the ring even though Winslow and Franny were wildly in love."

"Don't tell me this has something to do with the bars?"

"That's what I've been trying to figure out. But the part that doesn't add up is eventually Franny got a job in the kitchen here, presumably, so the two could rendezvous."

I give my shoulders a little shimmy.

Buck's lips quirk like he's thinking about kissing me.

I ask, "Do you think that has something to do with the secret passage?"

Leaning against the bookshelf ladder that refuses to budge, Buck scratches his head.

"By the way, do you think you could look at this thing soon? I can't get it to move." I give it a little shake.

Seizing the moment, Buck grips and jostles it, trying to knock the rust off.

"See, told you."

He examines the rolling mechanism and then flips a button on the underside before gliding it smoothly on the rails. "It has a brake so it can't go sliding willy-nilly."

Feeling dumb, I slide it all the way to the other end of the bookshelf, but as it slides past the carved frame on the left side of the shelf, I notice something I hadn't the many times I've been in here, trying to figure out what to do with the space.

"Buck, look at the carvings on the bookshelf's frame." I run my finger over them, pausing on one shaped like a heart, only it has a nearly invisible seam like it's not fully connected.

"It seemed to pop when I pushed the ladder past."

We repeat the process and the heart shifts a little. I hover my finger over it. Buck nods. I push on it and the bookshelf opens into what we thought was a dead-end passage.

He beams a smile. "Well, how about that, Cricket? You just helped solve a mystery."

CHAPTER 20
Buck

As Christina and I stand at the entrance to the passageway revealed by the bookshelf, the sinking feeling that we'll soon be wrapping up the project is like a punch in the gut.

I run my finger over the heart-shaped button triggered by the placement of the ladder. "If the ladder is on the left, the button appears. If it's on the right, it camouflages into the decor. But the button isn't wood."

She leans over me and studies it. "Looks like wood to me."

"That's to make it blend in better. It's metal and must be connected to this mechanism. The placement of the ladder must also be why we couldn't open it from the inside." I examine the opening to the passage, having a Sherlock Holmes moment.

"Do you think Winslow and Franny would meet up in the passageway?"

"There's a good chance, considering she would've had access to it from the storeroom. What about him though? He'd have to sneak all the way down here," I say vaguely.

Christina studies the bookshelf some more then looks up. "Did you notice how large the heating grate is?" She points overhead.

"I did because I had to repair part of it. There's a fireplace in the bedroom above so I imagined they wanted to keep the library toasty warm, but maybe it's oversized so he could shimmy through." I slide the ladder back to the right side, closing the passage, and gesture for Christina to climb up with me. I don't mind that it's a tight squeeze and wrap my arm around her waist.

"See that?" I point to a heart wrought in the swirls of the metal.

"It's another hidden heart. They're all over this estate."

I wink. "I thought you'd like that. John Quigley, Franny's father, was a blacksmith."

"Just like you."

I nod, eager to put together more of the story. "And my great-great-grandfather—on my mother's side."

"Wow. Do you think Winslow would sneak down here through the grate and then use the passage to meet Franny?"

I take Christina's hand in mine and say, "Let's role play." I creep down the ladder, slide it into position and the bookshelf opens, revealing the passageway once more.

"I'll go to the storeroom and wait for you there." She giggles as if there's something forbidden about our love, and we have to meet in secret.

I creep along the passageway and reach the dead end. I brush my hand along the wall, feeling for a handle or button. Like the bookshelf in the library, it must only open from the outside.

The floor on the other side creaks and the shelves shift.

Christina throws her arms around me as if we hadn't seen each other moments before.

"Okay, now what do you think they did?" she asks.

I draw her into the passageway and plant my lips on hers, unable to hold back any longer. From the moment I dropped her off last night to when I laid eyes on her this morning, I've wanted to do this—to feel her breath fall into sync with mine. Our hearts pound together as our lips connect and tell a story, one that's all our own.

A question creeps into my mind—will it last? It can't if she doesn't believe in a happily ever after. But there is no sense in thinking about that now. Instead, I immerse myself in the kiss, in Christina.

In the gentle push of her mouth moving with mine.

In her smooth skin against my scruff.

In the soft purr coming from her throat.

And in the way I truly, deeply want this to last forever.

When we part, Christina's lips and cheeks glow a faint rose, and she whispers, "Now what?"

I'm not sure if she means for us or Winslow and Franny, but I glance at the window.

"Now, we make our escape." I throw open the sash and clamber down then hold up my hands for Christina. She makes the short drop into my arms and slides down my chest before landing on her toes. She tips her chin up and I kiss her on the forehead.

"This is how Winslow and Franny would've made their escape under the stars. Then he would've taken the Sweetheart Stone and..."

Her eyes widen.

"He would've dropped to one knee, and presented her with the engagement ring." I demonstrate on bended knee and present an imaginary ring to Cricket.

She bunches her hands up under her chin, squealing excitedly before whispering, "They'd have to be very quiet so they didn't wake anyone up."

"And he'd have asked her to marry him," I say.

"And of course, she'd say yes."

I hold up my fingers as if pinching a ring between them then say, "But the only problem is, the ring, the Sweetheart Stone, went missing right around when Winslow and Franny publicly professed their love...and has never been seen since."

Just then, a round of cheers comes from the balcony on the

second floor where Louella Belle, Bo, Mae, Camellia and half the crew cheer shouts of congratulations.

For a long moment, Christina and I look at each other, baffled. Her cheeks shine red as if she realizes something a second before I do. Then we both start laughing.

"Wait, we weren't done," she says.

Taking my hand, this time she leads me back to the house and into the ballroom.

"If we're engaged, we have to celebrate."

"I think the others are going to be doing plenty of celebrating." I'm braced for them to enter at any moment, offering congratulations.

But for the next few minutes, it's just Christina, me, a large family tree that had been hidden for years, and the scaffolding that saved us yesterday.

We dance and glide across the floor, avoiding tools and sheets of plastic. But it's just us and I can't help but wish this were real.

When we're nearly out of breath, the doors open and our would-be well-wishers arrive minus the cameras—perhaps Bo had the sense to keep them out as if this was an actual private moment.

The three ladybosses chirp and chatter, reminding me of when they'd appeared uninvited at my house in the woods—I'd sworn off women at the time. Then again, I hadn't met Christina.

While I study the family tree, I let her do the explaining. She flashes her ringless hand then explains, "Buck and I were role-playing."

"Like Dungeons and Dragons?" Mae asks.

"I'm not that kind of dork goblin," I mutter.

"No, like the Easton Estate love story." Christina looks at me as if asking permission to tell them, and I give a little nod. She goes on with dramatic detail about Winslow and Franny's secret meetings and the Sweetheart Stone.

"What happened to the ring?" Louella Belle asks.

"No one knows. It was lost. The families fractured and fell apart," I answer.

"Over a diamond?"

I shrug. "More what it symbolized."

"True love," Christina says. "The Eastons didn't approve of the union between Winslow and Franny. When they stopped believing in true love, everything fell apart."

Christina gives me a look that sends me staggering back slightly. Everyone else is so rapt by the story that they don't notice, but I can't help but think she just realized something about her role in true love—or perhaps that's just the romantic in me. The one hidden under the tattoos, muscles, and grit.

"But did they get married?"

"I nod. I'm proof."

"Engagement or not, I think we need to celebrate," Louella Belle says.

"We have work to do," Christina says.

Bo waves his hand dismissively. "It's just about lunchtime. Work can wait a few more hours. If I've learned anything from Ella Belle, it's that when she says to take a break, you listen, especially when there's pie involved."

They both laugh, and she nuzzles his nose. "I like the way you think."

He slings his arm over her shoulders and squeezes.

I feel a boyish shyness come over me, but that doesn't stop me from doing the same to Christina. This time, she leans into me as we all leave the worksite for lunch.

We have to push two tables together at the Starlight Diner. Rhondy doesn't even take our orders. Before I know what's happening, plates with sliders, chicken wings, and biscuits get passed around. Then she rolls out the pie like she was waiting for just such an occasion.

Christina's eyes widen at the slice of peach pecan with a drizzle of chocolate and a dollop of whipped cream.

"I made that with you two in mind." Rhondy winks.

"You were right, Rhondy," Louella Belle says.

"When am I ever wrong?" she asks.

Paul hollers from the kitchen, "When you were yelling answers at the TV last night as if the Jeopardy contestants could hear you."

"I do love watching that game show."

"Watching? More like treating it like a participatory event. Nuh-uh. Half the time I can't hear what the host says."

The two lovingly bicker back and forth. They've been together for as long as I can remember, so they must be doing something right.

Christina stares at her plate of pie then points at the dollop of whipped cream. "Look, another hidden heart."

I kiss her temple and then scoop up a bite to feed her. Her eyes flutter closed and she says, "I'm dead."

I chuckle. "Can I steal a bite? Because if that's what dead looks like, I want to be dead too."

"You're supposed to share. It's part of the initiation." Louella Belle giggles.

"Initiation into what?" Christina asks.

"Happily ever after." Louella Belle and Bo exchange a knowing glance.

Never imagining that I, the guy who tracked down bad guys and brought them to justice, would be feeding a woman pie on a hot summer's day, I gather another bite onto the fork and hold it up for Christina. This beats the bad convenience store food Eddy and I would pick up on stakeouts. Let's just say the car wasn't pine fresh.

"I can't eat another bite," Christina says as I hold the fork poised for her.

"We're here to celebrate," Mae says.

"What is it we're celebrating exactly?" Christina asks.

"Your and Buck's engagement," Camellia answers.

"We were role-playing," Christina and I both say at the same time.

"Yup. Right. Sure. Now how are we going to find that ring?" Louella Belle says.

"It's been missing for years. Someone probably found it, sold it, or hid it away," Bo speculates.

"We've taken the house down to the rafters. It can't be hiding there." Louella Belle taps her chin in thought.

Christina and I exchange a private look.

My eyes say, *If we tell them about the passage, that's like revealing the coordinates to our tree fort. It's no longer a secret place all our own.* And it's acknowledging that there's something more between us.

Hers: *I'm not a risk-taker. If we take that leap, I need a safety harness, helmet, and some mattresses on the ground for protection.*

You always have me.

At least, I think that's what her eyes say. My hand finds Christina's under the table and I gently squeeze. We have to take this slow. One step and one secret revealed at a time.

"Tell us how you're related to the Easton family, Buck," Mae says.

I explain how my great-great-grandmother worked there and that my great-great-grandfather was a blacksmith like me.

"Would your parents know anything?" Camellia asks.

I frown. "Not likely. Plus, they're living that cruise ship life—having just left for the Caribbean last week. Anyway, I've heard their stories countless times and have done my own research."

"We need someone who knows about notable, local families. A historian. A person with a unique interest in wealth, jewelry, and that kind of thing," Camellia says.

"How about a matchmaker?" Louella Belle asks then shakes her head. "Never mind. Rhondy is more of a contemporary cupid."

Christina's gaze flickers like a lightbulb at half power. "I do know someone that may know a thing or two if there was wealth involved."

"The Eastons were the richest family in the state back in their day," Mae says. "My grandparents bought their farmland from them...along with the rest of the county."

"The rest of Georgia," Louella Belle adds.

"So who were you thinking of?" Camellia asks.

"My mother."

And that's why she and I end up on a flight to New York City first thing the following morning. Bo and Louella Belle's dog Bean and Gremlin are best friends so they're looking after my dog for the day.

"Are you sure you want to come?" Christina asks as we walk toward the entrance to the airport.

"On a day trip to Manhattan with you? It sounds fancy and jet-setting. As you know, I'm an iron bending, dragon loving, dork goblin, aka not that kind of guy. However, I wouldn't miss a minute with you. Not even a New York minute."

She laughs at the dumb joke as we approach security. I flash my ID, and they let me through while Christina struggles with the strappy sandals she insisted on wearing.

"Why didn't you have to take off your shoes like the rest of us peasants?"

"The privilege of being me."

"No offense, but with the beard and tattoos, I'm surprised they didn't pat you down."

"I told you that I'm a law-abiding citizen."

"More like a secret agent, international man of mystery," she whispers.

"That too."

A throng of travelers passing through security thrust us forward and toward our gate. When we're settled in first class, she asks, "Is this another perk of being you?"

"Nah. This is for us to enjoy. Also, selfishly, I cannot sit in the smaller seats in the back given my height. I pay for the convenience."

"Anything else I should know?"

"Parents adore me." I wink.

She tucks her chin. "Was this an official, third-party research poll? I thought you said you didn't date much."

"I'm just trying to calm your nerves."

"How can you tell I'm nervous?"

I lace my fingers through hers. "I notice everything about you, Cricket." I kiss Christina's temple and feel her relax beside me.

In a total of two hours, we're off the ground and then descending. It takes me a moment to calibrate with the pace of the city as we set foot on the sidewalk.

First, we stop at her apartment on the upper east side so she can grab some clothing she left behind when moving to Georgia.

I follow through the marble entryway to the brass elevator. It's all very posh. But would I expect anything less from the DomesticDiva? As we travel to the fifth floor, a troubling thought enters my mind. "How long do you plan to keep the apartment here? Do you rent it out?" I ask.

"No. I figured I'd keep it exactly as it was so if I ever need to come back I could just pick up where I left off. You know, if things don't work out in Georgia. Like a plan B."

Yeah, I know all about those. "Did you get your start in interior design while living here?" I follow her down a long hallway with a plush carpet.

Christina has seen my living space and I'm curious to see hers and if it's as put together as her photos online.

"Sure did. In Manhattan, there's only so much room for everyone and we're always in each other's space, so I wanted to create comfortable, inviting home spaces, havens for people. Places to gather, entertain, and be surrounded by beauty."

"That sounds very inspirational."

Struggling with a few bags, an older woman exits an apartment.

"Can I help you, ma'am?" I ask.

The woman looks me up and down. "Who are you? Some hooligan they let into the building? I don't want any riffraff on my floor." She looks at Christina with recognition. "Are you that girl that lives next door and never says hello?"

"I was busy?" Christina asks, more like a question than a defense.

The old woman sniffs and looks us both over as if taking sides, and says, "Figures you'd bring in a kind young man. Sure, you can help me."

I tote the older woman's bags to the elevator and then head back to Christina's door.

She unlocks it and says, "I'll only be a second."

I stand in the apartment's entryway and my jaw drops. There isn't anything on the walls except a thermostat. A simple couch sits in a corner along with a desk. A single stool sits in front of the bar at the kitchen counter. Not even a throw rug warms the floor. An open closet reveals a few coats and a heap of white fabric on the bottom—a wedding gown maybe?

Perhaps this is what Christina would call minimal décor.

"I'll just be another minute," she calls, sounding out of breath.

A garment sails through the hallway, hits the wall, and slides to the floor.

"Sorry. I can't find anything to wear."

"What about what you were wearing?" A second too late, I realize that was the wrong thing to say.

"When you meet with my mother, you get *dressed*."

I frown at my black T-shirt and jeans.

Christina reappears wearing a fitted light pink dress, pearls, and beige high heel sandals. Breathless, she struggles with a bag and says, "All set."

"Can I carry that for you?"

"Oh, uh, sure." She riffles through it and mutters. "Maybe the silk scarf would be a better look or perhaps I should go with the navy blazer, although it's hot out."

I grip Christina's shoulders. "You're in a tizzy."

"I'm not dizzy."

"No, but you're practically bouncing off the walls. The very bare walls. Did you get robbed or clean this place out and bring everything with you south?" I ask.

She laughs. "I brought my computer and some of my clothes and shoes."

"What about your *stuff*?"

"Oh right. I brought my toiletries, of course."

"No, I mean your things. Like curtains and carpets and do-dads."

"Do-dads?"

"Yeah. Stuff. Knickknacks."

She shrugs. "I don't really have those."

"But you're an interior designer. I've seen how you painstakingly select the perfect potted miniature series of succulents to display on a bookshelf. Or an array of spice jars. Throw pillows. Décor. You don't have any of that."

"No." She hurries ahead of me like she doesn't want to talk about it.

I stop her in front of the elevator, gripping her shoulders. "You spend your life making for other people what you don't have. What you want."

Sadness pinches her features. "I just don't have time...to get it right. To get it perfect."

"There's no comment card rating your performance."

"The world is watching...and so is my mother."

"Then leave it off your phone. Unless you like the world watching." I tap the air with my finger. "Also, you said your mother doesn't look at your social media."

"No, but she sees and notices everything. Every hair out of place. Every loose thread. We should probably head over to her place."

"You sure you want to do that? You seem flustered."

Christina takes a deep breath like she's trying to collect herself. "After you meet Sylvia Lancaster, you'll understand why."

It pains me that Christina doesn't see that she's already perfect. She has no idea. Clueless. I have a sudden, deep, unyielding desire to show her how great she already is. For her to see what I see. If she does, maybe she'll truly let down her walls.

CHAPTER 21
Christina

I wanted to say no to the pie yesterday at the Starlight Diner just like I want to refute what Buck said about my dedication to perfection. The thing is, he's not wrong. I feel as if all eyes are on me all the time and I have to perform to get a good approval rating. But the pie was deliciously worth it, so maybe if I let him be right everything will turn out okay...and be delicious because I'm pretty much done listening to my mother's voice in my head about what not to eat.

Sugar, carbs, and fat, here I come!

The only problem is, my hope that everything will be okay has never worked out in the past.

I've always expected that by creating comfort for others, I'll eventually find a place to call home for myself. It wasn't the penthouse we're headed to just outside Central Park where I grew up.

Home isn't only about throw pillows and scented candles either. It's about people. Whether a person is single, in a relationship, has a family, or in a community. I've just never felt that with my own parents.

But I do with Buck. However, I'm afraid that what we're building together is going to slip through my fingers.

"How long have you lived at that apartment?" Buck asks, drawing me from my thoughts.

"Twelve years. I'm thinking about selling."

I'm holding onto it because Butterbury is temporary, but the closer we get to completing the project—then moving on to a couple more to complete our contract for Designed to Last—the pull back to New York diminishes. Butterbury isn't so bad. There's pie. The Viking beefcake...

Buck looks dubious with his arms crossed in front of his chest as we descend the elevator.

"Before you say anything, I haven't had time to decorate. Haven't you ever been to a nail salon? The manicurists are usually so booked, they don't have time to do their own nails. It's like that."

"No, Cricket, I've never had a manicure."

"You're missing out."

He flashes me his nails. "You think so?"

I huff and hurry ahead of him as we exit the building's foyer. But I can't escape the truths he noticed:

- I've been so preoccupied with taking care of other people's spaces, I haven't tended to my own
- I've merely created the illusion of a home and lifestyle for the internet and people I don't know personally
- I'm afraid to dig in and put down roots because what if I'm left alone—the chubby girl no one wants

Buck says, "I was referring to your neighbor. That's a long time to live next to someone and not know them."

"I only have so much battery for people-ing."

"Can you translate that, please?"

I let out a short breath. "I spend most of my time interacting in-person and online. Having to add another person to my list felt daunting." I sink a few inches with guilt because I probably shouldn't have ignored Mrs. Clemson all these years.

"Part of creating a home is building community."

He has a point, but I stop on the sidewalk and cock a hip. "Okay, lone wolf, Viking, beast-man. Sure. Community. I see you have a lot of that on your compound in the woods."

He opens and closes his mouth. "I guess, uh, after I retired, my MO was to be an independent, lone wolf. Not rely on or get close to anyone. But—"

"But you agreed to do the show. Why?"

"There are two answers to that. One, I was curious about the Easton house for reasons you now know, including recovering the Sweetheart Stone and restoring my family's good name."

"And the other?"

"I couldn't just stay in my forge all day every day. People need people. I see that now. At the time though, I needed to get away. The truth is, I have a hard time trusting."

"Is that your other reason? To test out your boundaries of trust?"

He brushes his hands up and down my arms. "Not exactly. My second reason was you."

"Me?" I find that hard to believe, but the little shiver inside warms me up. "Well, brace yourself because my mother is like me on steroids."

"I've spent most of my life bracing for impact. Do you know those signs in airplanes that have the little diagram with the figure curled up in different positions in case of an emergency landing? Imagine a lifetime of that. Of me having difficulty letting myself be happy, playful, at rest. Trust me, I'm prepared."

"I can relate, but you've never met Sylvia Lancaster," I whisper as the doorman of my parents' building ushers us inside.

"Why didn't I know your mother is Sylvia Lancaster?" Buck asks.

"Shh. If you say her name too many times, then spin in a circle while hopping on one foot, you'll summon her."

He starts to laugh. "Aren't we going to *see* her?"

"It's best if we catch her unawares."

"This is starting to sound like a covert mission," he mumbles.

"Right up your alley," I joke.

Buck's posture changes slightly. Not like he's bracing for impact. Rather, like he's coiling for an attack. Like he carries an invisible sword and shield. I might be wrong, but his body language makes me feel protected like I finally—unlike with Dimitri and Les—have someone in my corner. On my side against my mother's subversive and often sarcastic attempt to make me feel one inch tall and one hundred inches wide.

The scent of expensive perfume mixes with cleaning products in the familiar entryway of the place where I spent my formative years. The hum under my skin is almost deafening as my anxiety ratchets up after the elevator door seals us inside and shoots upward.

"All this time, I thought of us as opposites, but does the fact that we've both been waiting for catastrophe to strike make us basically the same?" Buck asks.

"Like mine, is your mother known in some circles as the ice queen and a man-eater in others?" The hum gets louder inside as I countdown. T-minus one minute until contact.

Buck frowns. "No, she's a homemaker."

"You could say Sylvia is a home breaker."

"Do you mean she cheated on your father—a homewrecker?"

"Probably, but she's responsible for arranging more unhappy marriages than there are married couples in this town."

"Make that make sense."

"I could write a book and we have less than thirty seconds until we reach the penthouse, but in summary, my mother fancies herself a matchmaker, kind of like Rhondy, but instead of spotting true love, she pairs people off for reasons involving money and power. All wrapped up in a pint-sized presentation of cordial pleasantries and cutting remarks. She collects prized objects...and people. Name anyone rich or famous, chances are she had dinner with them, went to the theater with them, vacationed with them. Or arranged their marriage. The art, jewelry, antiques, and collectibles figure into the equation because she targets people based on what they have or have access to. My first husband for instance. He was connected to the largest art collection in Russia, including many lost renaissance pieces. It all fell apart before she got her hands on it." I stop to catch my breath. I've never told anyone this. "It's a game to her. It's all about who you know, being seen, and how you look—my failure that she's particularly hung up on. Like I said, brace yourself."

The doors to the elevator start to open, but Buck pushes the heel of his hand against the *stop* button. He cages me between his arms.

"Are you saying she's like the Easton and Quigley families who refused to let Winslow and Franny marry? Hung up on the way they want to be perceived rather than reality?"

"Sort of. She encourages marriages for the wrong reasons." My mouth feels suddenly dry like I've given all the warnings I can. It would be impossible not to see the plea in my eyes.

"Before we leave this elevator, I want to make two things very, very clear." Buck's voice is low, foreboding. "Everyone has a dysfunctional family to some degree or other. You're an adult now and can't let what happened in the past influence you now. If you hear her voice criticizing you in your head, don't listen to it. You are beautiful and anyone who tells you otherwise is lying."

His blue eyes spark and hold mine captive. I've fallen hard for this guy and I don't think there's any coming down from it.

"And the other thing?" I ask, almost breathless.

"I love you, Cricket."

He presses his lips to mine in the kind of kiss that could erase time. And I wish it would. But at least we have this moment. I get lost in the soft scratch of Buck's stubble, the lift of his cheeks as he smiles against my mouth, and the brush of his eyelashes on my cheeks.

Forget perfection, I have this—this man, this moment, this love.

When we part, I want to tell him that I love him too, but the doors slide open.

The corner of Buck's lip quirks and he grips my hand because we're in this together. Then I brace myself for impact because it's coming, whether I like it or not.

The penthouse is a veritable showroom of marble, glass, antique wood, and fine textiles. Gallery-quality art hangs on the walls. It should be a museum with little ropes reminding visitors not to touch or look or breathe.

I hold my breath now as heels click closer from the hallway.

"Christina? What brings you here?" Sylvia Lancaster's gaze floats to Buck, looming protectively beside me.

"Hi, mother."

"Are you employing a bodyguard, dear?"

"No. This is Buck. He's, uh—" I hate myself for hesitating. "He's my boyfriend." I wince when I meet his eyes, prepared for him to look disappointed.

Instead, I get the lip quirk that I love so much. And I love him. Standing beside him right now fills me with pride and joy and comfort.

"Nice to meet you, uh, Buck was it?" My mother uses her most patronizing tone as if talking to a wheat stalk-sucking hillbilly.

"Buckminster McDermott," he says as if that means anything to her.

Her expression changes from hoity-toity to focused curiosity like she's a hound that's caught a scent. "I knew a Buckminster once. A Scottish Lord, I think it was. I'll have to refer to my notes."

"Yes, he's a cousin."

At those words, she gets that glossy, crazed look in her eye—like she's already calculating how to use Buck to her advantage. "You're related to the Cargill family? I have a vase from their collection."

I wince because she pronounces the word *vase* like it rhymes with pause—*vahz*—and I'd like to press *pause* then *eject* on this visit right about now.

"Actually, we're here—" I start to say.

"Come in and have some tea. I'd love to learn more about you, Buck. Christina, I'd sure enjoy hearing about what you've been doing now that you're divorced." She turns to Buck. "Mr. McDermott, you do know that my daughter is a widow and left her fiancé at the altar, though we don't talk about that do we?" She speaks as if I'm to blame and that Dimitri wasn't involved in an art-theft ring unbeknownst to me and that Les is a card shark con artist.

"It's Buck and yes, I can assure you that I'm aware." Someone replaced the dork goblin Viking with a refined gentleman whose charm could hypnotize a cobra—or intimidate one.

Skills that could come in handy right about now.

My mother sighs, which sounds like it would be passive, but it really just means she's winding up to throw a punch—not literally but verbally.

"It's such a shame about Dimitri. I still can't quite get over how he died. Tragic, really." She leans in and whispers to Buck, "He was killed. It's been so hard to cope." My mother presses her hand dramatically to her chest, shakes her head, then straightens. She really could've made it on Broadway. "Then Christina had to run off with Les. What was his last name again? Oh, it doesn't matter. He isn't from one of the notable families."

I go stiff, afraid Buck will make the connection at the same time as I fight between turning red with embarrassment and rolling my eyes. "Mom, I don't think Buck cares about all that."

"Then what do you care about?" she asks.

"Your daughter."

I straighten a little, realizing this guy sees through my mother and has my back.

"I meant, what do you do for work?"

He clears his throat and says, "Formerly Central Intelligence, ma'am. Currently blacksmith."

Did I hear Buck correctly? He must be joking.

My mother blinks a few times as if processing the information and her lips fight against forming a little *O* of nervousness. It's not a stretch to suggest she could be connected to criminal activity given her art collection. "Central Intelligence like CIA?"

I'd like to hear his answer myself.

"That's correct. I retired. Lovely art collection you have." Buck gestures to the wall and then gives her a hard stare.

"Oh, thank you. It pays to have friends in high places."

"Does it?" There's an edge to his voice like he knows that all her connections aren't on the up and up.

My mother laughs flippantly.

Before any more shocks to the system, I say, "Speaking of friends, we came here to ask you about the Eastons."

"Ah, yes, a southern family. Old money. Textiles, I believe."

"Do you know of a Les Easton?" Buck asks.

I wince, wishing he hadn't used the name. Any second now, someone will make the connection and my secret will come out. I don't want Buck to know that I was ever with someone like Les. When I fled Las Vegas after he convinced me to elope, I promised myself I'd delete him from my past, just like a bad post on my Picto-Chat account.

"Can't you use your CIA connections to find out?" my mother astutely asks.

"This is more of an inside kind of job," Buck says. "But it's not really him we're curious about. We're wondering if you know much about Winslow Easton and Franny Quigley?"

"Quigley? That's not a last name you often hear in polite company." She shakes her head.

"Why not?" I ask.

"She betrayed her parents and married an Easton—a complete scandal."

"Yes, they got married." Buck bristles at my mother's insult since he's a descendant.

Here comes the million-dollar—or in this case, several

million-dollar—question. "Do you know if there was an agreement between the families? A dowry? If the Sweetheart Stone ever exchanged hands, as it were?" I ask.

"There would've been the engagement ring if the union was authorized. But it wasn't. So no ring. No wedding gift."

"Any idea what happened to the ring?" Buck asks.

"Why would you like to know?" My mother's eyebrow lifts with suspicion as if she called dibs on it—on anything valuable, sparkly, and sought-after.

"Because I'm Winslow and Franny's great-great-grandson."

My mother shakes her head. "That's a shame. I was just going to look up the last name McDermott and see if—"

See if she could find any benefit in manipulating him.

Before she embarrasses us both, I interrupt. "Mother, you don't have a say in who I marry anymore."

Buck eyes me warmly like the notion crossed his mind.

"Clearly, what with that Les Streckle character."

I want that oversized cardboard box I hid in right about now. "I did that because I thought—never mind."

My mother sniffs. "I don't think anyone would want to marry you at this point with those two failures behind you."

The muscle in Buck's jaw tics.

My eyes fill at her cruelty, but I won't cry here. Never in front of her. My voice is small when I say, "We'd better get going. Can't miss our flight."

"Too bad you aren't able to stay for dinner. I take it you have to get back to your little show?"

My lips form a flat line. "Yup. My little show."

Buck laughs genially. "You're so modest, sweetheart. By little, Christina means that it's the number one television program in the country. The world loves Cricket's interiors, her charm, her smile..."

Heartened and encouraged by his kind words, I stare blankly at my mother. "She knows that. She's just trying to undermine me as usual."

"Not true, Christina. All your life, I've merely been trying to teach you what's important."

"And pray tell, what is that?"

"Who you know," she says simply.

I nod. "We agree then. Who you know is important, but even more than that is who you love and how you love."

My mother flinches as if the L-word sprouted wings and stung her like a hornet.

"Say hi to Dad for me." I start toward the elevator.

"It was nice meeting you, Mrs. Lancaster. If you remember anything about the Sweetheart Stone, please be in touch. Oh, and nice Monet you have there." Buck nods politely.

As we exit, my skin doesn't hum, it buzzes. Usually, when I leave my mother, I feel deflated, but now I'm just puffed up with anger...and it's not only at her.

When we're in the elevator, I say, "Buck, you didn't tell me you were a CIA agent. What was it you said—you were a researcher for a governmental agency?"

"I figured you knew after the James Bond comment. And you should talk. Was your mother talking about the same Les who's been poking around the estate?"

I hang my head. "Yes. The same one."

"You were engaged to him?" His expression is a mixture of shock and disgust.

"I wanted to prove to her that I wasn't a dumb, chubby dork and that a high-roller was interested in me."

Buck grips my arms—something he does when he really wants me to hear something.

"I'll admit, I'm ticked off. I don't understand why you didn't mention it and why he didn't either for that matter. But you don't have to prove anything to anyone—least of all a woman who values property over people, including her own daughter." Anger at me or in my defense, I'm not sure, rolls off him like heat from a fire.

We exit the elevator, and this time, I have to keep up with Buck.

When we get to the street he stops abruptly, and says, "And definitely don't listen to people who use the snooty version of the word *vase*."

Confusion must flicker across my features because I get the one-sided lip quirk. Buck made a joke. Relief starts to rush through me but stops short because his easy forgiveness is too good to be true and I have to come clean so I get what's coming to me—him walking away.

"I was afraid to tell anyone about Les, mostly because I was ashamed that I'd been with someone like him in the first place. I bought into his lines about his glamorous life in Las Vegas. I was conned until he tried to get me in on one of his schemes, but first, we had to get married to pull it off. I thought he loved me, but caught onto him and realized it seconds before it was too late."

"Then he saw you on TV and wormed out of the woodwork." Buck grunts and stops on the street. "Well, this is a mess. You're a hot mess."

"Thanks for saying the quiet part out loud. I know I'm a mess, a wreck, failing at life."

He smooths a piece of hair out of my face. "Emphasis on hot. I lost someone I cared about once. After dealing with guys like that, I'm just glad you're safe."

My brow wrinkles with confusion.

"Guys plural?"

"Yeah, Dimitri and Les."

He must've picked up on the fact Dimitri wasn't the most savory character. "I didn't fully piece it together at the time, but it turns out that Dimitri smuggled art."

"Yeah." Buck is suddenly tightlipped.

"I'm sorry about my mother's arrogance. If we'd stayed any longer, she would've started dropping names—who among the elite she played tennis with this morning, the mega-millionaire she's meeting for dinner, the big event this weekend—"

"I can see why it's like you've been waiting for the other shoe to drop."

"What do you mean?"

"You're perpetually anticipating that something will go wrong."

Feeling attacked, I go on the defensive. "Because it will. Is today pick on Christina day or what?"

"It's like you're waiting for something to go wrong, for me to walk away, or disappear."

I bristle because that's exactly what I've been waiting for. Nervous laughter escapes. "What's with that expression, anyway? Who drops a shoe out of their hand? Off their foot? Maybe on a swing or carnival ride, it could fling off. But ordinary shoes don't drop off ordinary feet. They stay on and the person stumbles, walks, or runs—I literally ran to the airport in my wedding gown. Talk about a hot mess." I could be the one to walk away, right now. Cut my losses and flee so I don't have to face Buck's inevitable departure from my life.

"But step by step they get where they want to go and so will we." He uses his commanding tone like the shoe-dropping scenario isn't an option. "And if Les comes near you again, I'll make sure he'll be the one stumbling away, never to return."

I don't wish my ex harm, but he does have a dangerous edge and knows some sketchy people.

"So you're not mad at me?"

Buck pulls me into a hug. "No, sweetheart. A little disappointed you didn't feel comfortable sharing your past with me, but now that I saw and heard why you built those protective walls around yourself, I understand. As I said, I'm just glad you're safe."

I melt into his arms, feeling more secure than I ever have. For once, feeling cared for and appreciated.

He gazes down at me, eyes sparking blue in the summer sun. "Are you in the mood for pie?"

"Does that mean you're ready to head back to Butterbury?"

"If you are. If you'll come with me."

I close my eyes, imagining life in my empty apartment and my lonely relationships. Then think about the warmth and generosity and kindness of the man beside me. The friends waiting for me down south. The project that nears completion.

I glance up at the building, eager to get as far away as possible from it and my mother's snobbery. We can talk about his secret agent life later.

We're back in Georgia by dinner and at the Starlight in time for dessert. It's busy, but we get a booth by the window. At the beginning of the summer, I avoided this place because of the fat, calories, and carbs. Now, I feel at home and not at all afraid to dig into a meal that's going to nourish my soul—good food shared with good people makes for more than calories.

Buck orders the peach pecan pie and I go for blueberry. Rhondy bustles from customer to customer but quickly delivers our slices topped with extra whipped cream and a knowing wink.

"If I told you something, would you promise not to choke?" Buck asks after we dig in.

I swallow and set my fork down.

"Does this have to do with being in the CIA? Fair warning, I'm not into true crime shows or anything like that. I'd rather not hear about murders or assassins or anything."

He chuckles. "I came across both, but with my specialty in renaissance art history—college major before I dropped out—, my skills were best used in investigating high-end crimes—art, jewels, antiquities, and things like that."

"Can I ask you what on earth made a guy that looks like you, get into that line of work?"

He chuckles. "The tattoos came later. I went through a period when I was trying to erase myself with ink. When that didn't work, I attempted reinvention."

"How'd that work out?"

"It led me to you. But to answer your question, when I was younger, Bo, my brother, and I witnessed a bank robbery. It traumatized Theo pretty badly. I couldn't save him from the way it messed up his mind—while I was gone at school, he turned to drugs to escape. Engaged in reckless behavior. Overdosed. After that, I turned to the police force to protect others. That wasn't enough for me. I had to go all the way."

"So you joined the CIA and—"

The moment stretches tight because he has something big to tell me, I'm just not sure what. I don't want to know if he's ever killed someone or had to solve a particularly gruesome crime.

"I only put this together now, but I was involved in the investigation of your former husband. Dimitri Petrov. I showed up just after he and my partner, Eddy, had a gunfight. As you know, Dimitri died on the scene. Eddy fought hard but didn't make it. I couldn't save her…" His voice dips.

I blink slowly as my surroundings blur and tilt as the past I try to forget hurtles toward me. Realizing I've been holding my breath, my lips part, as I try to make sense of the bomb Buck detonated.

CHAPTER 22
Buck

The two plates of pie perfection sit on the Formica table between Christina and me. Even though the diner is noisy with customers, families, and Rhondy's favorite selection of oldies tunes, somewhere I can hear a clock ticking, counting down the seconds until everything between us explodes.

After all the secrets exposed and revelations earlier today, I thought perhaps we stood a chance. I wanted to make it work. But something nagged and tugged for my attention. I remembered where I'd heard the name *Dimitri* and more importantly why.

"Why didn't you tell me before?" Christina blinks slowly, shellshocked.

"About being in the CIA or—?"

"Any of it. All of it." Her expression craters.

"It's been a couple of years since I retired. I was different back then—I was afraid to bring that part of my life into my relationships now. I was grouchier, grittier..."

"I find that hard to believe."

"Ask Bo. But mostly, the only way I really knew how to keep everyone I knew safe from me was to remain distant. My mission was to capture the bad guys—to do that, I had to become like them. You said yourself that your first husband was a bad guy and while that was before I realized who he was, I didn't want to expose you to that part of me. Plus, I've changed."

"You're still pretty grouchy and gritty when you want to be."

"I'm sorry for that."

She lifts and lowers a shoulder. "Don't be. I liked the way you are because you also have a melty, marshmallow core."

I snag on how she used the past tense of the word *like* and I feel myself cratering, caving to what I deep down know to be true.

"My mother arranged the marriage with Dimitri. Whether she knew about his illegal dealings, I'm not sure. She can pretend to be naïve when she wants something—in this case, a gold clock that's supposedly from the Kremlin and in his uncle's private collection. Among other things. I certainly had no idea. We were together for three years. He was gone a lot and my main concern was how we were going to make a life together if he was abroad three-quarters of the time. Not, as it turns out, how he routinely broke the law and was wanted by the Central Intelligence Agency."

"Dimitri was part of the inner circle. We played the long game, got in deep cover, trying to smoke out the head of the crime ring. We'd almost brought him to justice." Buried memories claw their way out, scratching and wounding me anew.

"I'm sorry about your partner. Eddy, you said her name was?"

I stare at my hands for a long moment, wishing as I always do that I'd arrived on the scene a minute earlier. One minute would mean she'd still be alive. "She was a good woman, deserved a full life. Her so-called boyfriend cleaned her out. All I have left is Gremlin." My words are clipped, desperate to go back behind the safety of my iron fortress.

"That's so sad. Do you want to tell me about her?"

Christina stretches her hand toward mine, but I withdraw. The past is too close to the surface. It's better for my shields to be up, arms at the ready. That's how I can protect my position, myself.

"I guess you could say it's a small world. I'm still rocked by the fact that you knew Dimitri, but that was so long ago. I'd just turned thirty." She sighs. "Then Les was the failure of my late thirties. It's just like my mother to try to throw that one in my face. I'm sorry she was being so awful."

"I should probably get you back to your place. It's been a long day."

"We haven't finished our pie." She fools with the fork but doesn't take a bite. "Buck, since leaving New York, you've slowly closed off."

She's right and I admonish myself for getting caught up in a fantasy—in Christina. "It's for your own good. I try to forget about the past, but it has a way of creeping back in."

"Is this why you told me I have to be more worried about you than I do the bat?"

"I try to protect the people I care about but fail, every time."

"Do you mean your brother and Eddy?"

I grunt, desperate to get away from this conversation and the way it makes me confront the past and my shortcomings.

"You can't beat yourself up about that. You have to—"

"Christina, I'm not one of your projects that you can just fix."

"If we're counting our failures, I have a failed marriage and engagement that I could obsess over as if I hadn't already spent years doing so." She tilts her head from side to side. "I still do, but we can't use the past as a weapon against our future. You can't be bitter and blame yourself."

My fists clench. "It was a lack of control. I could've done better."

Christina snorts a laugh. "So we are exactly alike, always the watchmen on the wall, hyper-vigilant. Seeking control in your case and perfection in mine. I guess it was too good to be true."

My eyes flick to hers and I watch in real-time as we both give up.

Silence threatens to drown us as I try to get Rhondy's attention for the bill. Instead, I drop more than enough money to cover the cost of the untouched slices on the table plus a tip and get to my feet. "I'll bring you home."

She shakes her head. "You don't have to. I'll call one of the ladybosses."

"So I guess this is it." The words come out strained.

"Wasn't designed to last." Her voice shatters.

It's over.

Then I walk away. I leave Christina in the diner because it's better for me to break things off now than for them to get more intense. I'm doing us both a favor. She doesn't want a guy like me anyway—she'd be better off with someone like that city-slicker Les.

The notion of her with another man carves something out inside me, but that's selfish. She's safer without me. The fire within me burns my heart alive.

Abruptly, what feels like cold water douses the flames inside. All I'm left with is ash and a chill I can't fathom ever being able to shake. It's like ice works its way from my fingers and toes inward, freezing out the warmth Christina brought into my life.

She deserves to be someone's everything and I can't give her anything but my broken down past, my inadequacies, my shortcomings.

I'm simply not good enough for someone like Christina.

Lilacs scent the cab of my truck when I get in, and I roll the windows down. The warm summer night does nothing to defrost the chill that's worked its way into my chest. Forget iron bars, caging my heart. The thing is now frozen. The glowing green numbers on the dashboard clock say 7:59, marking this moment as one from which I'll never recover.

I won't be the same without Christina Abernathy in my life.

I rest my head against the steering wheel, feeling like I've made the biggest mistake of my life—worse than when I couldn't help Theo and when I couldn't save Eddy combined.

What if something happens to Christina? I couldn't live with myself.

I'm a failure. How can she trust me if I can't even trust myself?

Better to stick with the contingency plan. When things get intense, I always know where the escape hatch is, the nearest exit, Plan B—lone wolf in the woods. That's me.

A long beat passes as I sit in my truck, talking myself out of going back inside the diner. But I also wait for her ride to arrive so I know she'll get home safely.

The passenger side door opens. My heart leaps because Christina knocked the rust off the thing and I want her but can't have her.

"Hey, buddy," Bo says carefully as if approaching a feral animal. When I don't respond, he slides into the seat. "What are you doing out here?"

"I think the question is what are you doing in here?" My voice is a messy rasp.

"Happened to be in the neighborhood and saw the truck."

I scowl in disbelief.

"Okay, fine. You're right. The ladybosses called an emergency meeting because the word in Butterbury is that two love birds left their pie uneaten at the Starlight and no one ever leaves a crumb on their plate so it must be bad." He quickly lifts his hands in defense. "Don't shoot the messenger. That's what I was told."

I sigh.

"I know you're not a man of many words, but you must've said something to Christina to set off the chain of events that transpired in the last fifteen minutes."

"I told her about the CIA, Eddy, and Dimitri."

"Why on earth would she care about that?"

"They were married."

His eyes widen on cue. "Does that mean Christina is an international art criminal? We did background checks for Mr. Fix-It, but I didn't go that deep."

"No, she's not. Her mother arranged their marriage when she was still single at thirty."

"That was a long time ago...and so was everything that happened with Eddy. I applauded you for carrying on at the agency after her death, but I think it's time to move on emotionally."

I grunt.

"I know, I know. You're a tough, scary, man-beast." He speaks in a caveman's voice.

"Dork Goblin."

Bo angles his head in question but plows ahead without comment. "If you dwell on the past and remain closed off, you're going to miss out on your future...and it looked like things were shaping up between you and Christina."

"There's no way things could work out between us. She wants a glitzy life and I'm more wolf, metal, low-maintenance."

"I've seen the oils you use on that beard of yours. More like Diva Goblin."

A fissure cracks in the ice engulfing me. "Plus, I'm an outsider and she's an overachiever. We're not compatible."

"That's just a story you're telling yourself so you don't have to go out of your so-called comfort zone. Look at Louella Belle and me. There's a lot we have in common, but I promise you that I'm not Mr. Perfect."

"Nah, you're Mr. Fix-It." I almost chuckle.

"And I was trying to fix her when she didn't want help. We had to see a way forward together. Relationships are hard work, but being old, bitter, and alone is worse."

"I have Gremlin."

"Word on the street is Gremlin likes Christina more than you."

"He's a traitor."

"No, he just knows a good thing when it comes his way and you should pay attention because if you're not careful, she might just get away."

"I already screwed things up."

"The pie is still on the table, man. It's definitely not too late."

I glance up at the diner, lit from inside. Rhondy breezes past with plates piled high with delicious home cooked food. A little boy chases his brother around a table. Two older guys bicker back and forth—likely about some news event or other. An older couple leans across a table, heads inclined, talking intimately.

I scan for Christina but don't see her and the ladybosses. Perhaps they went next door to their headquarters. Maybe it really is too late.

"Bo, I appreciate your pep talk, but this is for the best."

"She changed you. Don't lose that."

"Did I need to change?"

He tips his head from side to side. "You were verging toward man-imal."

"Do I want to know what that is?"

"Half-man, half-animal. The beard was a bit out of control."

I smooth my hand along my jawbone. "Christina said she liked the beard."

"Which tells you everything you need to know. If I'm not mistaken, she loves you. That's a rare thing. Whatever belief about yourself or the past is holding you back, let that garbage go."

"She doesn't believe in a happily ever after though."

"Sounds to me like you're coming up with a lot of reasons to wimp out. The Buck I know never backs down from a fight."

"I'm not going to fight a woman."

He chucks me on the bicep. "You know what I mean. Don't fight her. Fight for her. Fight for love. Anyway, if she doesn't believe in happily ever after, that just means you haven't proved to her it's possible. Take it as a challenge. Figure out a way to show her that she's wrong. That's the key. Show her that love is everywhere if she looks."

"That's the thing, she's the biggest romantic I know. For instance, she sees hearts every place she looks—" I cut myself off as the mystery we were trying to solve suddenly comes into focus. I reach across the console and hug Bo.

He straightens his hat. "Glad I could help."

"Are you up for an adventure?"

"If it involves the swamp, baloney sandwiches, and a map your brother found in the basement, I think we're a little old for that."

I laugh and crank the truck, on a mission for love. Fifteen minutes later, I cruise up the driveway at the Easton Estate. The landscape lighting illuminates the newly planted columns of arborvitae, the rose bushes, and a few other ornamental shrubs.

A slick sports car sits in the driveway.

My senses sharpen in the particular way they used to when I was working with the CIA.

"Expecting anyone?" Bo asks.

I shake my head but recognize the car with the Nevada plate.

"Maybe one of the crew had to stay late," Bo says.

Remaining silent, I cut the lights and engine.

"I'm sensing that we're actually on a mission," Bo says.

"Be quiet and stick with me." I slide out of the truck and don't close the door all the way. My boots crunch on the gravel so I gesture for Bo to join me on the grass.

I lead him around the back to the window of the storeroom.

"We don't need to break into our own project," he says.

"It's best to use the element of surprise when possible." Using a drainpipe as a foothold, I clamber through the window.

Bo follows me and drops into the room. We both pause and listen. Footsteps echo through the house on the second floor. I open the passageway, hoping the ladder is in the correct position because if we can get upstairs via the library, the intruders won't know we're here until we're right on top of them.

"I didn't see this on the building plans," Bo says in awe at the secret passageway.

I shush him and gesture that he stay close. We creep through and sure enough, the bookshelf pushes open. Next, I position the rolling ladder under the heating grate.

"Dude, this is cool."

I press my finger in front of my lips because sound carries. I carefully shift the heating grate and hoist myself through. Bo follows at my heels.

"Okay, what's the plan when we confront the burglar? Who's the good cop?"

I chuckle low. "I'm always the bad cop."

"Good to know."

Once on the second floor, I assess the situation, but before I can make a move, Bo streaks past me beating his chest and yelling a battle cry. I sprint after him as he tackles a slender figure wearing a sports jacket.

"You're under arrest for trespassing." Bo's voice is muffled. "Buck, do you have the cuffs?"

I snort a laugh and pull him off the rumpled intruder.

Les pushes to his feet. "You'll be hearing from my lawyer."

"Uh, you're trespassing on private property so how would that work exactly?" Bo wags his finger then points at Les.

Straightening to my full height, I step forward. "You have one minute to explain then I'm calling the police."

"I was just checking out the project. This house is rightfully mine."

I grab him by the shirt collar and practically drag him downstairs to the ballroom. Pointing at the wall, I say, "Show me where you belong on that family tree."

Les's eyes widen. "Uh, I'm an Easton."

"No, your name is Les Streckle. Last known address 529 Prickly Pear Road, Las Vegas Nevada. Additionally, you're banned from several properties on the Strip, have more than nine hundred dollars in parking tickets, and just made the biggest mistake of your life—no, scratch that. The biggest mistake you made was conning and hurting Christina."

"How'd you know?"

"Moving forward, assume I know everything. Now, tell me what you're really looking for." If he says he's looking for *Christina*, I'm going to wring his skinny neck.

Les tears himself out from my grasp and straightens his sports coat. "I'm looking for the Sweetheart Stone."

Bo's eyes are full-on saucers. I guess I should've briefed him.

"Do you have any leads on where it might be?" I ask Les, appealing to his ego—he seems like the kind of guy who likes to brag.

"I know it's here somewhere in this house. Gannon said it has to be."

"Oh, so you're in league with Louella Belle's lousy brother?" Bo asks.

"We're acquainted."

I clench and unclench my fists. "Full story. Now."

"I owe him some money. He said if I find it, I can consider the debt paid. I didn't know Christina was here. I, uh, figured it best to keep my mouth shut about our past so I could keep a low profile and minimize the chance that she'd reveal anything about me."

Bo fumes and paces in front of the hearth.

"Also, I wanted to find it before the mayor floods this town and it's lost forever."

I tuck my chin. "What's that mean?"

Bo grumbles. "Stoll has the bad idea to partner with Hydro-pro, a hydroelectric company that has a solution for the area's non-water shortage problem. By that I mean, they're claiming there isn't sufficient water for the county, manufacturing a crisis, but that's not the case. They just want the land."

It's my turn to grumble because that would mean my parents' home, mine, and the entire town would be underwater. I recall Christina saying something about the mayor and a mystery but had dismissed it at the time, wanting to keep my detective persona separate.

"Is there really a ring?" Bo asks me.

"Definitely. Whether it's here or not is uncertain." I wink in his direction because I do have a hunch about where it might be.

I'm not going to reveal that to someone like Les. "Let's retrace our steps, but first, Les, it's time for you to go."

For a moment, Les looks like he's going to object to my order, but Bo and I stand shoulder to shoulder. Les backs down and walks toward the door but not before casting us a glare.

"And if I see you here again...I'll let you fill in the blank," I grind out.

He pales and scurries away like the rat he is.

After making sure Les leaves, I gaze at the hearth, running my hands over the carved wood—it's similar to the bookshelf frames downstairs with flowers, vines, and flourishes. One of the flowers jiggles a little when I brush it. Nope. That's a heart.

"Ah ha. I think I found it." I prepare for another secret passage or to find the Sweetheart Stone.

Instead, a little wooden box drops into my hand.

Bo looks over my shoulder and says, "Looks like you need a key to open it."

"Yep and the woman who has it also happens to have the key to my heart," I answer, hoping she'll take me back.

Bo lifts his eyebrow in my direction a la Mark Wahlberg.

"I had to slay my dragons and, uh, lucky me. I found the treasure." I think I know what's in the box, but the real treasure is Christina, my very own sweetheart.

CHAPTER 23
Christina

Louella Belle, Mae, and Camellia sit with me at the table at the Ladyboss Command Center. Rhondy must've recognized there was trouble when Buck left me, alone in the booth. My pie came with us and they brought reinforcements—chocolate, ice cream, and five boxes of candy.

As usual, my phone beeps incessantly with notifications. Then the incoming call jingle vibrates the thing clear across the table.

"It's Buck," Mae says, glancing at the screen.

"Also, he texted no less than a dozen times," Camellia says.

"He wants to apologize." Louella Belle bites her lip as if uncertain whether I'm ready to hear that.

The hum under my skin makes me want to arrange everything tastefully on a decorative plate even though I'm not supposed to eat it. Instead, I take a bite of one of the chocolates.

It reminds me of when Buck and I had S'mores. Then I think about dancing in the ballroom and how being with Buck was always a full sensory experience. There was the sparkle in his eyes, the rumble of his voice, his rough yet steady hands, and the press of his mouth against mine.

My hands drop into my lap and tears edge their way to my eyes.

"Do you want to talk about it?" Louella Belle asks.

"Or yell. Sometimes that helps me," says Camellia, the most soft-spoken of the bunch.

We all stare at her.

She shrugs. "You know, whatever works."

"If we're being honest, I punch my pillow when I'm upset," Mae says, definitely the smallest of us.

I wrinkle my nose and come clean. "I'm a stuff-it-inside and hope it goes away kind of coper."

"Sounds like we all have our issues," Louella Belle says. "But it seems like you and Buck are a lot alike."

That opens the floodgates. Around ugly sobs, I say, "I knew things between us would eventually turn into a big fat fail. They always do. I'd let my guard down and my greatest fears proved to be true. He's no different than any of the other men in my past."

"But you're different," Camellia says.

"Yeah, you eat chocolate now," Mae adds.

"And you loosened your grip on having to make everything perfect," Louella Belle says.

"I'm not sure if that's progress because as soon as I did it all fell apart." I cup my face in my hands.

"What exactly fell apart?" Mae asks.

"Buck and me," I sob.

"My guess is he got scared." Camellia sets a box of tissues on the table.

I wipe my eyes. "Are we talking about the same person? Have you seen Buck? He's six-five. I don't think he's scared of anything."

"Commitment," Louella says around a cough. "Relationships. Failure."

"Do you have a hairball?" Mae asks.

"No, but I'm treading lightly because I'd argue Christina and

Buck have the same, um, how to say this delicately? You have the same hang-ups."

My tears slow to a sniffle. "I do not."

"Says the lady who boasted about being on the No-Man-Plan."

I pout, feeling like having a pity party with all these snacks rather than picking apart my relationship shortcomings. "I've been hurt in the past."

"Did you ever think that maybe you were with the wrong guys in the past?"

"And you think Buck is the right one?"

"The perfect one," Mae says.

"The perfect match," Camellia agrees.

"Even Rhondy thinks so and she's never been wrong," Louella Belle says.

I frown. "The fact of the matter is he left me high and dry."

"But with pie." Louella Belle pushes the plate toward me.

"What does that have to do with anything?"

"He can devour a slice in three bites. No chance he'd leave it on the table if not for a good reason, proving my point that he got scared." Louella Belle smiles proudly like she rests her case.

"Scared of me?"

"You can be intense sometimes," Mae says.

Camellia dips her head. "Using your passion for interior design as a metaphor for your attempt at trying to order your internal anxieties applies in this case."

"But the good news is that you've changed so much these last few months. It's like you proved to yourself that you can delegate, let things be slightly askew, eat French fries, and that the world won't come crashing down." Louella Belle wears a soft and assuring smile.

"But it feels like it is." I whimper.

She gives me a side hug and rests her head on my shoulder. "I know. But as far as I can tell it's still spinning. You're still here and so is the project, us, and even Buck. He just doesn't realize it yet."

The others agree.

"You forced Bo into strong-arming him to stay put, huh?" I guess.

"Strongarm is a strong word. More like *forced.* It was do that, otherwise, I'd make sure Rhondy refused him service for a year. No biscuits, no pie—you have to use the leverage you can." Louella Belle laughs.

"Harsh."

"We've got your back. But so does Buck. He made a mistake, that's all," Camellia says.

"How can you be so sure?" I ask.

Mae sighs. "Because I've seen you two make eyes at each other."

I roll mine.

"And he proposed to you in the garden behind the estate," Camellia adds.

"We were role-playing."

Louella Belle lifts and lowers her eyebrows. "The look he gave you was real."

"Him walking away and leaving me in the diner was also real."

"You set the bar very high," Mae says.

"Lowering your expectations is much different than lowering your standards. You strive for perfection and people aren't perfect. None of us are." Camellia shakes her head slowly.

The corners of my lips dip in response. "It's not like moving a limbo stick. My grip on perfection goes deep." But as I speak the words, something comes loose inside. I relax on an exhale. A thought trickles in with a promise that from now on, my @DomesticDiva photos and videos will be unfiltered—no more showing the world highly polished versions of my reality. I feel instant relief.

Mae winces. "If we're talking about Buck, given his height, I don't know how low you could go with that limbo stick."

Louella Belle takes my hand in hers. Mae clasps my other one. Camellia closes the circle.

"It's just a matter of letting go, taking hold of something new, and trusting that it's all going to work out," Louella Belle says.

"And look, you're already three-quarters of the way there," Camellia adds. "You started eating sweets and treats, loosened up on the constant cell phone connection, and collaborated with us."

I think about the No-Man-Plan and how all I've wanted was a successful career. But for what? So strangers can admire me? So I can have more likes and followers. How many would be enough? I'd always be chasing an elusive number because there's no meaning or substance behind it. That comes from friendships and relationships with real people like the ladybosses and Buck.

A fluttery little sigh escapes. "He does clean up nice."

"He cleans up to perfection," Mae adds.

"I guess I can have a satisfying career and a successful relationship."

"You can have it all—all the cake and all the pie," Louella Belle says. "But sometimes not all of it at the same time, otherwise you might get a stomach ache and because relationships take time and attention and devotion."

"Buck did mention something that maybe you can give me your thoughts on. One of my big fears is rejection so I come off as being friendly but have protective walls up." My words are careful, measured.

"With a moat around them," Camellia adds.

"They're heavily fortified," Mae says.

"At first, you didn't let anyone get too close, genuinely close. But you've changed." Louella Belle beams.

"I blame Rhondy's pie."

We all laugh.

"And maybe your knight in shining armor."

"He does have a shield and sword at the forge." I think about his projects and how a relationship, but not a person, can be one. I let out what feels like the longest-held breath ever, one so strong it could blow down a brick wall or two. "Watch out Big Bad Wolf!"

"That's the spirit," Mae says.

"Are you ready to kiss and make up?" Camellia asks.

"Buck is waiting right outside," Louella Belle says.

My eyes bulge. "You're just as bad as Rhondy."

"I learn from the best."

I walk to the front door with the three of them trailing me then pause. "The training wheels are serving me well, but I think I need to do this myself."

"Do horses have training wheels?" Camellia asks.

"I think you broke the damsel in distress and knight in shining armor analogy," Mae says.

"Excelsior!" Louella Belle thrusts her hand in the air like she holds a sword.

I exit HQ into the balmy summer night.

Two men lean against the mailbox on the sidewalk. Ordinarily, I'd be intimidated, pull out my pepper spray, and run the other way. Bo tips his cap and saunters off.

Buck and I meet in the middle.

"Guess you didn't go far." The shiver that runs through me says nothing has changed despite our spat—I'm still as attracted to and in love with this guy as ever.

"Far enough." Buck looks shy, boyish for once. "I want to apologize. I'm sorry for running off." He scuffs the sidewalk with his boot.

I poke him in the chest. "That was dumb. I thought you fancied yourself a hero."

"More like a *zero* with a move like that. I don't know what I was thinking." He pauses. "That's not true. I was thinking about protecting myself from the past, but that can't hurt me if I'm living in the present...and if it hurt you, I'm sorry. So sorry." Pain fills his eyes.

I step closer, breathing in his familiar smoky, leather scent. Relief swoops through me. Buck is all man, my man. "Don't be too down on yourself. You're my hero. You helped save me from myself, so that's something. And if you have any more superhero moves, we could think about our future."

"Would you like a future with me?"

"I'm in this for Gremlin. He won me over, but if I had to choose a runner up..."

The corner of Buck's lip quirks. "I'm definitely not as loveable as Gremlin, but—"

"You're my bearded James Bond, Viking, blacksmith in shining armor, er, a black shirt and jeans."

"And you don't mind?"

"As long as you're okay with Little Miss Hot Mess."

"A hot mess? Hot, yes. But there's nothing messy about you."

My fingers splay across my chest. Hot? He thinks I'm hot. I tuck that compliment in my shirt pocket. "Glad you think so. In that case, um, the not-messy part, must mean that I'm winning at life." No-Man-Plan done. Dietary plan ditched. Viking beefcake with a beard clinched. Maybe I'm doing alright after all.

Buck bites his lip. "Are you sure you don't want to date a guy who's freshly shaven, wears a sports jacket, and drives a slick car?"

"Who said anything about dating?"

He sinks back.

"Furthermore, when we were at the diner and I said that I *liked* the way you were, I didn't get a chance to explain. I'm in this for the long haul, so yeah, we can date, but I'd like more than a casual encounter. And earlier, when I said *liked*, past tense, I wanted to tell you that it transformed into something bigger—love."

Buck wraps his massive hands around my waist and boosts me off the ground. Our foreheads press together.

"I thought you hated me, Christina. I hated me for walking away like that." Agony crimps his voice.

"If by hate, you mean you hate perfection, sure. I hate perfection. I'm done with it. People make mistakes. Accidents happen. We can lament and stew in a state of grievance or we can offer grace and forgive."

"I'm so sorry," he repeats.

"Let's forgive each other and start trusting each other."

His eyes sparkle. "I like that idea."

"Good because I love you and your beard." I give it a gentle little tug.

He kisses me on the cheek. "I love your face."

"I love your arms."

"I love your elbows."

"I love your earlobes," I say.

We go back and forth, pecking each other with sweet little kisses.

"You really like the beard?" he asks.

"I said I love it."

"But before, you hated it."

"I lied."

"I love it when you lie."

We both laugh.

"Speaking of liars, Bo and I were at the estate earlier and found Les prowling around. He was looking for the ring."

"Did he find it?"

"Not a chance." Buck winks.

I get the sense there's some subterfuge and criminal intent involved. The less I know about jewel thieves and the CIA the better.

"So do you forgive me?" he asks.

"I do. Guess the breakup didn't last very long."

Buck glances at his watch. "Only two very painful hours. If I built a cage around my heart and you had a fortress of stone walls around yours, how do we break through?"

"We already did."

Buck lowers me to the ground but doesn't let go.

"What's it going to be like in a relationship with you?" I ask.

"Is this one of your interviews?"

"Something like that."

"To answer your question, it's going to have its ups and

downs because that's life, but mostly ups because we're going to talk through our challenges instead of reverting to our old ways."

"I like that answer. Can you please define success?"

"Any day that I make my woman happy."

I giggle. "Are you happy?"

"I am now and I count success as every day we're together and we wake up excited for what's to come, spend time doing things we enjoy with the people we love, and going to sleep grateful for the time we've had together."

"That's it. You're hired and you gave me the name for the Easton Estate project." I explain that each of my jobs gets a special name. "Drum roll, please. Heretofore, I dub it, 'Happily ever after on the hill.'"

"That's a mouthful."

"True. It'll be HEA for short."

"We're going to be done in a few days. It's a little late to name the project, no?"

"It's never too late and we're never too old for anything, especially each other."

His eyes spark with hope. "Does this mean you believe in happily ever after?"

I nod. "If it means a HEA with you."

"Then my work here is nearly done." Buck leans in and plants a kiss on my forehead.

My brow ripples in question.

He winks as if the best is yet to come. Our gazes lock. My breath hitches. This man melts me on the spot as he leans down and trails kisses along my jawline before reaching my lips.

"I have to warn you, I'm swooning again." My voice is a breathy whisper and I remind myself to breathe.

"Swooning seems somewhat appropriate given we're working on a house from the late renaissance." He chuckles.

I draw a ragged breath as his commanding lips land on mine, and we kiss again.

Mae Fuller

I spend most of the day at Ladyboss HQ fielding phone calls, placing orders, and suppressing panic.

This afternoon is the official unveiling of the Easton Estate, more recently dubbed the happily ever after project.

The phone calls are fairly routine given the success of our show Designed to Last—brands want endorsements from us, events request our attendance, and friends and family members who're lost on their way to Butterbury ask for directions.

"Try the GPS. It's the button on your phone with the little map." I wince as an ear sprouting a concerning amount of hair and the size of my phone screen zooms ever closer. "Remember, we're on Facetime so you don't have to put your ear to the phone." I think this is one of Camellia's relatives. "Just look at the screen and push the button. There you go. Now, enter the address I texted you and follow the prompts."

Mercifully, I'm able to get off the phone without any further close encounters with ear hair.

The orders I've been placing are for the boutique we're opening in the front section of headquarters. As the show gained popularity, visitors from local towns and Savannah started to trickle in. Now, we're getting people from all over the southeast, and they want a destination experience. Louella Belle and Rhondy are heading up the bakery next door, slated to open in time for Christmas. For now, people want to say they've been to headquarters and walk away with branded swag and local handicrafts.

"Ladyboss," Camellia's voice singsongs from the backdoor. "You have thirty minutes left to get ready for the grand reveal. Am I going to have to stuff you in that dress?"

"Does it have pockets?"

"It's a floor-length gown so my guess is no," Camellia calls.

I close the laptop and slouch as the panic creeps closer.

"Come on, it's going to be fabulous," she says.

"Tell me again why Christina is making us get dressed up."

"Because it's fun to be fancy and we're having the post-home makeover reveal party in the ballroom and entrance into a ballroom requires a ballgown."

"Who made up that rule?"

"The ballers?"

I cringe at her use of the slang word. "I don't think you know what that means."

Camellia winks. "Let's get you ready."

Unlike Christina, I'm low maintenance. On an average day, I require a grand total of four products—face wash, toothpaste, moisturizer, and lip balm. That's it. No fancy glosses or polishes for me. My uniform consists of jeans, Ts, and sweatshirts. Basically, anything with pockets.

Camellia practically drags me to the apartment upstairs where we've been staying—at least until my project on the old family farm starts next week. Then I'll be bunking with the ghosts. Yay. That's another source of panic, but I'll face today first.

Twenty-five minutes later, Camellia has buffed me to a shine. She fluffed my hair with loose curls. Makeup transforms me into looking like an actual adult rather than the teenager I'm often mistaken for—an older teenager but still. The guy at the gas station had inch-thick glasses but most people don't believe that I'm in my early thirties.

My mother says I'll age well.

Considering no one takes me seriously no matter how mature I am, I'll believe it when I see it.

Oh, and I'm wearing a satiny gown in navy blue and teetering in heels with sparkles around the ankle straps.

"Good thing we bought workers' compensation," I mutter as I try to make my way downstairs, leaning heavily on the railing so I don't stumble.

"Officially, you're off the clock. Now, cheer up, we have a restored house to reveal to the world."

It was only about four months ago that I made my debut on television. I tend to avoid the spotlight and primarily work behind the scenes. And the fact that my brother is joining us for the reveal, which means he may bring his best friend Taylor, doesn't help matters.

Sleek black SUVs like the kind we're in and trucks alike line the road leading to the estate—the valet must've run out of room in the driveway.

Anxious bubbles form inside my stomach the closer we get. When Camellia and I pull up, a man opens the door, flashes pop, and voices volley questions about the project and show our way.

"This is so glamorous," Camellia whispers to me. "I feel famous."

"You are famous with thanks to HLTV." But she must not hear me because we're separated by a long line of people greeting us and tugging us each in different directions.

After walking along the red carpet, I enter the mansion and it's like stepping back in time to an age when the original owners of the estate hosted soirees. The only exception is the abundance of cellphones and the modern updates the crew made to the house during the remodel.

I smile and wave, keeping an eye out for my brother, Aiden, but I see Taylor first. I suddenly feel like an actual teenager all over again—I rewind to the last time I saw him in person and the era of my raging crush on a boy far too old for me.

Taylor is as tall as I remember and stands next to one of the arched entries to the ballroom with a glass casually in his hand. His hair is shorter than I remember but still goes past his ears. His tuxedo fits perfectly and he checks his watch. Now would be the time to go over and say hello.

The nerves inside threaten to bubble over. I startle when someone says, "Have you ever been arrested?"

I spin to see the mayor's lackey, wearing a suit that looks borrowed from an older and larger brother.

He waggles his eyebrows. "I ask because it should be illegal to look that good."

Leave it to me to attract the weirdo.

He juts his hand out and says, "Les Streckle. We met a couple of times before. I work for Mayor Stoll."

Of course, I remember this creep. Figures he doesn't recall meeting me. But more importantly what is he doing here?

"Excuse me," a deep voice calls from the microphone in front of the live band.

Friends, employees, and acquaintances all turn their attention to the front of the room where Buck stands. He draws something out of his pocket. "As some of you know, this renovation was a labor of love. In fact, I'd like to invite my love up here. Cricket." He motions in Christina's direction.

She stands on the edge of the crowd, beaming a smile. Louella Belle gives her a little nudge.

Buck's breath catches as she approaches. Christina dazzles in a sunny yellow gown. For the first time, her brown hair is down, cascading over her shoulders in a silky waterfall.

He reaches for her hand and squeezes. "You affectionately dubbed this project happily ever after and working on it made me realize that I want one with you."

She glows with a wide smile.

He continues, "You hold the key to my heart."

A few people around me *ooh* and coo at the romance of his proclamation.

Christina presses her hand to her chest. "You hold the key to mine too."

He smiles. "But you actually hold the key to my heart—the Sweetheart Stone."

She blinks a few times, gasps, and then hurriedly digs through her small handbag, producing the metal key she found in one of the second-floor bedrooms.

Buck goes on to tell everyone the story of his great-great-grandmother and grandfather, how the Sweetheart Stone, a family engagement ring, had been lost for decades. And how because their love was forbidden, the respective families thought the other stole it. They'd been feuding ever since.

Buck holds a wooden box. Christina slides the key into the lock. He opens it to reveal a pink diamond in the shape of a heart.

The entire room inhales with a collective gasp.

Then he lowers onto one knee.

I recall the day we spotted them outside in similar positions, role-playing. I thought for sure, they'd gotten engaged then. But this is even more romantic because he actually found the ring, and we're all here to celebrate.

"Cricket, will you marry me?" Buck asks, holding the ring up for her to see.

She bounces on her toes and hollers, "Yes! And my heart is no longer hidden. It's yours. All yours."

He gets to his feet and slides the ring onto her finger.

"It's the perfect fit," a woman next to me says in awe.

"They're the perfect couple," I say to no one in particular, feeling dreamy and happy for them.

Buck adds, "I'm glad you said yes because I already bought our house."

Christina tilts her head in question.

"Welcome home, sweetheart," he says, gesturing to our surroundings.

Her eyes bulge and she squeals. "Seriously? This place?"

"Home sweet home," Buck says.

How Louella Belle, Camellia, and I managed to keep that a secret, is nothing short of a miracle, but we kind of knew she'd say yes to his proposal so figured it couldn't hurt to help facilitate their future living arrangements.

The next few minutes are a whirlwind of cameras flashing, congratulations offered, and chatter before the music starts again and couples step onto the dancefloor.

I've never been to a ball before and linger on the sidelines. I work my way toward Buck and Christina and have to sidestep Les Streckle a few times. I can't fathom why he's here. If Buck spots him, forget a hole in the floor. There will be a spindly-man-shaped one through the wall.

I dodge around one of the catering staff's trays, trying to hide behind the tall glasses filled with bubbly liquid. Then I get stuck behind an elderly man with a walker. I try to blend in like we're here together, but he looks at me like I'm a few eggs short of a dozen.

"Sorry, sir."

"There you are, darlin'." Les corners me. "Would you like to have this dance?" he asks.

"No, she would not," a second male voice says.

When I look up, Taylor towers over Les, wearing a confident smile.

"She's here with me," my teenage heartthrob says.

I stammer, unsure if I've entered an alternate reality.

Taylor takes my hand, sending a zing through me. I stumble in my heels as we make our way to the dancefloor.

Homecoming, prom, and every fantasy I had are coming true right now. He plants one hand on my waist and the other grips mine firmly as we begin to waltz, flowing smoothly across the freshly polished floor.

"What a charming proposal," he says, referring to Buck and Christina who're still greeting well-wishers

"I'm so happy for them. By the way, thank you for saving me back there," I say.

"I noticed him tailing you for a while."

"And me trying to evade him?"

Taylor bites his lip. "Guilty."

Which means he was also watching me. My heart bounces in my chest and I wrinkle my nose. "Unfortunately for Les Streckle, he's not my type."

"What is your type?" he asks.

You. You're my type. Always have been.

"Six-feet give or take, fit, doesn't raid his older brother's closet for a suit."

Taylor laughs, sending a little thrill through me. When I was younger, I aimed to get him to laugh. Sadly, it was usually *at* me. But all the same, this feels as good as I hoped it would. As we continue to dance, I'd believe the parquet floor was made of puffy clouds if I hadn't helped refinish them myself.

"Speaking of brothers, have you seen mine?" I ask.

Confusion rolls across Taylor's features. "Your brother?"

I'm about to say *Aiden* when I realize something crucial. Taylor never acknowledged me or said my name. Chances are, he doesn't recognize me.

My heart sinks and I freeze on the dancefloor, panic commencing in three, two, one...

Not ready to leave Butterbury? Be sure to stick around for Mae and Taylor's romance in *The DIY Kissing Project.* Turn the page for a sneak peek of chapter one!

Sneak Peek!

As I cruise south on Interstate-95 in the hand-me-down Ford farm truck, I wiggle uncomfortably in my seat. If you've ever skipped exits because you're not sure how far it will be to the nearest bathroom or don't want to risk the types of public facilities that require a hazmat suit, you know the exact kind of wiggle I'm talking about.

"There has to be a rest stop coming up soon," I say to Pumpkin, my guinea pig. She rides in the backseat. Don't worry, I strapped her travel carrier in securely.

She *wheeks* in response. I smile, glad to be reunited after she stayed with my sister for the last few months while I got settled in Butterbury. As for the *wheek*, the noise is sort of like a squeak but distinct to guinea pigs. I think of it like a cat's meow or even a purr, but is an onomatopoeia, so it sounds the way you say it.

She double *wheeks*.

"We already have plenty of snacks," I say.

Sometimes the sound is a request for food. Pumpkin is a muncher. (Me too. My mother says I'm more of a grazer than a proper three-squares-a-day meal-eater.) Other times, the *wheek* is just a happy noise or one of contentment. I'm not entirely sure what she's trying to tell me since I don't speak guinea pig.

"Pumpkin, if you need the bathroom as badly as me, you know where to go," I hint. She has a corner in her travel crate.

A sign ahead indicates Savannah is one-hundred and eight miles away and Butterbury is just over a half-hour past that. No way can I wait that long for a bathroom.

My apologies if my current status is too much information, but I know everyone has been in this position—it's a universal human experience if there ever was one.

The traffic is light and I'm a seasoned road tripper, but don't want to stray too far off the paved path, especially since I'm eager to get Pumpkin set up in her new pen.

I've been staying in Butterbury for the last several months, but now that I have Pumpkin, I'm officially moving back to the small town in coastal Georgia. Growing up, we lived in several states for my father's job, but then we left New Hampshire to move in with my grandparents when I was in high school. No way did I ever expect to be heading back to live there. Especially not the farmhouse. Let's just say it's not *not* occupied—at least according to my older brother, who took it upon himself to spook me with ghost stories. While living there, I saw enough strange phenomena to be cautiously wary.

Nevertheless, I shall forge ahead because I happen to know that my parents, who are now living on retirement income in Virginia, still pay off my grandparents' medical bills and I have the opportunity to help them and breathe new life into the old place.

I shift again and try to distract myself from what's becoming a violent and painful need to use the bathroom. I look forward to putting this unpleasant experience in the rearview mirror as soon as possible.

"Pumpkin, you're going to love Butterbury. It's the quintessential small-town USA. Shops line Main Street, which runs along the central town square. Loads of families gather there after church on Sundays and just about every holiday in between. In fact, with the help of Rhondy, we ladybosses are opening a bakery in Butterbury later this year. Did I tell you that yet?"

Yeah, yeah, yeah. I'm talking to my guinea pig about Butterbury. Desperate times call for distracting measures.

Mmm. Butter. I think about Gramps' cows, churning butter with Gram and baking—anything to take my mind off the need for a bathroom. Her chocolate chip cookies were the best.

Since losing her and her famous recipe, I've been on a long-term chocolate chip cookie quest. It started in college when I'd study at different cafés and bakeries off-campus. It grew after my career as a Rockette ended—yes, I was a professional tap dancer. After that, I returned to my original field of study and found work as a graphic designer. Meanwhile, I was blogging, and it gained popularity. Several years ago, I took the cookie quest on the road in search of the perfect chocolate chip cookie in every state and overall in the country. Apart from Gram's, I thought I'd found the perfect one at a bakery in Alabama. But they closed up shop.

I could go for a warm, buttery, melty chocolate chip cookie right now. Even though it's only mid-September, a cold snap hit the eastern seaboard and I've been craving comfort foods.

A sign advertising a rest stop with a fast food place comes into view...or I could go for French fries. Those take second place to cookies as my favorite.

"Hold on, Pumpkin. This is bordering on an emergency." Scrambling to cross a couple of lanes, I make it to the left side exit without anyone honking at me.

As I pull into the parking lot, my phone trills with an incoming call. I grab the nearest parking spot and Louella Belle's name scrolls across the screen. I glance at the time on the dashboard and wince. We're supposed to have a conference call with the producer of our show, Designed to Last, at one pm.

What time is it? One pm.

Even though I'm on the road, Louella Belle insisted I couldn't miss this. Talking with a television show producer isn't the kind of call I can put off because I have to tinkle.

I squeeze my eyes shut, willing my deep urge to use the bathroom to subside for a few more minutes. The call can't take much longer than that—Hollywood types are busy, right? They have people to see and places to go and deals to make!

Drawing a breath, I answer. "Hello?"

"Hi, Mae. Conference call commencing in three, two, one," Louella Belle counts down in her southern accent that's twice as strong as mine, even though she'd vacated this part of the country for twice as long as I did.

"Hello, ladybosses," says a woman with an efficient and winning voice. "I'm Kendra Andrews, the executive producer at Home and Landscaping Television. My colleagues and fans alike have been singing your praises. Can you hear it all the way across the country in Georgia?" She titters. "The show is doing amazing."

That must mean our ratings have been good.

"They could not get enough of gruff Buck and the Domestic Diva. Ladies, you knocked it out of the park last season. Then with the footage from the proposal, well, *y'all* have been the talk of the town. It's amazing." She chuckles, presumably at her use of the common southern phrase *y'all*.

Christina mentioned that even though Buck isn't on social media, she's received a slew of posts by her followers tagging her with photos and updates inspired by Buck about their husbands and significant others growing beards and wearing flannel. They're single-handedly invigorating the beard oil and flannel shirt industries.

I make a mental note to suggest to Camellia that we create branded versions of both in our boutique storefront at Lady Boss Headquarters—the grand opening is later today. No rest for these DIY entrepreneurs.

Kendra says a few more things and punctuates them with how *amazing* they are. But I hardly hear because of what we'll refer to as my "particular situation."

Or pee-ticular situation.

No! I cannot think about it. I'm verging toward overflow.

Kendra is friendly, but I have to admit, the expression *y'all* sounds slightly forced coming out of her mouth like she's trying to coax a bunch of ten-year-olds into eating their vegetables.

"I know y'all will do amazingly during this second season. Just think, if we continue with this level of success, the sky is the limit." Kendra continues, detailing ratings and reviews.

I force myself not to think about how the spotlight isn't exactly my motivating factor. Instead, I focus because my "urge" to use the bathroom grows stronger by the second. I have to take drastic action.

I click *mute* on my phone and whisper, "Pumpkin, I'll be right back." I risk leaving the Ford's rear windows open so Pumpkin can enjoy the pleasant autumn breeze.

As I hustle across the parking lot, doing a jaunty little walk-jog-waddle, desperate for the ladies' room, I'm afraid the mute button fails and they can hear me huffing and puffing.

As I step foot on the sidewalk in front of the building, Kendra's voice crackles through the phone—the call breaks up.

Stepping back, I try to regain the signal. A car honks and I jolt, giving the driver an apologetic wave for not paying attention and thankful that they didn't run me over.

"If you had to pee this badly, you'd be distracted too," I mutter.

Christina's voice comes through the phone, saying something about the estate project and how important it was to maintain the classic style while bringing the home into the modern age. I lose whatever she says next. Like a Ghostbuster in the old movie, trying to detect ghouls, I hold my phone in the air as I work my way back to my car, hoping it doesn't break up worse. The voices through the phone become clearer—with Camellia chiming in about the winter season. She says something about Kendra's "temperature check" about the show. I only gather the producer requested a progress update from contextual clues. At least, I think that's what she meant.

Starting to breathe heavily because I don't know exactly

what's going on and due to my, ahem, situation, I glean that Kendra is surveying each one of us about our season contribution to the show Designed to Last.

Because this is a conference call, if Louella Belle, Christina, and Camellia have already spoken, that means I'm likely on deck next, considering we soon begin the fall season which will be my home improvement project.

"Mae, please tell us about your plans. Give us the forecast," Kendra says around a laugh. "I'd like to gauge what to expect beyond the outline and timeline Kim shared with us at our last review. This is important information for me to pass along to the rest of the team, including the marketing and publicity departments. Believe it or not, this season may be bigger than the last."

Thankfully, she doesn't use the word *amazing* because the only amazing thing that could possibly happen right now is me being inside the restroom.

As for my season of Designed to Last, I'm not exactly one for the spotlight. Sure, as a little girl and teenager, I envisioned my wedding day, complete with a gorgeous gown. Later, I lit up the stage with the Rockettes at Radio City Music Hall. But that was down to my love for tap dancing.

Throughout my life, if playing the *This or That* game, I'll always choose slippers over heels, movie nights in over hitting the town, and holding hands over bling.

My sister, Bess, jokes that someday I'll make a man very happy because I'm a cheap date. It's true. I often order off the kids' menu, shop sales, buy store brands, and will opt for a camping trip at a national park instead of a luxurious all-expenses-paid trip to an exotic location.

Bess also says that she doesn't understand me and that I'm built differently. I don't disagree.

My reply to Kendra will have to be short and sweet because of reasons I'm too polite to share over the phone. "Hi, everyone. I've been so pleased to see how, as the team and crew have gotten to know each other, we've found a rhythm that works nicely and have become friends. I think that comes across on-screen and I imagine the audience picks up on it." I continue, emphasizing how our offscreen chemistry translates to a quality show because everyone genuinely enjoys working together.

Louella Belle says, "Mae, are you there?"

My head drops back when I realize I forgot to unmute myself. I repeat the entire thing, though less eloquently because I legitimately feel like I might explode...or implode. I'm no longer sure.

"We're very lucky to have found such an amazingly cohesive group." Kendra discusses the upcoming season, stressing how amazing it'll be because farmhouse and rural-type properties are hot with the HLTV audience at the moment. "Y'all sure are amazing. Can you tell us about your vision, Mae? I have no doubt it's going to be amazing."

I have to pee so *amazingly* bad, my eyeballs feel like they're floating in their sockets. *Think fast, Mae.* "I appreciate your confidence in me. I don't want to give away too much because we're doing a big social media reveal for the season, so be sure to tune into our social media channels. I'll say this: imagine a farmhouse that was once beloved by a working-class family then fell into disrepair. Think good bones but years of neglect. A sweeping front porch that's sinking into the ground. A dark and dated kitchen. Think old-fashioned, clumsy construction, and bland design. An old barn that needs a lot of TLC. Well, leave it up to me, your DIY Darling, to restore and renovate the property to be an amazing showstopper."

Kendra raves, repeating the word *amazing* too many times to count. And on that note, I throw caution to the wind about losing the call, click *mute* again, and race to the restroom. With every painful step, I pray that there isn't a line, that the toilet isn't out of order, or that I get there at the same time as a pregnant woman with a bunch of children in tow.

Two minutes later: Prayers answered. Toilet visited. I've never been so relieved in my life. No pun intended.

"Butterbury, here I come!"

. . .

Keep reading...

Acknowledgements

I hope you enjoyed visiting Butterbury and the ladybosses. Exploring this small town and characters has been a lot of fun and there is more to come.

A big, warm cookie-filled hug from me to Amy, Joan & Melissa as well as all of my sweet and swoony readers, followers, and those of you who take the time to email, comment, and review.

Thank you for reading. You help bring these stories to life!

About the Author

Ellie Hall is a USA Today bestselling author. If only that meant she could wear a tiara and get away with it ;) She loves puppies, books, and the ocean. Writing sweet romance with lots of firsts and fizzy feels brings her joy. Oh, and chocolate chip cookies are her fave.

Ellie believes in dreaming big, working hard, and lazy Sunday afternoons spent with her family and dog in gratitude for God's grace.

♥

facebook.com/elliehallauthor
instagram.com/elliehallauthor
bookbub.com/authors/ellie-hall